Cthulhu & Other Monsters

Love

[signature]

Cthulhu & Other Monsters

Sam Stone

First Published in 2017 by Telos Publishing Ltd,
5A Church Road, Shortlands, Bromley, Kent BR2 0HP, UK.

www.telos.co.uk

Telos Publishing Ltd values feedback. Please e-mail us with any
comments you may have about this book to:
feedback@telos.co.uk

ISBN: 978-1-84583-122-6

British Library Cataloguing in Publication Data. A catalogue
record for this book is available from the British Library.

CONTENTS

*Previously unpublished

Cthulian Tales

The Vessel

Brent Jefferson pulled his hat down over his face and hurried through the dark and narrow streets of the French Quarter. Rain pummelled his head and shoulders. It was 10pm and a curfew had been imposed, which meant that all blacks were to stay in their homes after 6pm. But the Confederate military weren't interested in policing this area of New Orleans anymore. They had bigger fish to fry since the Federal Navy had opened fire on Fort Jackson. Jefferson knew it was only a matter of time before the Confederates fell and the Union Army broke through their defences to take over and occupy the city.

He knew he didn't have long before he'd have to flee the town and take with him the woman he loved. His biggest dilemma was that Carly didn't want to leave. She didn't even want Jefferson in her life.

Rain water dripped from the rim of his hat as he paused to look up at the tall building ahead. His eyes sought and found Carly's window. As usual she was sitting, semi-naked, flaunting her wares, even though on a night like this it was unlikely any trade would find its way into this dingy corner of the quarter. The soldiers were otherwise occupied, the local landowners were living in terror of losing their fine plantations, and the blacks were being whipped and locked up at night in desperate attempts to keep them from running away.

Times were changing and Jefferson knew that soon Carly's white owner wouldn't be able to force her to whore for him anymore. That was if the rumours of slaves being freed were entirely true. They only had the propaganda spun by the Confederates to back up any information on the war or the siege, but Jefferson suspected some of it was factual, if not all.

Despite the driving rain, Carly was cooling herself with a fancy Chinese fan. Jefferson recognised it as the one he had given her when she still let him visit. It gave him a strange kind of hope. Even from below he could make out the slender lines of her coffee-coloured thighs, as she sat, one leg crossed over the other.

'She's a whore, man. Why'd you even bother coming back here all the time,' said a voice from an open door a few feet away.

Jefferson turned to see his old friend Matthew, a former slave who had managed to buy his own freedom some years before. He now ran an illegal bootleg store from the basement of his small house.

'It's not her fault,' Jefferson said. 'You know that.'

Jefferson, Matthew and Carly had once belonged to the same plantation. The Beaugards had been cruel owners. Carly and Jefferson had wanted to be together, but fraternisation amongst the slaves wasn't allowed on Beaugard land – not unless they wanted you to breed more slaves. When their relationship was discovered, Michel Beaugard sold Carly on to the whore house. By then Matthew had bought his freedom and he thought it the cruellest punishment ever to both Jefferson and Carly. He had tried to raise the money to buy Carly's freedom from the pimp, but the white man wouldn't deal with Matthew. He saw the potential in Carly's half-caste looks and knew that the soldiers would like her. He would earn more from her by working her than by merely selling her on.

Even so, he kept Matthew dangling for a while: if the girl burned out quickly, he would probably let her friend buy her freedom. But Carly didn't burn out. In fact she took to prostitution so well that she was soon the best girl in the house. She was capable of dealing with twice as many johns in one night as any of the other girls. And they all left satisfied, and came back for more.

When Matthew realised he couldn't help Carly, he helped Jefferson buy his freedom instead. Carly was some whorish princess now in an ivory tower that neither of them could climb.

'I don't understand what happened,' Jefferson murmured as he stared up at her window.

'She weren't never what you thought she was,' Matthew said.

Matthew invited Jefferson in out of the rain and handed him a glass of cheap brandy. Jefferson took off his wet coat and hat and sat down in a chair by the fire. The heat was welcome, but it couldn't touch the cold that sat inside him.

'The city's about to fall,' said Matthew. 'It won't be no bad thing for the likes of us. We have good times ahead. Carly will be freed then – if she wants to be.'

Jefferson shook his head. He knew what was likely to happen – what should happen – but wasn't convinced the white soldiers from the north would treat the blacks any different than they did in the south.

'You knows I got a job at the Pollitt Plantation,' Jefferson said.

Matthew nodded. The Pollitts were good white-folks who radically freed their slaves some years before. All of the blacks that worked the cotton plantation were paid. It meant that the Pollitts were infamous among the other landowners, but that they were also the only thriving farm in the area. There were no disputes or runaways only happy families working, and living with the white landowners.

'The head house servant, Isaac, you know of him?'

'I knows him,' said Matthew. 'He the houngan.'

'He says he can help me.'

'If anyone can. He can.'

Jefferson stared into the flames. Maybe Matthew was right. Maybe he should sit things out and see where it led. Carly would be free to make her own choices wouldn't she? But then, Jefferson wondered, would she choose to remain working in the whorehouse anyway? She certainly didn't look unhappy where she was.

Jefferson returned to the plantation and fell exhausted into his bed.

Despite the late hour sleep was slow to come. Jefferson found himself tossing and turning, thinking about Carly and the hurtful way she had rejected him.

'I don't need no black boy in my life when I can play with all these white ones. They worship me, Brent. They buys me jewels and clothes and all they want is something I find so easy to give,' she had said.

Jefferson knew that a life with him, the dream they once had of owning a ranch, would mean hard toil for both of them. But it surprised him that Carly found her new life to be so 'easy'. She had always been so shy, so reserved, and now it appeared that she was completely the opposite. He tried not to think of her spreading herself for other men: it hurt too much. But sometimes when he lay in his bed at night he couldn't believe she was the same women he had loved so fiercely and risked so much for. Every scar on his back had been received because of his defiance, and his refusal to let her go and be used by the white overseers.

One time Beaugard's men had beat him so badly he nearly died. Even now he couldn't remember why they stopped.

He had a flash of Carly coming into the barn, the six overseers turned to look at her and Jefferson had blacked out cold. When he woke he'd found Carly pressing water to his lips, and felt the sting of salt on his back.

'You is such a fool sometimes,' she had said. 'Always comin' to defen' my honour. You gon' git yourself kil'.'

But it wasn't cold, or distant. All her words were spoken with pride and love.

Carly was smart. She could read and write but she kept this mostly to herself, even though Jefferson knew about it.

'My daddy was a white man,' she had told him. 'He let me learn with his other chil'ren sometimes.'

'What happen to him?' Jefferson said.

'Uprisin'. He had a taste for black flesh. Some of the men on the farm didn't like him messin' with their wives. The overseers beat the rebels down but by then they'd slit his throat. His widow sent me to the auction the very next day.'

'She wanted you gone ...' Jefferson said. He had taken her hand and kissed it to show how bad he felt for her.

'Yessum. She always hate how he paraded me around the house. How he bought me nice things, just like his other chil'ren, even though my skin was still too dark for him to ever admit I was his. She took all those fine presents back too. Sent me out in rags.'

Jefferson had always felt Carly was a lady but Beaugard's men had treated her like fresh meat from the start. It didn't matter how you were brought up. All that mattered was the colour of your skin.

'Jefferson ...'

Jefferson jumped awake to find Isaac standing by his bedside. The Pollitts' manservant was a large man, and his dark silhouette was an unnerving sight.

'You want to help your woman still?' asked Isaac.

'Yes.'

'You knows the sacrifice you has to pay?'

'Yes.'

'Come with me. The congregation is waitin'.'

Jefferson pulled himself from his sweat-soaked bed as he heard the drums pick up in the distance. He didn't ask what it meant. Even though he had been born on American soil, he knew something of the old ways by instinct. They all did.

He followed Isaac from his small shack and out towards the edge of the land. It was still night, but the dawn was tinting the sky and Jefferson could see the big old white house that belonged to the Pollitts up on the horizon. Nothing stirred over there. If the white family heard the drums they showed no sign of it.

'Isaac, how come the Pollitts free you all?' Jefferson asked as they plunged into the dense forest that formed a part of the plantation.

'That is 'tween me an' Masser Pollitt,' Isaac said.

Jefferson swallowed any further questions and quelled his curiosity as Isaac led him into a wide clearing just as the sun began to chase the night away.

They began a ritual. A dance of sorts, while Isaac, clad in a long white robe, shook a tall staff, covered in bone shards tied on with cord. The bones rattled together in rhythm with the drums. Jefferson saw no one playing them though, and even here the sound seemed distant, but part of the ceremony.

Bare-chested, Jefferson kneeled by a blood-soaked altar while a young woman danced forward holding a live chicken. Within moments Isaac had taken the bird, cut its throat and splashed the still-warm blood all over Jefferson's face and chest. The rest of the blood was drained off into a round bowl.

As the last twitches of the bird ceased Isaac stared down into the bowl and began to talk in the old tongue.

Jefferson listened to the lilting language, unable to recognise a word because his parents had never been allowed to speak it on Beaugard's land.

'I sees somethin' here ...' Isaac said.

'What you see?' asked Jefferson.

'I sees Carly. She ... *No!*'

Isaac's sudden gasp brought Jefferson to his feet. He looked into the bowl that Isaac held and for a moment he thought he saw Carly's face in the blood, only it didn't seem like her at all. She held the same, cruel, sneering expression she had worn when she sent him away the last time. There was a darkness crowded around her. Carly's lips moved, even though Jefferson heard no sound. A huge monstrous bulk that appeared to be gathering momentum from the words she spoke.

Isaac abruptly tipped the blood out of the bowl and the vision was lost.

'What was it?' Jefferson said.

'You don't wan' to know what I seen. She ain't no good Jefferson. She into some bad voodoo. Somethin' like I never seen 'fore.'

'You said you'd help me,' Jefferson said.

'I can't. I never would have said so if I knowed what was goin' on ...'

'Tell me what to do,' Jefferson said.

'She gone to you,' Isaac said. 'You best for'git her.'

No matter how much he pleaded, Isaac wouldn't change his mind. He sent the gathered congregation of semi-naked men and women away. And all evidence of their ceremony was removed including the remains of the dead bird.

A few hours later the same people stood side by side with

him in the cotton field, but no one spoke of the ritual.

The failed ceremony made Jefferson even more determined to save Carly. If something bad, some form of black magic, was responsible for the change in her, then maybe he could help. Maybe he should just steal her away, out of the city, as he had planned to do the night before.

When the work day ended, Jefferson gathered his possessions, his freedom papers and the small amount of money he had managed to save and set off from the plantation for the last time.

New Orleans town was in chaos.

'What's happenin'?' Jefferson asked as he saw a group of slaves running from the dock.

'The Union Navy done broke through the boom,' one of them said. 'They is firing at anythin' that move. Git outta here fella or you is gon' git kill'.'

Jefferson hurried away, but not in the direction that the slaves went. He carried on his journey to the French Quarter. Tonight, no matter what she said, Carly was going to listen to him. And, if he could, he would persuade her to leave with him.

As he did the previous night, Jefferson looked up at Carly's window. This time the balcony doors were closed, the room was in darkness. Jefferson felt a pang of anxiety as he hurried towards the building.

The building had once been a fine and expensive house, owned by a wealthy Creole family. Now this former regal home had been turned into a brothel. This dwelling housed girls and women on all levels of the spectrum and fees. Some catered to aristocracy, others – the basement whores – lay in cots underground and serviced the white-trash. White men, no matter how rich or poor, always seemed to need whores. Even so, girls like Carly were in the minority. She was favoured by the wealthy, and had entertained a fair amount of Confederate senior officers too.

Jefferson pushed the thought of all those wealthy white men

away. Her words still stung him but he couldn't give up on her. Not yet. Not until he was certain she was really where she wanted to be.

Heading around the back of the building Jefferson found the entrance to the basement rooms unlocked. Carly had told him about this entrance on one of the few occasions she managed to slip out to meet him. That was before the brothel changed her, but even then she had difficulty in being around him.

'Bein' with you makes me feel bad,' she had said once. 'You is everythin' I *thought* I wanted.'

'I love you, Carly. I'm gon' git you outta here,' Jefferson had promised.

'That's a nice dream Brent. I'd like to believe it could happen. But you try takin' me from this place you is gon' git yourself strung up. I'm white man's property. You knows that would be stealin'.'

Her words were intelligent like always, but Jefferson didn't want to hear them. It was on their second to last meeting when he had been the most insistent. Begging her to come with him then.

'You don't wan' somethin' that's been all used up,' Carly said. 'You deserve better'n me. Don't come back here. Forget about me. This just ain't gon' work out how it was s'posed to.'

Jefferson couldn't forget though, and all the times she'd been kind, juxtaposed with the one time she had rejected him, made it harder for him to let her go.

Now, he paused at the back door wondering what had gotten Isaac so spooked. What was it he had seen in the chicken's blood? Jefferson pushed away the weird and blurred image, convinced it was all his imagination – brought on by his desire to find the help he wanted. The thing was, Jefferson was a practical man. He didn't believe in heaven, hell or voodoo, he had just been so desperate he had hoped for a miracle.

A creeping doubt entered his mind when he recalled Isaac's reaction during the ritual. The houngan had been truly afraid of something.

Pushing down the nervous adrenaline that flooded his body,

Jefferson tugged on the door, and as he expected, it opened effortlessly.

Once these downstairs quarters would have belonged to privileged serving slaves of the Creole household. Now, the interior of the basement smelt like hot sex and perspiration. All the time he was certain someone would see him there. One of the white pimps, or maybe one of the whores would raise the alarm. But no one came out of the rooms, and though Jefferson listened outside one of the doors, he heard no sounds from within.

There was litter and spillages of unknown origin underfoot. His shoes felt tacky as he traipsed quietly through the narrow corridor, past the whore's dormitory and up the staircase that led, he hoped, to the inside of the house. At the top of the staircase, Jefferson opened another door. He found himself in the main lobby.

Light poured in through a tall feature window illuminating a large circular hallway with an ornate marble floor and a grand staircase in the centre. Jefferson looked around at the many doors that came off from the hallway and up to the staircase and balcony that spread around the top. He could see several rooms in the gloom above and it didn't take him long to work out what direction Carly's room would be in.

The house was quiet though. Too quiet. Though he had timed his visit to coincide with the end of business, he had expected some customers, servants and whores to still be around. He went to the front door; found it locked up tight as though they expected the siege outside to surge inside. Maybe there had been no trade that evening. Maybe the whore house had remained closed while outside the world went to hell.

A surge of panic consumed him. What if the white man had taken all the best girls and fled? Forgetting caution now, Jefferson took the stairs two at a time. At the top he turned right and followed the doors around to the one he thought was Carly's. Then he paused. What if she was in there now with a customer? Could he bear to see it?

Jefferson floundered for a moment then he grabbed and

turned the handle.

The door was locked.

Of course. It would be. They wouldn't let their best girl roam free would they? But then … how did she manage to meet with him in the past.

Jefferson pressed his ear against the door then tapped lightly. No sound came from inside at all. Then he heard a strange chanting coming from the floor below. He turned and walked back to the balcony, looking down hallway. The sound was coming from one of the doors to the left. Though he had no idea what he was going to do Jefferson hurried back down.

He could hear music now. This must be a ballroom. Perhaps some kind of debauched party was just beginning. He didn't know what to do. He couldn't just walk inside and take Carly. He wouldn't get within ten feet of her before some white man would shoot him down.

Jefferson heard a door creak somewhere behind him. He sank back into the shadows beside the staircase just before a group of people emerged from the room opposite. Three men wearing robes approached the door and Jefferson pressed himself deeper into the gloom for fear of being seen.

The doors to the ballroom opened releasing a flood of light into the stairway. Jefferson looked in, his eyes adjusting, and then opening wide. There in the centre of the room was Carly.

She was surrounded by several people all kneeling in a circle on the mosaic ballroom floor. She was wearing a long black dress and she stood before a tall table on which was opened a thick leather bound book. Her hands were raised, palms upwards as though in supplication, but her eyes remained fixed on the pages of the book.

As the other men joined her, two standing either side, one joining the kneeling congregation, Jefferson was reminded of the ceremony that Isaac had performed. Only Isaac had said something about daylight and dawn being crucial to keeping evil out of their magic. Carly was clearly involved in something more here than mere prostitution.

Jefferson realised he was trapped now in his hiding place

unless someone closed the doors to the ballroom. But the open doors didn't seem to worry these people. Jefferson wondered if everyone in the main house was now gathered in this room and this was why there was no need to keep their activity secret. He cast his mind back to the whore den below. He hadn't seen anyone down there, his entry had been easy. Too easy.

'On dis night ...' said Carly, 'when the enemy is near, we call upon the Old Ones to help protec' dis house. Hide us, your servants, oh Great One.'

Carly began to read directly from the book. They were like no language Jefferson had ever heard. The robed congregation shivered in unison as the idiom seemed to vibrate in the air. There was a substantial echo after each word, far more than the space should have created mixed with the low timbre of Carly's voice.

Jefferson felt the hairs stand up on the back of his neck. He sensed power. Real magic: nothing like the feeling he had experienced that morning in the clearing with Isaac. This voodoo was different. It was black magic: just as Isaac had said. It terrified him.

Jefferson felt an urge to run. An unnameable fear sent blood pounding through his veins. He felt like a buffalo cornered by hunters. It was a moment of clarity, that made him realise he needed to get out of there before ...

Jefferson swallowed. He forced his panic down and away. Before what? This was all just strange to him. What could the magic do to him or anyone else?

'On dis night ... when men die for their belief ... we ask the Old Ones to protec' this house ...' Carly repeated. 'Destroy all those who enter dat do not belong here.'

Carly slipped back into the strange tongue once more and the gathering raised their voices in a rehearsed response, not unlike the Christian chants that Jefferson had endured when he was a slave on the Beaugard Plantation.

Jefferson felt as though the words had pierced him. Whatever magic Carly was summoning – and he couldn't help but wonder how it was even possible after years of deliberate atheism – was presumably dangerous to any and all intruders. Himself included.

Once more he began to wonder if he should leave before things went too far. He felt a real and genuine terror, though, that froze him in his hiding place while he watched the woman he loved.

The chanting suddenly stopped. A sense of anticipation rippled through the room. Jefferson could smell it, taste it; almost like the sexual energy he could sense in the basement.

'Bring in the sacrifice,' Carly said.

A young white girl, face heavily painted, was brought in from a side room that led off from the ballroom. She was subdued but afraid. Her thin arms trembled as she was brought before Carly.

Jefferson knew about forfeits from Isaac. Other than the death of a chicken – which Isaac had explained fulfilled the magic's need for life energy – the voodoo priest did not condone the taking of human life. *This*, he had said, *was black magic and it had no place in the rituals of good men*. Jefferson realised that this girl was, in fact, the equivalent of Isaac's chicken. Jefferson didn't know what to do. He had no responsibility to anyone but Carly. He couldn't risk being discovered for some white whore who meant nothing to him.

The girl was forced to lie down on the floor. The robe she was wearing was pulled open, and Jefferson could see that she was completely naked underneath. He wondered how she had come to be in the hands of these people. She seemed so young and he suddenly he wasn't convinced that she was the whore she was made-up to be either. What if she were just some poor innocent who had been taken by these mad men? And how could Carly be involved with this?

Carly walked towards the girl. Now she was holding a dagger which glinted in the light from the chandeliers.

'You know what you have to do?' said Carly looking down at the girl.

Four men held her spread-eagled on the floor, each holding a wrist or an ankle.

The girl didn't struggle but from his vantage point Jefferson could see tears roll down the sides of her face into her blonde hair.

'Dis is my sacrifice to you, oh Great One!' Carly announced. 'My own blood sister, given in tribute. Give me the power to free dis city. Give me the power to seek revenge on those that have used me.'

The girl squealed as Carly ran the sharp blade over her wrists, cutting viciously into the arteries.

Two more whores appeared with bowls. They placed them under the wrists of the girl and her captors twisted her arms viciously to ensure the blood seeped into the containers. Jefferson knew it wouldn't take long before the girl bled out. He had been shocked to see Carly inflicting the wounds but had forced himself to remain still and unobserved. Jefferson had heard of Carly's white sister. She had been close to her. Jefferson had even believed that Carly loved her. He couldn't believe that she had now, effectively murdered her for some obscure power.

The men and women were disrobing and all stood before Carly in their naked glory. As the bowls filled the girl's captors let go of her arms and ankles and left her to bleed on the mosaic floor. Two of them brought the bowls over to the table and placed them before Carly. The knife was now lying beside the book, and Carly turned the page with a blood-stained hand. The blood stains disappeared as though the book was made of blotting paper and it had sucked in the blood.

Carly then dipped her fingers in the blood and began to perform a baptismal ceremony on the congregation. She daubed blood on the naked breasts of the women and smeared it on the erect penises of the men. When she had finished, she slipped the black dress she was wearing off her shoulders, dropping it down onto the floor.

Jefferson had never seen Carly naked before. He had wanted to marry her, have her as a wife and lover for life, not use her like a whore even though he had thought she was no virgin: none of the slaves were, the overseers saw to that. Now he was

21

fascinated with her beauty. The slender thighs, the full buttocks, the pert and round breasts that were so perfect he felt hypnotised by them. And so did, it seemed, everyone else in the room.

Jefferson began to think that this ritual was all some staged drama that would lead to sexual debauchery. It didn't though. And there was no doubt that the girl on the floor was a genuine sacrifice. Even so, Jefferson felt drawn from his hiding place, towards the ballroom and Carly. Her striking nakedness was like a magnet whose pull he couldn't resist.

Unable to stop himself, Jefferson stood and walked forward towards the open doors and into the room.

Carly was smearing blood on her own breasts and loins now. She paused to look up at Jefferson. Her eyes narrowed but she didn't stop the ritual and none of the white or black men present even acknowledged his presence.

'I'm here to take you …' Jefferson said. 'The city is fallin' to the Union Army. Soon all black slaves will be free.'

'I knows,' said Carly. 'I bin callin' this power to free us all.'

'This dark magic?'

Carly nodded. Jefferson looked around. The rest of the horde appeared frozen, as though they were statues, posed in a garden of insanity.

'I knowed when we met that you were right for me,' Carly said. 'I seen it in your eyes.'

'I love you, Carly.'

'You went to Isaac to try and help me …'

'How did you …?'

Jefferson tasted blood as Carly pressed her fingers against his lips to silence him. It woke him from his confused trance. He looked around at the people again. They were like clockwork dolls that had run down.

'What is dis?' Jefferson asked. 'Carly? It ain't right you kil' yor sissa.'

'I had to kil' something I love in order to bring the power.'

Carly backed away to the table. She stood before the book once more, arms held up, exactly as she had earlier.

'It's almost time,' she said.

Outside Jefferson thought he heard musket shots. The army would be near. What would they do when they discovered the dead white girl? What would they think of Carly working her spell, covered in blood, like the men and women around them, standing paralysed like abandoned puppets?

'They ain't frozen,' Carly said as though reading his mind. 'They is in a dif'rent time from us right now.'

'How?'

'I open'd a doorway … you might say … in another worl'. This is the worl' of the great ones. The ancient gods that hide in and around our worl' waitin' to be invited in.'

'I don't understand.'

'This book,' Carly said. 'My white daddy had it in his library. He had no idea what it was or of the power inside. I knowed. I seen it. I read it and unnerstood.'

Jefferson looked at the book for the first time. He couldn't read, the words meant nothing to him, but he approached the table, looking down at the hand-scrawled patterns that filled the page.

Jefferson stared at the markings and he too began to understand. Carly's father hadn't been killed by an uprising but something she had done using this book. It all seemed suddenly clear.

He looked back at the body of the white girl. Carly's half-sister. Whiter now that she had bled to death than she had been in life.

'You wanted to free everyone?' Jefferson said. 'Why don't I believe that is all you is doin' here?'

Carly smiled but her face wasn't the cruel sneer that had eaten into his soul nights earlier. It was warm and happy, the Carly he had fallen for.

'I done this for us to be truly together. I can't be with no ordinary man, Brent. I ain't no ordinary woman.'

'What you sayin'? All these white men … All those overseers you went with … you think I don't knows what you did to stop me bein' beaten?'

'I couldn't let them ruin a perfect vessel,' Carly said.

'*Vessel*? What you sayin'? Carly I come for you … you gunna leave with me now or not?'

Carly's eyes fell back down to the book and the text. She began to chant those alien words once more and then time seemed to restart. Around him the people were moving again. Two of the men caught hold of his arms, pulling him back from the table. Jefferson struggled and fought against them, but the words that Carly continued to speak made his limbs weak, his mind full of a deep thrumming sound and a heavy fog and choked off the sound from his voice.

The men pushed him to his knees. Head bowed, all Jefferson could see was Carly's bare feet beneath the table. The air around him shimmered as though it were above the flames of a camp fire. The temperature became unbearable. Sweat ran down his forehead into his eyes. Jefferson felt an impulse to rip away his clothing. He felt as though the fabric was suffocating him.

Carly stepped out from behind the table. Jefferson raised his head and looked up at her perfect thighs, then her sex, and finally her face. She touched his shoulder and then his head as though bestowing some strange blessing. All the time her lips moved, and that peculiar guttural language poured out, hanging in the air and burning into his soul.

Jefferson didn't feel like himself anymore. He felt disembodied, and yet the pain he felt in his skin still reached out to him. He remembered the priest on Beaugard Plantation preaching every Sunday about fire and brimstone, the heat of hell, and he thought that somehow he had found his way there. Only Satan wasn't a man, it was a woman disguised as a human.

He saw through that façade now. Carly wasn't what she appeared to be and never had been. But how this had happened he didn't know. Maybe she was some demon born in the body of a child.

'My mamma knew the old ways,' she said. 'When my daddy forced his way into her, she cursed him and me. I wasn't born

24

with a human soul. No human man can ever force me … I can only be given to a god.'

Jefferson heard her words float to him through a miasma of choking sulphuric air. His body coughed, he felt a vague discomfort as the poison choked his lungs but his spirit was separate, gone from the physical form and only attached by a vague umbilical cord of light.

He looked down on the scene. Saw Carly for the demon's whore she really was. In this state he knew so much of what had been going on. There were flashes of memory.

Carly stopping the overseers beating him, Carly going to the master and telling him to sell her to the whore house. The master was so confused by her soft voice, eyes glazed over by her hypnosis. Then Jefferson saw Carly in the bedroom upstairs. He knew this wasn't possible, but he was certain he was seeing her with her first client. The man came in, excited by her half-naked body. But Carly just touched his forehead and he stopped moving. For a whole hour the man remained sitting in a chair. Then he left, saying she was the best whore he had ever had.

Jefferson tried to call her name but his ethereal body had no capability to make the sounds his physical form could and now that was so far, far below, still kneeling at her feet.

He saw the darkness gathering around her. The words of magic still poured from her mouth like maggots swarming from a dead body. They ate at his soul and they pushed him farther away from the world of the living.

The black, roiling shadow thing that grew around Carly was now dwarfing Jefferson's body.

Carly looked up and smiled. Jefferson wondered if she could see him there, if she wanted him to see everything that was happening.

'It'll be you in body only …' Carly said. A rapt, fanatical grin spread across her face.

The darkness stretched over Jefferson's form. He felt a stabbing pain as the thing swarmed him. Then it was as though a thousand bees stung his skin simultaneously. His body jerked in protest. The thing squeezed him, forcing his mouth to open as it pushed the air from his lungs. But as Jefferson's body heaved in new air, so it drew in the essence of this demon shadow.

Jefferson tried to yell once more, but he was growing more distant from the world of the living. The shadow disappeared inside him. Jefferson felt pain once more. This was the awful agony of his soul being expelled from his corporeal form.

He floated as high as the ceiling now. Carly picked up the blood-stained knife and pointed it upwards towards him.

Jefferson screamed inside as he felt the last tie sever and knew that his body was no longer a part of his existence.

The Jefferson-demon stood now. It looked around, as though seeing the men and women around him for the first time. It took the knife from Carly's fingers, and without warning, plunged it deep into one of the men nearby. As the man fell, the demon latched onto the wound, drinking and lapping at the blood.

When the blood stopped flowing, the demon attacked another worshipper, and another. Bleeding them all dry.

Carly stood, waiting until the demon was satisfied. Above, silently weeping, Jefferson watched his own body committing the atrocities. His mind screamed in denial as, having fed, the creature turned to Carly and forced her willingly over the table like a dog taking a bitch.

Carly screamed as the demon used Jefferson's body to pleasure her. She laughed and cried until her own orgasm shuddered through her, and at that point, the demon poured his seed inside her.

Jefferson wished his mind would go elsewhere, that he could stop seeing the woman he loved being violated by something using his own form. This wasn't what he had wanted for her, or himself.

When their violent mating was done the demon took Carly's hand and led her naked towards the foyer. Jefferson tried to follow, but sensing him still there, Carly paused, looked up and raised her hand towards him.

'Stay,' she said.

Jefferson tried to fight her will but he found himself unable to move.

Frozen in this one place, he could sense that Carly and the demon had left the house but there was nothing he could do but stay where she had left him.

Around him, the air seemed to boil and move as though, separated by a thin veil, monstrous gods held him in place with their unknowable powers.

Time slipped. Jefferson became aware of movement below. A group of union soldiers entered the room. They looked at the slaughtered bodies and shook their heads.

'Looks like some sort of madness went horribly wrong,' said one of the soldiers.

'Bad voodoo,' said another man as he entered the ballroom. Jefferson recognised Matthew. The black man seemed to be helping the soldiers.

'Sorry,' said the first soldier. 'We would have saved these poor slaves if we could have.'

'I knows it. We is glad you're here anyways,' said Matthew. 'I only hopes my friend managed to get his girl outta here before this went down.'

Jefferson watched them go.

There was nothing he could do. He was trapped and held there, incorporeal, powerless and hopeless. In his mind he screamed and screamed.

But the Great One, the elder god which had empowered Carly, and which had allowed his own body to be possessed by one of its nameless creatures, just tightened its grip.

Forever.

Of Gods and Blood

For Teri Sears

'My name is Teri. Teri Sears,' said the woman.

Lucy Collins looked up from the computer screen and met a pair of intense brown eyes.

Teri had shoulder length red hair, with a tantalising wave that reminded Lucy of the style of Hollywood movie stars of old. Teri had a young and beautiful face, chiselled cheekbones that any supermodel would die for and large eyes that exuded a strange amount of warmth mixed with a dark intelligence that Lucy likened to that of a predator.

'Can I help you?' Lucy asked.

'I was told you could,' Teri said.

Lucy waited. She was not accustomed to leading conversations. No she preferred some else to do that.

The silence was awkward for a moment then Teri, predictably, broke it.

'I was told ...' she began. 'That you are an expert on blood.'

Lucy blinked but did not reply. Underneath her calm exterior she was growing impatient. What did the woman want?

'You *are* Doctor Collins?' Teri said.

The previously confident expression was now nervous, as though Teri was afraid that she had made a mistake after all.

Lucy mulled over how predictable humans were. It hadn't taken long to rattle this seemingly confident woman.

'I am Lucy Collins,' she said but not because she was taking pity on Teri, but more that curiosity – her greatest weakness – was finally getting the better of her.

Teri sighed. 'Good. I thought I was speaking to the wrong person.'

'What can I do for you?'

'I have a blood sample for you to analyse,' Teri said.

She rooted about in her purse for a moment, and produced a small phial. Lucy realised immediately that this was something she would be interested in. The blood – unless this was some kind of joke – was blue.

She took the sample from Teri's outstretched fingers.

'Blood?' she said playing the game of surprise. She unstoppered the phial and sniffed. There was the strange metallic tang that was always the tell.

'Found at a crime scene,' Teri said.

'You're FBI then?' said Lucy.

Teri nodded.

'Who else has seen this?' Lucy said.

'Just our lab. They did enough to identify it. But your name came up as the specialist.'

Lucy looked down into the liquid as though her gaze could unravel its mystery.

'Have you ever seen anything like this before?' Teri said.

Lucy didn't answer.

'Only, my colleagues were definite that you should see it.'

Lucy's mind cast back to some years earlier. Yes, she had seen blue blood before. A small splash at a crime scene where a young man had been ripped apart by some unnameable force. That investigation had ended with no real result. The death, and the perpetrator, remained a mystery and the case remained unsolved. But Lucy had the data and it would be easy to cross check that sample with this, considerably larger one.

'So much of it …' she murmured.

'Yes,' Teri said. 'It was a veritable blue blood bath.'

Lucy gave a tight smile in response to Teri's attempt at humour. If this was taken from the same killer as before, then this was indeed no laughing matter.

'Leave it with me,' Lucy said.

Teri placed her contact card on Lucy's desk.

'Send the report to my email address, but call me if you want to know more.'

Teri left and Lucy looked up to stare after her. She was wearing a smart skirt suit, sensible heels, but Teri didn't walk like an FBI agent. She walked like a fashion model – one foot crossing in front of the other.

In the lab Lucy prepared the first sample of the blood for examination using a high quality clean glass slide 75mm by 25mm and with 1mm thickness. She placed the blood drop 1cm from the end of the slide and then covered it with another sterile slide before placing it under the microscope. Her computer screen filled with the zoomed in image of the blood: it showed no sign of coagulation. She searched for the usual red and white blood cells – found none. This was, she already knew, not human blood.

Lucy picked up her mobile phone and dialled Teri's number.

'Agent Sears? This is Lucy Collins. I'd like to see the crime scene.'

The building was tall. As big as an aircraft hanger, and on the upper tier a ring of broken windows surrounded the building. Lucy suspected that the top floor had once been office space for the owners of this building, but what it had been used for she could only guess.

A black sedan was parked near an open door. Teri must already be here, perhaps with some of her other colleagues, to ensure that Lucy did not contaminate the crime scene.

Lucy opened the door of her car and climbed out. It was a small European vehicle, easy to park in the city, unlike the local monstrosities that Americans favoured, and it was right hand drive. She closed the driver's door and went around to the boot – *trunk* – she corrected herself. Then she removed her forensic bag and extracted her coveralls from a holdall. She pulled them on over her clothing, and placed covers over her shoes. Once ready she picked up her bag and walked around to the open entrance of the building.

She passed through the door and a peculiar tingling sensation went up her back. The door and the threshold felt *alien*.

'Agent Sears,' she called.

Lucy walked confidently into the building. The space was huge, derelict. A warehouse space in the middle of nowhere. She had researched the address, but could find no record of a previous owner, or what the place had originally been used for. It was as though it didn't exist in the real world, though it was clearly visible on the satellite mapping system.

'Ah, Doctor Collins!'

Lucy turned to see Teri emerging from an office space at the other side of the building.

'This way,' Teri called.

Lucy's nerves twitched. She was not given to flights of fancy, or phobias, but this place unnerved her and she felt like a fly being beguiled by the gleam of diamond raindrops on a spider's web. Even so she walked forward with confidence.

'I was surprised to hear from you so soon,' Teri said.

'It's not every day that I'm brought alien blood,' Lucy said.

'Alien?'

'Not human. Ergo alien at this point.'

'The blood isn't human? Then what is it?' Teri asked.

'I don't know,' said Lucy. 'Perhaps this crime scene will give me some clue. You didn't tell me the circumstances in which it was found.'

'No. I didn't,' Teri said. 'Through here.'

Lucy followed Teri over yet another threshold. This one had the same essence as the first, but stronger. Lucy was beginning to wonder about the warehouse. Its location, on a ley line in the middle of the desert, was certainly unusual. But Lucy had never felt the ley line energy so enhanced before. So obvious. As though each doorway was an entrance to another time, another place. A void that should not be crossed.

'How did you know a crime had been committed here?' Lucy asked.

'It was reported by a local sheriff.'

'Talk me through it.'

They were walking through a former office. A broken table rotted in the corner beside a metal filing cabinet that was more rust than metal. The drawers were all half open, as though the occupants had left this place in a hurry. Lucy could smell rat piss and faeces and rubbish and the remnants of office furniture were scattered about.

'Well, he – the sheriff – called in that there had been a murder and his people couldn't handle it. That's the very circumstances that bring the FBI in,' Teri explained as though she thought Lucy had no understanding of their procedures.

'And you were the agent sent to investigate.'

'Yes.'

They crossed another doorway. Lucy shuddered. They had entered another part of the warehouse. A large open space, not offices like the central rooms had been. She looked up at the cracked and broken windows: very little light filtered in from outside. To the casual eye there was nothing unusual to see, but Lucy's senses were assaulted by the metallic smell of fresh blood. Blood that refused to react to the atmosphere. Blood that did not congeal.

Her eyes fell on the darkest corner. There. Yes, this was the place where something strange had happened. Something that Teri appeared to be reluctant to explain.

'Talk,' Lucy said.

'Over there,' she pointed. 'We found *something* over there.'

Lucy's eyes had adapted quickly and she could now see the charred wall. She sniffed the air pushing back the overwhelming blood smell in order to distinguish something else. Sulphur. Oh yes.

'Must I investigate or are you going to explain Agent Sears?' Lucy said.

'We … found a creature. You see your comment about *alien* wasn't wrong.'

'Where is the corpse now?' Lucy asked.

'Corpse? Oh I see. You think it was dead? No the creature is very much alive, Doctor Collins.'

'There's another smell here,' Lucy said. She had taken in the information that the thing still lived, but did not respond with surprise while she processed everything she could see and smell.

'It just smells like … filth to me,' Teri said.

But of course it would. Teri was human, of that Lucy was certain, and of course the FBI agent had no clue that Lucy herself was anything but.

'I have a keen sense of smell. There's the blood, sulphur and …'

Teri had been further in the room than Lucy and now she turned back to look at her.

'And?'

'Human fear.'

Lucy moved away from the office door and closer to the dark corner. She peered into the shadowy depths trying to make out any shapes, but her usually perfect sight could make nothing out of the foggy gloom.

Moving away from the corner, at the centre of the room, Lucy felt the chill. The cold seeped into her bones through the concrete floor and a frosty wave of air blew around her legs. She squinted into the darkness, then let out the breath she had been holding.

The murky air shifted: something moved.

'It's still here …' Lucy said.

'Yes!' gasped Teri.

Lucy was aware of Teri backing away from the black void in front of them. Unlike the FBI agent she was not afraid.

Lucy stepped forward in a calculated decision to show her strength. There was a ripple of movement, and now Lucy could make out a bulbous shape, and long, thick appendages that moved in a sinuous flow as the creature shifted. Like a giant octopus, or some creature from the deep. This could not be a land dweller …

Lucy moved closer, ever mindful of those tentacle limbs. Now she could see the pulsing suckers at the tip of each one. She saw the crease of the throbbing gills, sucking in something from the Earth's atmosphere that was somehow feeding this monstrous thing whatever it needed to stay alive.

Her foot slid on something wet. The smell of red and white blood cells, newly coagulated, assaulted Lucy's sensitive senses. She glanced down at the floor. There was some indescribable gore underfoot and it grew like a gruesome blanket covering the concrete and the creature. The remains were most definitely human.

She glanced quickly back at Teri. The agent stayed back. Her arms were wrapped around herself as though she were trying to keep the cold from entering her.

'This is a trap,' Lucy said. Then she gave a harsh cynical laugh.

'Yes Doctor Collins. I'm sorry. You're just collateral damage.'

'For what? At least tell me that?' Lucy said.

'A god!'

Teri's voice was full of exultation. Lucy risked a glance away from the creature and back at Teri, whose hands were now clasped before her as though in prayer.

'This is no god, no higher being,' Lucy said.

'It is. One of the ancient gods. I brought it here through time and space, from another realm. Another dimension. Its purpose, when it is fully healed, will be to grant my every wish.'

'Oh Agent Sears, you are not the first to believe in gods and I'm sure you won't be the last. This one will trick you. One day you'll be the fodder, just as surely as all of the victims you've fed it so far.'

'No! He speaks to me. He tells me of his other world. He'll rule our planet; I will be by his side.'

'Whatever floats your boat,' Lucy scoffed.

She turned and ran then, back towards Teri and the exit, but the Agent, foolishly, blocked her way.

Lucy halted when she saw the gun. So that was how it would be. She must walk willingly to her death, or be shot trying to escape.

'Have you ever met a devil?' Lucy asked.

'No more stalling,' Teri said. 'Turn around. Go to your

destiny with dignity. Know this Doctor, your death shall not be for nothing.'

Lucy smiled. Her teeth were whiter than Teri recalled ever seeing, and sharper than a human could have. It did not faze her however. She had a god on her side.

'I'm no innocent,' Lucy sneered. 'An unfitting sacrifice for any god, or demon. This one though ... he is an old one, as you say. Man once worshiped such as he. Then the gateway to their hellish dimension was lost. How did you find the way in?'

Teri wanted to share her secret: after all Lucy would never live to tell the tale.

'An ancient book – once owned by H P Lovecraft. Oh his tales were not entirely fiction. Lovecraft wrote of the things he worshipped but feared to raise.'

'His words were warnings. Anyone knows that. Howard was a wise man I always thought.'

'You speak as though you know him, when really you waste my time.'

'When you have lived as long as I, you meet many people.'

Lucy's smile widened. There was no denying the teeth now, long fangs that draped over her bottom lip.

Teri took an involuntary step back.

'I'll give your god indigestion,' Lucy said. 'Are you sure you want to risk that?'

A movement, the slivering of a thousand snakes, drew Lucy's attention away from Teri.

The creature was becoming impatient.

'How can it even survive here?' Lucy asked.

'With ever kill it evolves. One day soon it will take on the form of a man,' Teri said.

'Or woman ...'

The thought was inconceivable to Teri's jaded mind. 'He shall be king of the world ...'

'Yes. And you his queen. As you've said.'

Lucy grew bored of the game. She would have to make her move soon. The creature behind her, be it god or alien, would not wait forever, but she still wasn't certain how to send it back.

'I don't believe this thing is really from another dimension,' she said. 'Where is this book?'

As Lucy had hoped, the book was near, and Teri's eyes betrayed its location with a flick of uncertainty.

'Don't you realise nothing good comes from releasing a genie from its bottle?' Lucy said then she dived aside towards the very place that Teri's gaze had fallen: a rickety old stool at the other end of the warehouse.

Bullets fired, some found their mark, but Lucy did not stop until she had her hands on the ancient grimoire.

It was thick and leather-bound; one touch confirmed to Lucy that it was covered in human skin. Teri screamed and ran forward, her gun still raised.

Bullets pounded into Lucy's chest. She was flung against the wall with the impact. The derelict structure rattled. Glass fell from the windows all around her.

Lucy lay in a heap, the book clutched to her chest.

Teri was stronger than she looked; perhaps the beast had already endowed her with some special power. She picked Lucy up, carrying her across her arms towards the beast as it shifted and roiled in excitement. The book was still clasped against the unconscious woman's chest.

'You said she was special. Will her blood complete the transformation?' Teri asked.

A tightening behind her eyes indicated that the creature was about to communicate and she heard his answer inside her head. Its words brought pain, and ecstasy, a combination that sparked a flow of sexual energy through Teri's body.

She fell to her knees, weakened by the connection. Lucy's body tumbled from her arms and rolled.

Lucy watched Teri through her eyelashes. The woman was writhing about as though in ecstasy and Lucy briefly wondered if this was why the woman had been so foolish. For the several hundred years that she had lived, Lucy had learnt that humans would do anything for sexual depravity.

The book lay half under her and she touched it with a bloodied hand, trying to ignore the sting of her healing flesh as it worked the bullets out of her chest.

The creature obviously did not understand what Lucy was. She was an immortal, but above all a predator in her own right, and Lucy's fascination with blood was not merely a hobby, but an essential part of her life, for she needed it to live on.

Certain that Teri wouldn't move, Lucy shifted her weight, pulling the book free. It opened at her touch. She used her telekinetic skills to connect with the grimoire. After all, a vampire was a close cousin to a witch.

The pages flicked with a whirl of air and then the book fell open to reveal the required spell.

For this was indeed a spell: the creature had been summoned from another dimension by Teri's reading. Not that Lucy expected the Agent to have completely understood what she had done. In reality the book would have seduced her, just as it had tried years before when Howard Lovecraft had first laid his unsuspecting hands on it.

Lucy and he had been lovers at the time, and she had recognised it for what it was. As one of her Renfields, Howard had the ability to resist the call. He had been a fitting keeper for it at the time. When Lucy had tired of him she had given no more thought to the grimoire, just as she had never thought of Lovecraft again once that she had moved on – until now.

But of course the book had to have fallen into receptive hands after that. Lucy wouldn't have cared either way, she was not the protector of humanity, and cared little for their foolish endeavours. However, the creature had sought her out. Therefore, the grimoire had not forgotten its brief contact with Lucy.

'Ish r'y. Th'm m'r,' she chanted.

The cold wind she had briefly experienced began to pick up. Lucy glanced at Teri. The woman was in some form of trance, eyes rolled back into her head, arms outstretched as though she were about to be crucified. Lucy saw her as no immediate threat and therefore continued her chant as she read for the first time from the book.

'In anima. Thr'er. Dulas, I'm ich.'

Teri slumped as the creature's hold on her mind released. Lucy felt the monstrous life form now shift its weight. It was being drawn back into the sulphur-covered wall – its previous entry point – but it would not go without a fight.

A long thick tendril lashed at Lucy. Grabbing the book, she flung herself aside.

The words were flowing from her lips unaided now as the spell began to work itself. There was no going back as long as her mouth moved and the chant reversed the opening of the portal. Then Teri began to move. She pulled herself up, crawling towards Lucy, a maniacal laugh on her lips. White foam pooled around her lips. She was a rabid beast, a victim of the cruelty of her master's hold and the insanity wrought by contact with the book.

Lucy raised the leather bound book between them as though to ward her off, but Teri came at her, gun raised.

Bullets burst from the barrel, the loud shots hurt Lucy's ears as the noise was emphasised in the turbulent wind. The warehouse rattled around them, more glass fell from the windows. Doors flew off creaky, rusted hinges. The wind swirled around Lucy, pulling at her blonde hair, ripping at her clothing. But she stood her ground. The bullets hit the whirlwind around Lucy and fell to the floor, failing to reach their mark.

The creature heaved itself forward, away from the now open void. It had to go back, yet still it railed against, as though its crimes were not an injustice to humankind. It screeched its fury as its expulsion. And as it did so, Teri hurled herself at Lucy.

The wind caught her, buffeting her backwards towards the void and the creature that wrapped its appendages around the warehouse's supporting girders to hold onto this dimension despite the spell that wouldn't be denied.

Teri was blown off her feet, her body crashed against the monster; the thing released one of the girders and grabbed at this unexpected morsel, pulling her towards its gaping maw.

Teri screamed. 'Not me!'

The creature's greed was its ultimate downfall. As it released its secure hold, the power of the spell prised it away from the remaining girders. Then the wind did its work. It swirled away now from Lucy, and scooped up the crushed body of Teri, throwing its full force against the creature as it fought it backwards towards the void.

Lucy stopped chanting. She fell to her knees. She felt battered and bruised even as her incredible body healed itself.

The wind had dropped as the creature fell back into its own world, taking with it the helpless body of Agent Sears.

Lucy drew in a hard breath. Her ribs had been broken as the bullets had ripped into her, but now they were healing and the fresh air she sucked in refilled her collapsed lungs. It was just as well that a vampire didn't really need to breathe to continue living.

She closed the book and stood once more. The warehouse was a shambles, its structure undermined by the turbulent power that had opened and then closed the portal. Lucy leapt to her feet and dived aside just as one of the steel girders broke awake from its moorings. The roof fell in soon after but by then Lucy was outside and back in her car.

Lucy patted the soil back down on the grave before glancing back at the headstone.

Howard Phillips Lovecraft
August 20 1890
March 15 1937
I Am Providence

'Look after it Howard, there is no safer place for this book than with you, dead or alive.'

Fall Out

Chris pulled the ribbon from the windshield of his brand new 1953 Chrysler New Yorker. The car was polished shiny red with a canvas soft-top that dropped back into the boot space. A matching leather protector clipped over the back of the vehicle and the dash was real mahogany. It shone with the newness of recently varnished wood and Chris could smell the soothing aroma of the leather as he opened the door and climbed into the driver's seat.

'What do you think?' asked his Dad.

'I can't believe it. Really? This is for me?'

'Sure, son. Happy Birthday. It's not every day that my first born turns sixteen. Why don't you take it for a spin?'

The engine was loud as it burst into life. Chris released the brake and pulled out of the driveway, taking the car carefully out onto the street. Chris loved the car. It cruised smoothly, almost as though it was driving itself. He knew he would be the talk of the high school and – even better – he was now certain to get the girl of his dreams.

Ever since his father had started a new job at the base, out in the Nevada desert, they had seemed to have money to burn. In recent months his mother had completely redecorated the whole house, changed the furniture, and she was also driving a new car. Chris wanted for nothing and now he had friends and a social life that he had never believed possible.

Sometimes it seemed as though overnight he had gone from spotty geek to Mr Popular: all because they had money. And Chris was generous with it too. Buying cokes at the local diner, handing out dimes for the jukebox, and even on occasion passing out cans of beer he had taken from his father's stash in the ice-box in the garage. No one questioned what he did, least of all his folks. They were all glad that the dark days had ended.

After touring his neighbourhood, Chris drove the car back into the drive, locked the door and headed to the house. There, his father was talking about his favourite subject. He was obsessed with the Russians and the potential threat they posed. Chris supposed it was because he worked for the government.

'Almost a decade since the War,' Dad said, 'and the country is thriving again. But I wouldn't trust those Reds. That's why my work is so important.'

'What do you do at the base, Dad?' Chris asked.

'That's classified, son. But maybe one day you'll find out. Maybe one day you'll join the team.'

Chris's mother frowned, but he barely noticed it as he walked past her to switch on the new television set. He loved watching the evening programmes, that and the fact that they were the only people in their street to actually own a TV. He settled down on the couch as the news started.

Mom and Dad went out on the veranda, sat down on the wicker two-seater and looked out at the new car as it stood, gleaming in the drive-way.

'Well, at least he's happy,' said Mom.

'Gotta keep your kids happy,' said Dad.

It was a warm evening and Mom sipped home-made lemonade while Dad chugged a cold beer. After a while Chris came outside and admired his car too. The sight of it brought him joy, but also an odd feeling: a kind of worry that burrowed deep into his stomach.

'Dad?'

'Yes, son?'

'You know all this talk about another war? That the "A" bomb could be dropped on us at any time? Do you think that will really happen?'

Dad was quiet for a time, then he looked up at Chris over his beer can. 'I don't really think so. But just in case, that's why we have the shelter.'

Chris cast a glance over his shoulder at the house. From the front he couldn't see the lead-lined shutters that covered the entrance down into a blast shelter, but his mind's eye visualised it. He imagined the shutters opening as the family raced across the lawn. He saw them all cramming inside: Mom, Dad and his sister, Myra. The weeks, months, or even years might have to pass before it was safe to emerge because Dad said that radiation was something to fear even after the devastation of an explosion. Chris didn't know what worried him more, the concept of a nuclear explosion or the thought of passing through the fallout shelter doors and heading down into the deep, dark bowels of the earth.

'I'm going to the drive-in tomorrow,' Chris told them, trying to take his mind off his morbid thoughts. 'I'm taking a date. I'll need some money.'

Dad reached into his pocket and pulled out a roll of notes. He peeled off five twenties and held them out.

A hundred bucks, Chris thought. That was enough for several dates.

'You have to treat the ladies right,' said Dad.

Mom said nothing. She sipped her lemonade. Chris noted that she never drank beer but sometimes, when they had a dinner party, she would like to drink fancy wine that made her giggle like a teenager. At those times he would go to his room and play his 45's on his Victrola because he didn't like to see her like that.

'Thanks, Dad,' he said as he took the money, but his heart hurt a little: it almost felt like he was losing a piece of his soul. He stuffed it quickly into his trouser pocket and tried to ignore the burn that seeped through the fabric into his leg. He couldn't explain the oddness of the moment or the feeling of anxiety that accompanied every gift. It was as if he felt that he would have to pay some awful price for their current happiness.

'Who's the lucky girl?' asked Myra.

Chris turned around to see his sister lurking in the doorway. She barely surfaced from her room these days. She was younger than him by a year, but Chris always felt as though Myra knew more about the world than he did. He didn't know why.

'Elizabeth Penrose,' Chris said.

'Fancy,' said Myra.

'Yeah. She is.'

'I'm so proud. My boy courting a Penrose,' said Mom. 'This is worth celebrating, don't you think, Charles?'

Dad nodded. 'Sure, Lucy. Whatever you want.'

'We'll have a dinner party. Maybe we can invite the Penroses …'

Chris went back inside the house and left them planning his future. He didn't point out to them that this was only one date. Nothing more might come of it. Although he did like Elizabeth. A lot. And he was hoping that the new car would impress her tomorrow.

'Chris, don't you find it odd sometimes?' asked Myra following him into the kitchen.

'Find what odd?'

'How good things have become. Why, I remember only last year Dad could barely pay the bills and now suddenly …'

Chris felt that knot in his stomach again. A sick, dark fear scurried around the recesses of his subconscious. The answer to a riddle that he just couldn't find but knew all the same, hid somewhere there. He tried to shake the feeling away. He opened the fridge and took out a beer, snapping open the top.

'You know that's illegal, right?' said Myra.

Chris couldn't even bring himself to tell her to shut up. He was rapidly learning he could do as he pleased. No one stopped him. In fact his father encouraged him by indulging his every wish. His new car was proof of that. But still.

The thought of the car made his heart lurch and not in a good way. It was the sinking feeling of the drowning man who is waiting for the final moment to take away the screaming pain in his lungs. It was the inconsolable cry of a frightened infant in the night. It was the dread of death that faces the dying.

Chris shook his head, sipped the beer and the fear receded but Myra didn't leave him.

'I just feel …' she said.

'What?'

'Scared somehow,' Myra shrugged. 'I guess you think I'm crazy.'

Chris said nothing but his eyes fell on the kitchen window. The yard was lit up all night with security lights and they illuminated the shelter. Chris shuddered.

Myra moved next to him and looked out. 'You feel it too. I know you do.'

'We have everything to be grateful for, and nothing to fear,' Chris said, but he didn't believe his own words.

Myra didn't answer and the two of them stood there looking out the window until the lights suddenly went off in the yard. Their trance broke. Dad was standing at the door, his hand on the outdoor light switch.

'Myra, don't you think you ought to go to bed?' Dad said. 'School tomorrow.'

Myra slunk away, but not before she cast another glance at the window. It was too dark to see the shelter but somehow Chris knew she felt its presence there. Just as he did.

Chris and Myra had never seen inside the shelter. All they knew was that one day, soon after Dad started his new job, a team of workmen arrived and began to dig up the ground at the back of the yard.

'It's a fallout shelter,' Dad had explained. 'When this is done we'll have enough space and supplies down there to last for months if the Reds jump the gun and send out the "A" Bomb.'

Chris had been excited at first; he saw the shelter as a new place where he could hang out. Maybe he would be able to use it as a den when his friends came over. But as the structure began to take shape, he started to feel odd.

One time he went out into the garden as the workmen laid the foundations. A deep hole had been dug into the ground at least 30 feet down, and Chris could see a pattern that resembled a spider or octopus taking shape. Most of the yard was exposed, but he had heard his father say that once the shelter was built the lawn would be laid again on top of it.

'Why's it like that?' he had asked one of the men.

The men all turned their heads in unison and stared at him. They had blank, empty, expressions on their faces.

'Come away from there, Chris,' his mother had called from

the back door. 'You shouldn't bother the men while they are working.'

Chris stayed long enough to see the men return to work. He never heard them chatter or laugh and joke. He thought they were the oddest construction workers he had ever seen. Of course they were all probably military and sworn not to talk to anyone during the work. After all the fallout shelter had to be some perk of Dad's job, didn't it?

Sometimes in his dreams he found himself in the garden looking down into the foundations. He would be standing swaying at the edge, a terrible vertigo sweeping up like an invisible claw that wanted to pull him down into the dust. He would try to back away but his ankles felt as though they were held by some imperceptible force. He felt that he had lead feet and knew somehow that this always happened in dreams when you tried to escape something horrible, or run from some imagined terror. So he rarely fought the feeling. All he could do was gaze down into the pit.

Sometimes in the dreams he would see something slowly moving down there, a dark shape that was more shadow than it was form. At those times he would half close his eyes, squinting down into the gloom. He saw ... he saw ...

After he woke up screaming Chris couldn't bring the creature's image up into his mind, but he knew it was monstrous. He stayed away from the workmen after that, but the dreams still haunted him.

Chris had felt ill and sick during most of the construction. He even noted how pale his mother looked, how Myra began to stay out more at her girlfriend's house, and how his dad, usually patient, had become snappy and irritable. It was as though a thick fog of misery floated around the house and land. The open hole held such terror for him that he couldn't even bear to go into the yard anymore.

There was a palpable change in the atmosphere when the iron doors were fitted on the shelter. Dad turned the key, locking the doors before the workmen had finished packing up their equipment and tools.

After that life returned to some semblance of normality, but Chris didn't get any permanent relief. The discomfort was always there. The fear of some unknown bogeyman sat permanently in the pit of his stomach, and choked him while he slept. His Dad and Mom returned to normal, but Myra didn't: she distanced herself still further from the family.

The strange thing was Chris had never seen his parents open the door again. He even wondered if they had bothered to put emergency supplies down there. He sure hadn't seen them do it. But of course he didn't know what his mother did when he was out all day at school.

It was easy to forget his fears though because the benefits of their new position outweighed any of the strangeness he felt. The money was a big issue. They quite literally wanted for nothing and this did seem to make his parents happier.

'You okay, son?' asked Dad.

Chris snapped out of his reverie only to find Dad standing by the fridge, beer in hand.

'Yes,' said Chris because this was the expected answer.

'You happy?'

Chris nodded. He couldn't choke out another 'yes' no matter how hard he tried.

Dad frowned, then turned and walked away.

The next day, on his official birthday, Chris drove his new car to school. As his friends gathered around the convertible in the car park, he briefly forgot his worries and fears and enjoyed the feeling of owning the vehicle.

'That's a cool car,' said Elizabeth sliding up to him. 'I'm looking forward to our date later. And I have a birthday present for you too, but that can wait until this evening.'

'You're a lucky guy,' said Eugene, one of his new friends who happened to be the captain of the football team. 'Here you go buddy. Happy birthday.'

Chris took the gift from Eugene. He opened it up to find a football shirt.

'You're our new quarter back,' said Eugene patting him on the shoulder.

Chris was on top of the world for the whole day. He shook away the craziness that had followed him for the last six months. His life was changing so rapidly that he could barely keep up. No sooner had he done the try-outs and he was in the team, in the favoured position. He had always thought he was no good at sports, but the try-out day proved him wrong. When he had gone out onto the pitch he could just play. It was easy. He just couldn't believe his luck.

He thought back to the night before and realised that today he would have no trouble saying 'yes' if his dad asked if he was happy. He was. All that he had ever wanted was miraculously coming true for him.

It's ridiculous to be worried by our good fortune, he thought. *Things happen because they are meant too.*

He went into History Class and sat down to take the test. As he turned the page, and glanced down at the first question, Chris knew the answer. In fact the test went extremely well. He knew ALL the answers and he finished long before everyone else. As the bell sounded, he packed up and the thought crossed his mind that his paper would be graded an 'A'.

I feel that lucky today.

In his next class his Math teacher took him aside. 'Chris, I've noticed how hard you've been working lately. You seem to have natural talent with figures.'

It was all so easy. Maybe he did have talent and had only just realised it. Everything he did that day just went right, without any apparent real effort. So, when he got into his car and drove home, he was on a high that he had never experienced before.

'So what's this movie about?' asked Elizabeth.

'It's called *The Beast from 20,000 Fathoms*,' Chris said.

'Sounds scary.'

Chris put his arm around Elizabeth's shoulder, 'Hey ... I'm

here if you get scared.'

The movie started after twenty minutes of adverts. During this time Chris bought popcorn and soda for them both and they were settled and ready when the credits began to roll.

He noticed how Elizabeth tensed silently when the creature first emerged from the sea but other than that she wasn't really scared. Chris, however, found the concept to be utterly terrifying. He couldn't quite place why, but the idea of a government experiment creating a monster seemed to be such a possibility.

Chris's mind drifted away from the film for a while. An idea formed in his mind, a terrifying thought about his father's job. What exactly did they *do* out there in the desert? His mind's eye imagined the base even though he had never seen it and his father working in some sterile lab, experimenting on a large creature in a huge tank.

A surge of panic rushed into his face and cheeks. His heart began to pound and he had a brief flash of memory of the monster in his nightmares: it was a large tentacled being of grotesque shape and size.

'You okay?' asked Elizabeth.

Chris snapped back into the now and realised that he had fallen asleep during the film. He hoped he hadn't been snoring.

'Sure,' he said sitting upright.

Elizabeth smiled at him and turned her eyes back to the screen.

After the film finished, Elizabeth let Chris kiss her lightly on the lips before they followed the other cars out of the drive-in.

'Do you think our government would be capable of that?' Chris asked her as they drove back through town.

'No, of course not. I wouldn't put it past the Russians though,' she said.

Chris noted that she spoke like his parents when discussing the government. They all felt that President Eisenhower could do no wrong and that the enemy still lived overseas. Since the War patriotism was the norm. The movie showed a different view though, one that made him think that their world may not be so perfect and it had fed somehow into those ridiculous dreams he was having.

'We're so lucky,' Elizabeth said. 'We live in a great country that cares about its people. My dad says times are better now than they have ever been. He thinks we're going to "prosper".'

'What do you mean?' Chris asked.

'Well I heard him say something to my Mom, about how almost all the sacrifices have been made. Now we're all going to reap the rewards.'

Chris felt that odd prickle that irritated his nerves and sent a shudder up his spine. He didn't like the way she had used the word 'Sacrifice'.

'Did your folks mind that you were coming out with me?' he asked changing the subject.

'No. Dad said that somehow it was fitting,' Elizabeth said.

He parked up at the Penrose house and walked Elizabeth to the door. It was ten pm, the time her father had said he wanted her home and Chris didn't want to make the mistake of upsetting him on their first date. He wanted to be the perfect boyfriend. Elizabeth deserved that.

'Goodnight,' Elizabeth said as she opened the door. Then she was gone and Chris was left standing on their porch looking at the screen door.

He was somewhat deflated as he climbed back in his car. It was only a short journey home but he noted how quiet the streets were. He had never seen them this empty before.

His mind flashed back to the movie, his short sleep, and the dream creature. The image of it hadn't faded like it usually did. Chris could see it clearer the more he focused on it. He tried not to think about it, but failed.

As he turned the car into his street he felt a strange and irrational terror. *I should turn around now. Drive right out of this place and never come back.*

He pulled the car over to the curb and looked down the street at his house. He could see a light on in the lounge as he might expect at this time. His folks weren't on the porch though and the rest of the house was in darkness. Even Myra's window was in full darkness and she often stayed up late reading.

Palpitations, anxiety and total panic rushed through him in a matter of seconds. *What's wrong with me? Am I losing my mind?* He knew his fear was irrational but he couldn't shake it.

He waited for a few minutes longer. The street was eerily quiet. He turned his head to look at the house beside him. It was in total darkness and it was only ten fifteen.

Mentally shaking himself Chris put the car in gear and slowly moved forward towards his drive, but again an unreasonable panic consumed him. Sweat poured from his brow as he parked the car. He was paralysed with terror as he looked up at the porch screen. He couldn't understand why the thought of being home frightened him so much. Surely he had nothing to fear here? Despite his rational thoughts he was incapable of getting out of the car and walking inside the house and he just didn't know why.

He placed his head in his hands and wept.

'Come on son,' said Dad from the door.

Chris looked up, but his eyes were misty and the shape in the dark didn't quite look like his Dad.

'Come on, Chris,' said his mother.

'Don't fight this,' said another voice and Chris turned his head to find Abraham Penrose at the side of his car.

They were wearing strange clothing. Long black robes that had hoods and as Chris looked around he found he was surrounded by all of his neighbours.

Penrose opened the car door and took his arm. Chris didn't have the strength to fight, even though he didn't understand what was happening on some level he still realised that this whole thing was wrong, unfair. He hadn't done anything to deserve it.

They didn't go inside the house as he expected, Penrose led him round the side and Chris came face to face with his mother as she opened the gate.

'Mom …?' he pleaded but she turned away and said nothing.

They walked over the lawn. Chris thought he could feel

something under the earth, a vibration. His anxiety increased to brain snapping levels. He was surrounded now by all of his neighbours and as they entered the yard they spread out into a crescent around the front of the fallout shelter.

Chris tried to resist when he realised that Penrose was taking him towards the heavy lead doors; he didn't want to see inside the shelter. That curiosity had long since passed. But Penrose wasn't letting him go. He tugged and pulled, bruising the skin on Chris' arm as he all but dragged him over to the doors.

'Brethren. We are gathered here to honour our god and to make good the promise we gave,' said Penrose as they reached the doors, he turned around making Chris face the rest of the neighbourhood.

Chris could see that his neighbours were all wearing black robes, some of them had pulled up the hoods, but most hadn't bothered and they stared at Chris with eager expressions, their eyes gleaming with something akin to madness. He recognised the old widow from number three, the newly-weds from number twelve and an array of other people who he had known for most of his life.

'This night is an important night for us,' Penrose continued. 'It is the start of the next phase and a completion of the old one. All of you will reap the rewards for your efforts.'

'Dad?' said Chris as his father joined the row in front. 'What's going on? Is this some kind of joke?'

'Sorry, son,' said Dad. 'You've had your fun and now we have to pay the price.'

'I didn't … I haven't done anything wrong …'

Chris turned his head and looked at Penrose. He had never noticed the insanity in the man's grey eyes before and it was reflected in all of the faces that watched the proceedings.

'Time to go into the shelter,' said Penrose.

Penrose pulled Chris round once more. This time they were facing the doors and, as if by magic, they were opening up on their own. *I'm dreaming*, thought Chris. *I'm still at the drive-in.*

There was a dull greyish-green light shining from the depths of the shelter and a sickly stench floated out on a thick miasma of mist.

'What is this?' Chris cried. 'I'm not going in there.'

A fanatic's smile widened on Penrose's euphoric face. 'But you have to Chris, you belong to the god.'

'What are you talking about?'

'We entered into a pact with a new and powerful god. He will give us everything. We are safe from war, will have unending prosperity for as long as we uphold our part of the bargain. We give him our first born, on their sixteenth birthday.'

'*What?*' Chris gasped.

'*Alomoth rehath elimore dyseth.* I call on the god to come to us and accept our sacrifice,' said Penrose.

'D ... Dad?' Chris said trying to look back over his shoulder. He was shaking now. His legs buckled beneath him but Penrose and another robed figure lifted him back up to him feet. They pulled him towards the door.

The stench was worse than ever. It stank of stale sweat and rotten fish tinged with sulphur. Chris gagged on the fog that rushed up into his face. It was as though an invisible hand was exploring his features. Cold fingers prodded and poked his cheeks like an adoring grandparent.

The smell was all over him now. He felt that he had become one with the fog, dissolved into the rot and he noticed that Penrose and the other man were no longer holding him. They had backed away as though they were afraid of the mist.

The strange, foul gas pulled back and away into the depths of the earth, and Chris found life returning to his limbs. He turned around slowly to face the people. They were laughing and smiling now, the insanity seemed to be gone and Chris felt a tremendous relief.

It's all some kind of joke. Any minute Myra will come out and start laughing at me for being taken in. Sacrifice indeed!

A smile broke out on his face. He wouldn't let them win. He would pretend he hadn't been scared but had guessed all along.

'Very amusing, Dad. I didn't realise you had such a peculiar sense of humour.'

Dad's sad eyes turned to him at the same moment that Chris tried to step away from the fallout shelter doors. Then the nightmare restarted. The mist rushed up at him again. It surrounded him, grabbing at his ankles, his arms, his neatly trimmed hair. He saw the slight frown on his father's face, the guilt that danced in his eyes and then his Dad turned away and walked back to the house.

Chris tried to scream but the sound strangled in his throat. His eyes bulged as the air was squeezed out of his lungs. Blood pounded into his ears. He thought he heard his mother crying but the sound was lost in a rush as his ear drums burst. Red moisture poured from his eyes, nose and mouth and his internal organs exploded. His stomach seemed to be forced up into his mouth. White bile, mixed with blood seeped out between his lips. His teeth crumbled in his mouth and then, mercifully, he was pulled back into the shelter, his body too crushed to fight anymore, and the doors slammed shut with a sonorous crash.

The robed figures stared at the doors as Penrose hurried forward and turned the key in the lock. They were shocked into silence. They had expected it to be more symbolic and less horrible, but the creature from the other world had clearly wanted them to see what they had done. It was a message. No – it was a warning.

'Prosperity will be ours,' said Penrose, raising his arms to the sky but he was afraid.

The creature would be satisfied, for now. But more sacrifices would have to be made or each one of them would pay the price. And his daughter Elisabeth, his own first born, turned sixteen next month.

Food

The party always started at dusk.

Rose, Jen, Lara and Lucy exited the monorail onto the platform. They were dressed in flamboyant club wear. Rose was wearing a short skirt that barely skimmed her thighs, with a diamante bra top, over which she had thrown a sheer lace vest top. Her hair was black with bright red streaks flowing through it. Lara and Lucy were twins and so as always they wore identical outfits. Shiny black satin shorts, gold boob tubes and their bangs were up in two pigtails at the front, while the rest of their hair cascaded down their back and shoulders in electric blue waves. Jen was the most conservative of the four of them. She wore tight black jeans, and a loose fitting white shirt. Her hair was pulled back in a mousy brown bun, but the others didn't criticise because this was an effort for Jen, even down to the addition of pale pink lipstick.

They followed the exit sign and came to a line of eager females waiting to cross the barrier, but the station guard wouldn't open up until it was exactly the right time.

'Okay folks, step forward. The party is about to begin,' said the station guard. 'Remember you can't leave until dawn.'

'Come on Jen, it'll be fun,' said Rose. 'About time you let your hair down.'

'It's not my thing,' Jen protested.

'It's my hen party,' Rose said. 'So I think we all need to have as much fun as possible.'

'Yeah, once that ring's on your finger the fun stops,' laughed Lucy.

The turnstile began to move and the girls entered and passed through.

Outside the adult theme park waited for them. They

crossed into a street that was lit up by neon signs. Bars, clubs, beauty salons. Anything you wanted was here for the ultimate bachelorette party experience because anything you did in Party Town stayed there, with no fear of future recriminations. No guilt.

The girls walked down the street, glancing in at the shops. A candy store which sold exotic ice-creams, candy and cookies, was full already with the first wave of women. Across the road a French-style patisserie had a line growing outside and then there was the beauty make-over spa. This was emptier than the other shops; most had prepped before they arrived to save time. They had so few hours that they didn't want to waste any of it.

'Come in ladies,' called a bouncer at the first club. 'All night dancing to 1980s club music.'

'Is he one?' asked Lucy.

'All of them are. There's no *real* guys here, remember,' Lara said.

'Yes,' Rose said. Her eyes gleamed with excitement. 'One last fling. And all guilt free.'

'Just like masturbating really,' said Lucy.

Jen lagged behind as the other girls entered the club. She glanced down the street. The neon lights didn't excite her, it left her cold. But it was Rose's night. She had a job to do and Rose had to enjoy herself no matter what.

She gave the bouncer a wide birth as she passed through the club door and walked into the club. Already the music was blaring. Women and men littered the dance floor and hung out by the bar, drinking, Jen assumed, real alcohol. Some of the women wouldn't be human and she knew that *all* the males were artificials. It was the only guarantee that the park offered.

'Hey,' said one of the men at the bar. 'Let me buy you a drink.'

'No thanks,' Jen said.

It was a ridiculous conceit. Guests' credit cards were stored in the system. Everything was being charged to them all as soon as they entered the park. Jen went to the bar and ordered a coke, then she turned and watched Rose dancing with a half-dressed 20th century movie star (*John Travolta* – she thought it was) lookalike. Trivial information popped into her brain about the star. Wasn't *Saturday Night Fever* in the 1970's? Jen shrugged. It was a nice touch nonetheless.

Jen sipped her coke and found a seat in a booth near the dance floor so that she could watch the others. Lara and Lucy saw her, then dropped their purses onto the table in front of her. There was no money, phones or any other items in the girl's purses - only makeup - because these weren't permitted in the park. Complete privacy had to be guaranteed at all times and cell phones – with their cameras – were anything but private.

Jen mourned the loss of her cell just then and wished she could have checked her work emails at least. The evening was going to be a boring one for her with no access to the outside world, and all of this noisy partying. She glanced at her watch. Only 11hours left until dawn, then they were out of here. She wondered how she would stand it.

Rose was being pawed by the artificial Travolta. It was obscene. Jen looked away.

'You look about as interested in this as I am.'

Jen looked up to see a young woman in front of her booth.

'Friend's bachelorette?' the girl said.

'You too?' asked Jen.

'I'm Anna,' she said.

'Jen. Wanna join me?'

Anna slipped into the booth then waved to the bartender who came over with a drink for her.

'What's that?' asked Jen.

'A little Jack and coke. Takes the edge off the boredom.'

'Why'd you come?' Jen asked.

'It's hard to say no to Rose.' Anna said. She nodded over to where Rose, Lucy and Lara were dancing surrounded by beautiful males.

'Oh. You came with Rose too!'

'Yeah. She's my sister. I'm sworn to keep her on the straight and narrow but you know what, I'm kinda fed up with always being her nursemaid. She can screw an artificial tonight if she wants. And drink herself sick. Why should I care?'

'I thought *my* job was keeping her safe tonight,' Jen said. 'She never mentioned she had a sister.'

Anna laughed. 'That doesn't surprise me. She treats me like the black sheep. Says I'm boring. But seriously, I'd rather be me, than be a party girl. Know what I mean?'

Jen nodded.

'Look there is a pizza bar here ... all part of being decadent for a night ... wanna leave these three to it and go and eat?'

Jen agreed.

'Going for pizza with Rose's sister,' Jen said to Lara who was sitting at the bar with a buff looking guy. She was plying him with drinks which seemed ridiculous when he probably wouldn't be able to enjoy it.

'Meet you back at the turnstile at dawn,' Lara said. 'We'll be finding a private place to take some of these guys soon.'

Jen and Anna left the bar and went out onto the street. Outside was like New Orleans *Mardi Gras* before it was banned for being an unsafe activity. Half naked beautiful men and women gyrated through the centre on floats, while spectators set off party poppers littering the sidewalks with multicoloured streamers. Over head, fireworks exploded from the rooftops of the buildings, lighting up the night sky in a colourful rain of luminosity.

'Beautiful,' said Jen looking up.

'It's not the real sky, of course,' Anna said.

'Nothing is real here though is it?'

'Only the food and drink,' Anna said.

'Where's this place ... I have a map somewhere,' Jen said.

'No need. I know where to go,' Anna said.

She turned left and Jen followed. Soon they were off the noisy main street, and walking down a quieter side street.

'I guess all of the entertainers are artificials?' Jen said.

'That's what the guide book says,' Anna said. 'They look so real though, don't they?'

'I can't tell the difference.'

The pizza restaurant was down a completely deserted alley.

'You sure it's down here?' asked Jen.

Anna paused and looked back at her. 'Oh God. Sorry. You're worried. Hey ... didn't they tell you, there's no crime here. That bouncer at the club was just for show. You're perfectly safe. Look. Here's the place.'

Just around the next bend the pizzeria sign was bright and welcoming.

'Wow. This place looks great,' said Jen.

'Yes and it has all *real* ingredients. None of that synthetic healthy stuff. This is proper fattening cheese and dough. Wait till you taste it.'

Jen was excited for the first time since she had entered the park. One night of unhealthy eating and drinking wouldn't kill her after all. She followed Anna into the restaurant and they took a seat at a table near the window.

The place was authentic. Dull lighting. Italian map hanging from the wall. Real candles in used wine bottles were the centre pieces for the tables. It screamed nostalgia of perhaps a hundred years ago.

The waiter brought them a starter of artichokes. The taste was amazing. Jen had never tried real food before.

'You've gotta have pizza here, though I expect the pasta will be great too.'

They ordered one pasta dish and one pizza with practically everything imaginable on top to share.

'I'm starting to see the appeal of this place now. I mean it's not all parties and sex with machines,' said Jen.

Anna laughed. 'Only if you're into that. Some people come just for the food. Though as you know, there's a restriction on how often you can eat stuff like this. The *Health Bill* and all that.'

The waiter returned with a bottle of wine but as he went to

SAM STONE

pour some in Jen's glass she stopped him.

'Give it a try,' Anna said. 'Live a little.'

Jen nodded and watched as the waiter poured a small amount of the red liquid into her glass.

Then she picked it up and sipped. It was nothing like the healthy wine they were permitted as part of the national lifestyle: it was rich, full bodied and potent. Jen felt its effects rush to her cheeks immediately. It was a good sensation. It made her feel freer, happier and more relaxed in a long time.

'Good huh?' said Anna.

Jen sipped more, and faster.

'It tastes so nice and the buzz is great,' she said.

'Slow down there,' Anna said. 'You don't want to peak too early.'

The pizza and pasta arrived then. A bowl of something called penne with pesto and genuine chicken, and the pizza had all kinds of toppings, cheese, tuna, shrimp, anchovies and black olives.

'I ordered the fish one because I know that the synthetic fish just doesn't taste like the real thing,' Anna said.

Anna picked up a slice of the pizza and took a huge bite out of it. Jen followed suit. Her mouth was assaulted with rich flavours. In one bite she realised how bland synth seafood was: all designed for the health and nutrition of the body but not even the deliberate flavours could compare to this real produce.

'This is … delicious,' Jen said even though the word did no justice at all to the food.

The pasta was equally good.

'How can this be bad for you?' Jen said after eating half of the bowl. 'Oh sorry. I should hand this over to you.'

'That's okay,' said Anna. 'I prefer the pizza anyway. And we can always order more. Eat what you want. This is one chance in a while to do as you please.'

They ate all of the pizza, but instead of getting more Anna recommended a special desert called Tiramisu.

'An Italian classic,' she said. 'You'll like it.'

Jen *loved* it.

'Lara, Lucy and Rose will all be in some seedy hotel room with those awful males,' Jen said. 'What a waste of their time here. They could be eating this wonderful food instead.'

'They aren't like us Jen,' Anna said. 'They wouldn't appreciate it.'

Jen ate the last mouthful of her dessert. Then she signed her bill receipt.

'Where to now?' she said.

'Another place off the beaten track,' Anna said. 'Just the right thing for people like us.'

They went to a quiet bar just around the corner. It was still retro in style, plush red velvet seats and booths around a grand piano. A pianist played and sang relaxing ballads.

'I'm a bit of a "foodie",' Anna said. 'At least, I would be if I was able to be. I'd probably weigh 200lbs if I had my way.'

She laughed.

'So what does this place offer? Other than the pianist. Which is really nice,' Jen asked.

'Fine wines. Cognac. A thing called Irish coffee, which you should try actually.'

Anna ordered them more wine, promising the Irish for the end of the night.

'Chateauneuf Du Pape,' Anna said sipping the wine. 'This should be savoured.'

Jen enjoyed the wine, the buzz had levelled out now, and Anna ordered a selection of nibbles for the table. She tried peanuts for the first time. Something called nachos with cheese and guacamole. Jalapenos that burnt her mouth, making her gulp the wine faster. The waiter brought her a yoghurt drink to kill the heat.

'Wow! That was new!' Jen said. 'I liked it. But it burned!'

'Chilli takes some getting used to after our bland diet,' Anna said. 'I'm really enjoying this though Jen. You're good company. And it is way more fun tasting these things with someone else.'

'Well, the evening has worked out way better for me than I

thought it was going to as well. Party Town isn't as bad as I thought it was.'

Midnight approached and passed as the two women talked and sampled as much as they could of the various wines, brandies and finally the Irish coffee.

'We should get back to the eighties bar,' Anna said. 'Check out how my sister is faring.'

They walked back through the wild streets. Jen and Anna were frequently approached by males of varying types. Each declined the offer of company.

They reached the bar at 4am and the bouncer greeted them with the same speech he had when they had arrived earlier. But as they crossed the threshold the bouncer called them back.

'Rose, Lara and Lucy are here,' he said and for a moment he went into such a cold unnatural pose, that both women became acutely aware of his inhumanity. He gave them a card with a location printed on it.

'Thanks,' said Anna.

She looked down at the card and read it.

'The high school gym,' she said.

'High school,' said Jen. 'There's a high school on the site?'

'She's gone to the prom to get laid. Rose is so weird,' Anna sighed.

They left the Eighties bar and caught a cab across the town.

'How do you know so much about this place?' Jen said. 'Have you been here before?'

'Once or twice,' Anna said. 'You know how it is. You're not allowed to over indulge too much. I came for my twenty first. That's when I discovered the food and wine. Then again for Rose's 30th a few years ago. It was good to have an excuse to return this time too. And even better, Rose is paying for all of it, or I said I wouldn't come.'

The taxi pulled up outside of the gym. Anna signed for it then they got out and walked towards the open doors.

Music blared from inside and strobe lighting bounced in colourful waves across the high windows.

'The party's in full swing,' Jen said.

'I never did prom. Couldn't get a date,' said Anna.

'I'm sorry,' said Jen.

'What about you?'

'Me? No prom.'

They entered the hallway to the gym and discovered the doors ahead into the main hall were closed.

'Wonder what we'll find in there?' said Anna.

Jen didn't reply.

They passed through the corridor, the doors were all closed. The changing rooms, the bathrooms, the coach's office. All in full darkness. As they reached the gym the doors opened. The music stopped and the strobe lighting switched off as they crossed the threshold.

The gym was empty.

'I guess the party just ended,' said Anna.

They looked around. There was no sign of anyone there. No prom. No teachers or DJ. No artificial or real people.

'Come on,' said Anna. 'Let's get back to the main strip. Only two hours to go. We can eat a little more. Maybe ice-cream. You ever tried the real stuff?'

They turned to leave the building and found the corridor in complete darkness.

'What time is it?' Anna asked. 'Maybe we've overstayed.'

'It's 4.15am. Less than two hours till dawn,' Jen said.

'Okay. We had better just go back to the main strip. Be near the exit. There are fines if you don't go out in a reasonable time. And I can't afford to get one.'

Outside there were no taxis. And so the women began the long walk back, following the exit signs.

'Don't worry, we still have time to leave,' Anna said. But Jen didn't appear to be too concerned.

'Look at that!' Jen said as they entered another dark and deserted street.

'Jeez, they are shutting everything down early this time. Normally there are ten minutes warnings and a row of cabs to get you back in time. There's none to be seen at the moment and we aren't even late.'

They hurried through the dark street.

'It's eerie as fuck like this isn't it?' Anna said.

'I'm not worried. You told me there's no crime here. So we're safe, right?'

'Sure,' said Anna, but she didn't feel safe. She was nervous and scared but she didn't want to freak Jen out so she put on a brave face.

They turned a corner and found the main strip.

'Finally!'

The lights were still on but the *Mardi Gras* was gone and so were the people. Maybe Jen's watch was wrong? Anna pulled her own timepiece from her purse. It was now 5.30am.There was fifteen minutes left to the start of lockdown. What was going on? Perhaps there had been an evacuation? Something that she and Jen hadn't heard or noticed. But no, Anna remembered that there were emergency protocols and exits everywhere in the park if there was a problem. None of those protocols, like the warning alarm, had been activated.

'Maybe both of our clocks are wrong,' Anna said. Though she thought it unlikely.

They approached the exit and saw the guard on the other side.

'Hey,' said Anna. 'You wanna let us out?' The guard was in sleep mode and therefore didn't answer. 'What the fuck is going on?'

'It's okay,' said Jen. 'The park doesn't close for half an hour. They don't open up until then.'

'What now then?' Anna said.

They decided to go back to the eighties bar since that was the closest place. Maybe Rose, Lara and Lucy would be there now getting a final drink before leaving.

The bouncer was still by the door as Anna and Jen entered. He didn't invite them in, or acknowledge their presence.

'He's in sleep mode too,' said Jen.

They entered the bar. Music was still coming from the DJ booth. The bartender was clearing glasses away from the bar but no one was around.

'Okay. We need "Help" mode,' said Anna. 'This just isn't right.'

She walked to the bar and spoke the complex code to the bartender.

'How can I help you?'

Anna turned away from the bar and stared at Jen. Jen's voice had changed. It was no longer natural and had that quirky sound that the artificial had when they were in help mode. She was so abnormally still, that Anna realised there was no way she could be human. Why hadn't she noticed the strangeness of this girl?

'What are you?' Anna said her voice quiet.

'Jen6. Mousy friend model.'

'But ...'

'What can I help you with?' Jen6 said.

'I want to find my sister and leave,' said Anna.

'Your sister, Rose is not here.'

'She's left already? What about Lara and Lucy?'

'They were never here. The town was open just for Anna.'

Anna took a step back. Her elbow bumped the bar. She rubbed it. 'This isn't funny. What do you mean?'

'Rose1, Lara1 and Lucy1 were animations of the people you know,' said Jen.

'I don't understand. How can the park be only open for me? Did my sister set this up?'

'You were invited. You accepted and signed the forms,' Jen6 explained.

'An invitation from Rose ... she's getting married ...'

'Does that sound like Rose?' Jen6 asked.

Anna stared at her. 'No. It doesn't. But I hadn't seen her for a while and the food in the park ...'

'Yes. We know you love the food Anna,' said Jen6. 'It's why you were invited back.'

'This is a joke isn't it? You're not artificial are you? My sister put you up to this. Any minute she'll come in and say 'Fooled you'. Only I'm not fooled. This is a stupid sick joke and I don't like it.'

'We never joke about these things. You signed the forms Anna. That relieves the town of any responsibility for food related diseases and sickness ...'

'There was nothing wrong with the food. It was all perfect.'

Jen6 stepped forward and took Anna's arm. She pulled her firmly away from the bar.

'You can't do that!' Anna said. 'You're hurting me. You're a real person. You have to be.'

'I'm artificial.'

'What about your code?'

'Code deactivated for Anna.'

Jen6 pulled Anna across the dance floor towards a door that said STAFF ONLY. The door opened and the bouncer was waiting on the other side. Jen pushed Anna forwards. The bouncer caught her.

Anna used the help code again, but it had no affect on the bouncer or Jen6. The bouncer and Jen6 took an arm each and led Anna through the kitchen. Several artificial chefs and kitchen staff were frozen mid activity. Once was bent over a dishwasher, plate in hand halfway inserted, another was poised before the oven, cleaning cloth lightly touching the smooth cool surface. Another was reaching up into a cupboard with a set of pristine pans partially placed on the first shelf. But Anna had little time to register this, other than the abnormality of it, as the bouncer yanked her roughly toward the back door and out into the alleyway beyond.

The ground outside was littered with trash cans. The artificials pulled Anna down the alley towards a dark doorway. As she approached she saw the sign 'No Admittance'. The bouncer ran his free hand over the keypad and the door opened. Anna was led inside. By this time she was struggling hard against the hands that held her, but to no avail.

Her mind denied what was happening: this had to be some form of elaborate joke her sister had set up. After all Rose had come into large wealth recently. It was why she had chosen to pay for everyone to visit the theme park. Could she have paid for this too? Just to scare her? But why? They didn't always see eye to eye but they weren't necessarily enemies ...

She barely noticed the empty warehouse open up into a dark cavern until it was too late.

'Where are you taking me?' Anna cried through ragged breath.

'The City,' said Jen6.

Then the bouncer and Jen6 propelled her forward and let go.

Anna was falling. It felt like an eternity as she tipped into darkness. There was no sense of depth, or speed, she just knew she was falling down.

Below the earth, she thought. *To the nameless city.*

Solid ground was beneath her feet with a crunch of gravel and dirt as old as time itself. Anna knew all this but not how or why she knew it.

She was standing, no longer falling and the artificials had gone. For this at least she was grateful. They had always scared her, though she had never admitted it to herself before. There was something insidious about them: always a glitch away from doing something to a human. And now they had done something.

But what exactly. She ran her hands over her arms. She was unhurt though bruised, but the dark place in which she stood was as cold as the grave. She shuddered and peered into the dark, trying to make out anything at all. But it was so dark she could barely see her hand in front of her face, and the claustrophobic vacuum paralysed her.

Mist formed ahead of her, like morning smog over damp fields. She felt it before she could see it. There were no fields, no water, no earth and no light around her. There shouldn't be fog. Her rational mind told her this, but facts were facts: it was before her eyes.

'Where am I?' she tried to say, but the empty place swallowed the sound as it left her lips.

Except ... there was sound. Noises that belonged here

could be heard, and Anna heard movement now. From the mist, or perhaps behind her, something moved.

A sound like a thousand angry rattlesnakes echoed through the space, revealing the vastness of the cavern.

Anna froze. Fear made her bladder turn to sludge. She turned on the spot. A million eyes watched her. Malignant, voracious gazes that devoured her.

Anna took a step backwards but she felt the mist wrap around her reducing her limbs to powerless flesh. She couldn't scream or move. And then she knew why she was here.

The information was fed to her, just as the pizza and pasta and luxurious wines had been. Anna was being fattened up for the kill. She had been chosen by the ruler of the nameless city to feed his starving minions. *I'm food!* She thought. The horror of it sent her mind reeling.

Anna's mind screamed. Her fear and torment fed them. Greedy. Glutinous. Monstrous things. The mist squeezed and pulled at her wringing out her physical and mental agony until Anna was nothing more than an empty shell.

It released her when her mind was gone and she flopped to the ancient dirt a wet and broken mass of meat. And then, the final creatures crept in.

A light breeze blew over Party Town as the sun came up. The neon lights flickered out as the street cleansers moved in and began to sweep away the signs of the party. The artificials were in storage.

Only another twelve hours to go until the doors opened once more and the next influx of party goers arrived. But the place would reset, as it did every day, with no human effort needed.

Below the surface the creatures were no longer restless; they waited in silence until their next meal arrived.

Sonar City

In the hot smog I could barely make out the solar panels and the steam converters: ugly mechanisms positioned like external guts on the fronts and sides of the giant high rises. The gadgets attached to the buildings appeared to be floating in the polluted air as though they weren't part of the buildings at all. A café bar had a clockwork windmill, turning slowly on the roof. It was like some vile parody of the *Moulin Rouge* but without the class. From the corner of my eye I could see Selfridges. They prided themselves on being eco-friendly but at the back of the shop I knew there was an outlet pipe spewing a black, stinking ichor into the sewage system from their *negative*-footprint generator. On the opposite side of the street one of the converters halted with a clunk. There was a vibration, a high pitched hum that rippled through the smoke not quite above human hearing. White noise vibrated through the filthy air. My ears throbbed.

The old antiquarian's shop was the only building in the city that hadn't changed in the last few years. The little parlour carried none of these monstrosities but it was wedged between two ugly towers. The beasts either side appeared to be conspiring to crush the old building between them, yet still she held firm. She looked like a battleship racing against an armada, and as I crossed the road, walking through the polluted air, the place felt like the only safe haven in the whole of the city.

Jonas was stood in the doorway holding the handle with one hand while a fat bunch of keys jingled in the podgy fingers of the other.

'I saw you from across the street,' he said.

'I'm surprised you can see anything in this,' I said, following him inside.

The shop hadn't changed at all since the last time I had been there. It was still full of weird curios: antiquities from many a bygone age. Jonas loved his collections. He had always felt a connection with the past. I looked up at the ceiling. The lightning rod was still hanging in its leather pouch, out of reach from the mauling hands of customers. This relic would never be for sale as it had always meant too much to Jonas, but he still proudly displayed it.

In the cabinet behind the counter was a gun – the type that used bullets. The ornate silver handles were polished to a sheen and a box of gleaming; matching bullets were decorously placed to one side. The weapon was a rarity and a novelty in this age of laser and steam weaponry. To the left was another cabinet, this one contained a real china tea set with pale roses painted around the edges of the cups and saucers. A gauntlet was displayed on the counter, spread out on a piece of red velvet cloth. I paused beside it. It was supposed to have belonged to a medieval king, but Jonas and I both knew differently. Once in place, the gauntlet couldn't be removed from your hand until death. It contained clockwork bionics and gave the wearer superhuman strength. The glove, however, was a parasite: it drew its power from the life-force of the wearer.

'Dangerous place to leave that,' I said.

Jonas shrugged. 'It needs a host.'

The shop was full of dangerous and powerful objects. I glanced again at the lightning rod. Who knew where this *really* came from? Jonas said the mythos surrounding the weapon was that it had belonged to a sea god, but I wouldn't have been surprised to hear that the lance had been owned by Zeus himself. As I stared upwards the rod began to glow.

Jonas took my arm. My head snapped back into the present. The lightning rod was powerful, that was for certain.

It had been ten years since I had last seen my old mentor, Jonas. The fault was mine of course; I had been travelling in beautiful and exotic climes. It made the return to civilisation all the more shocking. When I left, the city had been normal – sure I knew the fuel crisis would change things, but I never expected quite how much. The new systems were supposed to be an improvement – carbon-neutral even – but from what I could see the place was worse.

'So you're back,' Jonas said. 'Let me look at you.'

'I'd twirl but you know I'm not that sort of girl. This place hasn't changed much. The atmosphere is better in here than out there.'

Jonas closed the grille and locked the door. 'It's safer too.'

'Street gangs, I presume? The poor visibility certainly makes it easier for them.'

Jonas shrugged. 'There's worse out there than teenage thugs.'

I followed Jonas into the back room and we sat like civilised people drinking neat whisky from china cups: Jonas always was quirky that way.

'What's been happening here?' I asked eventually.

'You know about the fuel crisis?'

'We finally ran out of coal?'

'As you can see there have been all kinds of experimental options,' Jonas sipped his whisky and I noticed for the first time that his once fierce blue eyes had a thin white film over them. It could be cataracts, but I knew that wasn't the case: he had seen me even through the smog.

'I didn't see you, I *heard* you,' he said. Jonas was the only person who was able to read my mind and I was glad the talent was still there. 'I'm blind.'

I closed my mind up. I didn't want him to know how bad his words made me feel.

'When did this happen?' I asked.

'It's a bi-product of the smog. The city has been in this state for almost five years. Most of the residents are going blind from the pollution.'

I didn't know what to say. Jonas had taught me all I knew. I had always thought of him as invulnerable.

'We survived because we adapted. We do see, in a way, but it's not through our eyes any more. It's a kind of sonar …'

I stared at him. 'And added to your other skills …?'

Jonas nodded. 'I get by just fine.'

I let out the breath I'd been holding. The old mage had his faults but I knew he was fine, despite the state of the city around him.

'You called me back,' I said. 'Why?'

'I know you hate pollution, Lucy. I know you hate crowds, and I suspect that your exploration of the world has brought you to the few remaining places where there is no civilisation. But … there have been some strange occurrences here.'

'Civilisation?' I repeated. 'Mmmm. This world is not what I call civilised despite your efforts to retain the old values, Jonas. Anyway, I can't help you. My detective days are over.'

Jonas nodded, sipped, and proceeded to tell me about the problem anyway.

It seemed there had been several disappearances. Jonas' daughter, Mai, among them.

'She's always been a difficult girl,' he said. 'Subject to disappearing at short notice, going away on a whim, but this was different. She's changed recently. I thought she was finally maturing.'

I learnt that Mai was involved in a new wave of revivalism. Like her father she enjoyed the old world: its gadgets, its philosophies, its clothing and its bizarre unusable mobile phones. Revivalists walked around accessorised with parts of the old world. They used wrist watches instead of pocket watches. They had designer phones, touch pads that didn't work but they played with anyway. They wore jeans, leggings and mini-skirts. They abhorred formality. They rebelled because they could. The revivalists didn't smoke opium like the modernists did; they considered it unclean which was somewhat ironic when they were piercing their faces and bodies with pieces of metal. Revivalism was a recurring fad though, and it came and went with each new generation which was why Jonas wasn't concerned at all when Mai became involved with the group.

'I suppose you've tried to find her?'

Jonas glanced at his pocket watch, and then placed it back in his waistcoat pocket. He removed the cups and the whisky decanter, taking them into the small kitchen. He returned shortly with a roll of parchment which he spread on the table in front of me. It was an old map of the city. I recognised the ghettos and the market streets, even though they were now filled with the clutter of modernist technology.

'This is the sewers,' Jonas said, spreading a large piece of transparent film over the top of the map.

The sewage map fitted perfectly over the parchment, and I noticed the lines depicted a specific pattern but the criss-cross shape meant nothing to me. Jonas unrolled another film map, laying this over the top of the other two. The words 'Ley Lines' were written neatly in the far right corner of the latest addition. It matched perfectly with the centre of the sewers and fell on the very street Jonas' shop occupied.

'I've always known it was here,' he said. 'It was one of the reasons I bought the shop.'

'I don't understand.'

'Lucy. This is a potent source of ley line magic. It's like living near the fountain of youth.'

'The city looks aged and so do the people in it,' I pointed out. 'What do you mean the fountain of youth?'

'Ley power is the magic of the Earth. It's pure energy. If we could tap it, we'd be able to clear this smog and throw away our gadgets. It would give the city a new lease of life.'

'Jonas I don't understand what this has to do with the revivalists or with Mai.'

Jonas sighed. 'The thing is, I think someone has been tapping the ley, but I don't think they've been using it to help: rather the reverse.'

Jonas wasn't given to wild flights of fancy in the old days, but he was a mage and I knew he understood about nature and magic better than anyone I'd ever known. He was also an ardent supporter of 'leaving well alone'. I thought back to our last adventure together. The image of the burning book was forever etched into my mind. The first three letters of the title, *N E C*, were the last to surrender to the flames. I recalled Mai begging her father to let her use the magic the book held. Yes. Jonas was not one for using magic unnecessarily and to even suggest tapping something as powerful as the ley made me wonder just how bad things really were here.

'There are rumours that another book exists,' Jonas said, reading me again. 'That someone used it to summon an ancient evil from the bottomless depths of time.'

'You mean …?'

Jonas shook his head, 'I doubt we'd still be alive if it were one of the Great Old Ones. But a lesser god maybe …'

'You think Mai could be involved? Or has she fallen foul of some mage's spell?'

'My tracker indicated that Mai was down there,' Jonas said, his index finger landing on a point on the map right in the centre of the ley lines. 'I suspect she's working with the revivalists and that they are behind whatever is lurking down there, and what has befallen the city.'

'She's always been attracted to *wrong* magic.'

Jonas nodded. His white-filmed eyes were sad.

I changed my clothing in Jonas' pokey bathroom. It had an old-style plastic bath and toilet seat, even though the toilet was still made from porcelain. They hadn't changed through the years but the flush mechanism had and it was the first punk tech I'd seen in the place. I didn't ask him about it – a man, no matter how eco-friendly, had to have some comforts.

Once in a pair of jeans and tee-shirt I felt peculiar. I missed the restriction of my corset and my breasts felt exposed despite the old-fashioned bra which pulled me in as tight as possible. The steel underwire dug into my skin. It was a most unpleasant and uncomfortable outfit and I really couldn't see the appeal at all. I stared longingly at my fitted brown velvet jacket and the matching knee length culottes, thrown casually over the side of the bath. Then I picked up the rucksack. The bag didn't contain the tropes of the twenty-first century though. It held the things I'd need if I was heading down into the sewer to find Mai.

I met Jonas outside the shop. He was looking around with his strange foggy eyes.

'Street's clear,' he said looking directly at me.

'So. Why am I dressed like this?'

'If the revivalists are down there, you can pretend to be one of them.'

It seemed a ridiculous idea to me but I shrugged. If the revivalists *were* in the sewers I thought it unlikely that they would believe I was a new member, but stranger things had happened in my years as a PI.

I felt the sonar then: a ripple in the air that wended its way through the fog and wrapped around me. It was curiously invasive. A lick of energy swept over my head and down my back. It was as though a glove of vacuous sound had enveloped me. I could hear nothing from the noisy engines or the slow moving traffic. I took a step back. The sound waves fell flat and away as Jonas looked down. The noise of outside came crashing back in.

'Sorry,' said Jonas. 'I was checking out your disguise.'

If *everyone* could do this would they see through the costume, I wondered?

'Most won't look so closely. Revivalists are treated a bit like social pariahs.'

I wasn't on the street long and didn't come in contact with anyone, so the disguise proved somewhat pointless. I slipped down into the sewer with a pair of night-vision goggles firmly in place. I wasn't one for carrying lanterns: too easy for an assailant to knock from your fingers, besides I needed both hands free for this job. I was carrying a holographic imager for a start; Jonas wouldn't let me take his precious parchment and besides the imager gave me light and direction indicators that a map just wouldn't have. I switched the imager on and looked down into a virtual picture of the sewers. The centre wasn't too far away. All I had to do was turn left, walk down this main shaft and then take a sharp right at the end.

The goggles cast a green light over the tunnels and made the walls look sick. Somehow the green glow intensified the smell. It wasn't the odour of faeces and urine that came to me. I could smell iron, salt, and some other unidentifiable sickly sweet aroma. I followed my nose even though it was in a different direction to the centre that Jonas had identified on his map.

The tunnels narrowed and then opened out into a crossroads. I found myself in a central chamber and the source of the smell became evident. A tunnel of shallow water converged in the centre, fed from four different gullies. A strong waft of sewage came from the right hand side. I peered down each tunnel in turn, seeing nothing unusual and then as I turned, my trainer-covered foot slipped on something I didn't care to identify. *It would never have happened if I'd been wearing my regular boots.* I caught myself against the wall of the chamber with my free hand and the holographic imager slipped from my fingers and clattered down onto the tiled floor. The sound of the instrument falling echoed through the empty tunnels and I experienced that strange phobia one feels in a tomb: a fear that any noise will wake the dead.

The wall felt cold and wet and as I pulled my hand back I saw that my fingers were covered in a greenish slime. My first instinct was to wipe my hand on the revivalist jeans but I sniffed the gloopy substance instead. It smelt of bile, roses and the sharp tang of sea salt. Sweet, vile and overpowering.

I shrugged off my rucksack and, opening it with my clean hand, I reached inside and searched for my sample dishes. *A good scientist never leaves home without them.* Using my handkerchief I wiped the slime from my fingers, and then opened one of the dishes and scraped some of the substance into it. The gunk was similar in consistency to snail mucus but thicker. The walls of the cavern were covered. I pressed the lid firmly in place then dropped the dish into a clear plastic envelope and sealed it. Once this was done, I packed everything back into the bag and turned towards the right hand tunnel. The smell was stronger there and I wanted to know what was making the slime. I couldn't imagine there was a huge snail living down there but then pollution was at an all time high; even the residents of the city were evolving so why not a gastropod?

I looked back the way I came. Jonas had been specific. I was to follow the map to the centre and go nowhere else, but my curiosity was piqued. My instincts were telling me to follow the slime.

I was halfway down the tunnel when I remembered that the imager had fallen on the floor in the chamber. If I didn't find it, I could potentially have difficulty finding my way back out of the sewer. I turned back the way I came.

A low whining, like cogs in need of oil, echoed down the tunnel towards me. I threw myself against the wall as the sonar wave moved past me. Someone, or something, was down here with me and they were searching with the only eyes they had. I knew that all kinds of creatures used sonar to see. Bats being the obvious one. I could feel the sonar probing like a searchlight looking for intruders.

It spooked me. The hairs stood up on the back of my neck, my heart beat so loud in my chest that I was sure that the creature could hear it. I ran back to the chamber, forgetting to look for my imager. It was sheer luck that brought me back to the ladder through which I had entered the sewer. I climbed the steps, my feet and hands slipping on the metal. The clothes and shoes I was wearing really weren't practical at all and I couldn't understand why I had let Jonas talk me into changing.

At the top, I pushed the manhole upwards and climbed out into the thick, smoggy air. I felt the sonar probe reaching for me and I slammed the manhole back down cutting it off. Once outside I was slightly disorientated. I couldn't place where I was in the street. My heart was still thumping in my chest. The fear was irrational: I hadn't seen anything. But an intense claustrophobia had consumed me down in the tunnels and continued to suffocate me now I was up in the city. I took a deep breath and coughed the smog back out of my lungs. It wasn't good. I could feel the poisonous air eating at my insides. *How long did it take to go blind in Sonar City?*

I withdrew a scarf from my rucksack, wrapping it over my mouth and nose and as I began to filter air through the makeshift mask, my head cleared and I was once more able to think.

It took Jonas a long time to answer the door. He wasn't looking out for me this time and so I rang the bell and waited like any normal customer might. When he opened the door he was surprised to see me.

'I didn't expect you back so soon,' he said.

His words surprised me as I felt like I had been gone for hours.

'What did you find?'

'Have you got a microscope?' I asked.

He went away, returning quickly with an old style scope that required batteries instead of clockwork to run it. Fortunately Jonas had some of those too, and they still worked.

'Memorabilia,' he shrugged.

I placed the rucksack on his table and extracted the sample dish. Jonas watched but I noted that his eyes widened when he saw the slime. In the gaslight it looked a darker green. It was like the infected mucus coughed up from the chest of a consumption sufferer. I smeared some on a slide and placed it under the hot light of the microscope.

'What do you see?' Jonas asked.

It was hard to describe the vileness of the substance and because Jonas could no longer see in the traditional sense I found myself wishing I could show him. The slime was moving, it was shying away from the light, but it had nowhere to go. A thousand microbes jumped and twitched and fought with each other. Then, they combined and multiplied, spreading out under the slide cover.

'What is it?' asked Jonas.

'Infection,' I said.

'Where from?'

'The bowels of the city.'

Jonas stared at me for a long time then poured himself another whisky into a rose patterned china cup.

'It's worse than I thought,' he said.

I changed back into my own clothing. The crisp shirt, brown leather corset, velvet jacket and long culottes felt comfortable after the flimsiness of the revivalist clothing.

'I lost my imager,' I said as I came back into Jonas' parlour. 'I'll need to take the map this time.'

'You're going back down there? Even though you know the city is infected?'

'Yes.'

'Why?'

'I promised to try and find Mai and now I need to know what's causing the poison. There has to be a reason and without proper equipment there isn't much more I can do to analyse the slime.'

'If Mai is still down there,' Jonas said. 'What will this poison have done to her?'

I let the thought hang between us. I didn't want to speculate. I reached for my own satchel this time and rapidly switched my equipment from one bag to another. I had an intense feeling that I would find more than I bargained for once I went back down into the tunnel.

'The map?' I said.

Jonas was reluctant to part with his treasure, but the thought that his daughter was stuck in the sewer, slowly being poisoned, made the ache of parting with the old parchment less painful.

I grasped it, tucking it down into my waistband, and then turned, heading back through the shop.

'Wait!' Jonas said.

He pulled a stepladder away from the wall and positioned it in the centre of the room. Then he climbed up and unhooked the lightning rod and scabbard.

'But this …?'

'I don't know what's down there, it may be nothing more than the poison leaking out from the machines, but if ever anyone needed this weapon right now it's you, Lucy.'

I took the rod cautiously. It had always held too much fascination, too much seductive power, and I had found it hard to resist. Jonas helped me strap the scabbard to my back. The rod was only the length of a short sword and it was light and easy to carry.

'Reach back and draw it,' Jonas said.

I reached over my shoulder and slid the weapon easily out

of its sheath. It lit up in my hands as though it recognised me. I had no need to ask how to use it. Instinct filled in the blanks.

The smog was worse when I finally made my way back down through the manhole and once more into the tunnel. I felt more secure this time, knowing I had the lightning rod. At the bottom of the ladder I pulled out the roll of parchment. Placing the goggles over my eyes, I opened the map and this time turned towards the centre. Jonas had said that his tracker spell had located Mai at the core of the ley lines. I wasn't going to let myself be distracted this time. If something awful was down here, then I had to get Mai out as soon as possible.

The left tunnels were identical to those on the right and I found myself in a similar chamber to the one where I had lost my imager. Faced with four routes I consulted the map once more. The centre was directly ahead and so I walked on, my heels clicking lightly on the tiled floor. The stench of sewage was worse in this direction but I pushed all thought of the nauseating smell from my mind. I had to find Mai. I'd wasted enough time already.

I turned the corner, following the route to the ley line centre, stopping to glance down at the map each time. On the next turning, the tunnel narrowed down and because there was no walkway I was forced to follow the path of water that ran along the centre. The tiles were slippy, but my feet were surer in my own boots.

I felt the sonar wave again but it was far away, back in the direction I had come from. This time it was accompanied by a mournful wail. It was a sound I couldn't identify, but it was similar to whale song. Perhaps a sea creature was somehow trapped inside the sewer?

I reached the end of the tunnel. Directly ahead was the central chamber. Even with my night-vision goggles the chamber looked excessively dark. I stepped cautiously forward, drawing the lightning rod. I paused at the doorway. The light from the rod was sucked down into the darkness barely illuminating more than two feet in front of me. The goggles were no help and so I switched the setting to direct light ahead of me.

'Who's there?' said a voice.

'Mai?' I whispered. 'Is that you?'

I heard a soft scrape, like a snake slithering across dry sand, as the person moved in the darkness.

'Who are you?' said the voice again.

I spoke softly. 'Lucy Collins. You remember me don't you? I worked with your father.'

'Go away.'

'Mai, I can't leave here without you. I promised Jonas.'

'I'm no longer Mai,' she said and again I heard that awful susurrant movement which sent shivers up my spine. It sounded as though several snakes had entered the grotto and were writhing around her.

I held up the rod, turned the full beam of my goggles into the darkness, but Mai skittered back and was swallowed by the darkness that consumed the chamber.

I heard the cry again. A lonely, wretched whimper.

'He's coming,' Mai said.

'Who?'

'Leave now!' Mai's voice became urgent.

'Let me help you,' I said. 'Mai?'

'I remember you, Lucy,' Mai said. 'Go back to my father. You can do nothing to help me now. It's too late.'

I stepped forward and Mai hissed and gasped, throwing herself backwards against the wall of the chamber. The dull thump gave me perspective on the depth of the cavern and so I shambled blindly forward. In the distance I heard the call once more and felt the weak pull of sonar. It was getting closer.

'Who's holding you here? Who is it that's coming?'

'You can't fight him. He's a god.'

'Mai. Talk to me. Why did you come down here?'

The snakes in the dark rattled and skidded as I reached out for Mai, sure that I was within touching distance.

My hand fell on a cold, damp surface. I heard Mai gasp and I realised I had touched what had once been her arm. I felt along the slime-covered skin, the reek of pollution wafted from her skin and I forced back the urge to gag.

'What happened to you?'

'I'm no longer Mai,' she said again. 'But I still retain some of her memories.'

'Then … what are you?'

A wave of sonar hit my back and paralysed the air around me. As it drew back I heard another wail, only this time it wasn't of sadness and loss, but of anger and the creature emitting the sound was now heading rapidly towards us.

'It's too late,' Mai gasped. 'He's here.'

I fell back against the wall beside what was left of Mai, and the chamber lit up as a creature filled the narrow doorway by which I had entered. It was hard to make sense of the monstrosity before me. A huge, bloated body squeezed itself into the opening by elongating. Large disc-like eyes focused on me as the creature opened its mouth. Tentacles poured forth from blackened lips, and they whipped out towards me. My back was pressed against the side of the chamber and I had nowhere to go.

'No!' gasped Mai, pushing me behind her.

Light filled the cavern now and I could see Mai in all of her mutated glory. Her skin glowed black green, her arms, now numerous, draped down to the floor and into the shallow depths of the water that led into the tunnel. Her eyes had all but consumed her face. Large discs of white and black that reflected the beast that was almost inside the tunnel now. She still had some semblance of humanity left though. Her height remained the same and she had a thick black robe draped over her contorted body.

'Behind me,' Mai gasped. 'There's another way out. Go Lucy!'

'I can't leave you.'

'There is no place for me above now. I've been changed to be his mate.'

'Who … what is he?'

'A god,' she said. 'Yh'menyhua is his name.'

She pushed me towards the door and as I reached it, Yh'menyhua's tentacles gripped Mai and she began to chant the strangest words. It was a language I had never heard and had no hope of understanding. I turned to see the creature pulling Mai forward and was left with the memory of her face glowing with ecstatic religious zeal.

I drew back and away from the sounds of their monstrous love-making. I didn't want to witness the mating rituals of this particular couple. I staggered down the tunnel, withdrawing the map once more from my belt. Behind me I heard the sounds increase, only Mai seemed to be crying now. Whatever the beast was doing to her was causing her great pain. I paused. I couldn't leave her there no matter how much she said she didn't belong. I turned back.

Mai was naked now. Half-human, half-cephalopod, Yh'menyhua had her gripped by two sharp hooks that he buried into her former arms. The tentacle arms attacked her, piercing her over and over in different places as the monster attempted to complete his mating ritual. She bled green, not red. The sight of her blood was both frightening and compelling. He moved her around in the air as though they were in water. Powerful throbs of sound filled the chamber, the air buffeted and moved, elevating Mai into the right position. Then another arm protruded from the centre of what could only be described as the monster's face, and penetrated Mai's stomach. The creature spasmed and jerked and Mai screamed as his alien sperm poured directly into her womb. The alien began to glow. It was then that I realised how very serious this was.

Yh'menyhua was trying to reproduce. What impact would this have on the city above? Surely all of these creatures would need to feed?

I looked around the chamber. In the corner I saw a pile of rags. Human bones, skulls and remains were visible in the sickly illumination. Yh'menyhua had been feeding on those who failed to mutate. How many women had been brought down into these murky depths? How many women had this monster mated with, and then killed when his attempts failed.

The vast being released Mai. Her body fell to the cold, damp floor and she lay there still and cold, but her stomach glowed and twitched, swelling immediately as the creature's abominated life took hold inside her. Yh'menyhua slid back towards the entrance. He didn't detect me lurking in the shadows as I watched the proceedings. Mai came out of her stupor and sat up, pulling her altered body up into a sitting position. She rested against the wall of the chamber. Her surplus arms massaged her swollen stomach in a way that was too grotesque to be human. Her flat, fully black, eyes were expressionless.

The lightning rod glowed in my hand, reminding me it was still there. I re-entered the chamber, sure of what I had to do.

Yh'menyhua rose to his full height, filling the space as his arms lashed out. One struck the wall by my head, and the slime there hissed as it was dissolved. The end of each tentacle was primed with some sort of acid or poison. I ducked as another swung towards me. His appendage smashed hard into the wall behind me and he roared.

'Mai? Can you stand? I'm getting you out of here.'

Mai staggered to her feet, her bloated stomach squirmed and bulged. I wasn't sure what I was going to do with the offspring but I couldn't leave her here to be used as breeding stock for this monster.

'It's too late for me …' Mai hissed. I glanced at her and saw a new metamorphosis was occurring. Snake-like tendrils emerged from her lips and down over her chest. A thick mucus poured down her legs and the first of the monster's progeny crawled down her thighs. Mai screamed with the pain of the birthing and wrapped her tentacles around her body.

I rushed forward as the creature tumbled to the floor and skittered blindly through the water towards its hideous father. I raised the lightning rod and pointed it. Raw electricity shafted out towards the alien child. It stopped in its tracks, shivered and trembled as the lightning hit. Its small body danced and Mai screamed behind me as the grotesque baby exploded splashing the walls with thick red gunk.

Yh'menyhua rushed towards me, arms lashing out. A black bile spewed from his hideous mouth. I dived out of the way as a tendril hit the ground narrowly missing me. I turned and pointed the rod. The monster froze but nothing happened, the lightning had not yet recharged and I had wasted the first bolt on the alien baby who had been less of a threat than its father was. *Foolish.*

Mai screamed again. Her stomach was contorting but she managed to hold herself up against the wall. More alien babies poured from her, scattering like a disturbed nest of spiders out towards the dark corners of the chamber. They hid as I faced the monster.

The rod vibrated in my hand and I pointed again towards Yh'menyhua as a deep and raucous laughter shuddered from his hideous bulk.

But the lightning rod disagreed. This bolt was stronger, more intense and the blinding light that bounced from the green body of the creature forced me to turn my face away and to cover my eyes. I dived for the doorway again, throwing myself out into the cool dark of the tunnel as a fireball burst inside the chamber. Mai screamed. I wasn't sure if the blast had killed her too, and maybe it would be better if it had. The rod dropped from my hand, my fingers were burnt and blistered. The rod was singed and no longer usable. A sixth sense told me that its power was dissipated and gone from it forever. I wondered if Jonas had known how much there was left in the rod. Had he used it once? Had he, in his youth, fought alien monsters to save the city?

I crawled back along the wall and looked into the chamber. The place was black again. The light that the monster had generated was now burning out. I saw the creature's body smouldering in the dimming light and glanced around to see the glowing embers of his misshapen issue.

I hurried across the chamber to where Mai had been. She was not there.

I looked around, prodded the simmering body of the alien fiend with my boot. It didn't move. Good. A thin tendril wrapped around my foot and yanked me. I stumbled against the wall, pulling back and found the half-dead body of one of the babies spasming in its final moments. I looked down into almost human eyes as its life-force finally slipped away. I stamped my heel down hard on its distorted head just to make sure it really was dead.

I sniffed. Blood. Mai had made her way out, but left a trail for me to follow.

One of my night-vision goggles had shattered but I could see enough to find my way back to the stairs and the manhole. I climbed up, noting splashes of blood on the rungs. The trail continued – red now, rather than green – heading upwards and out into the city. Mai's blood led me back to Jonas, and at his shop I found her naked body, shivering on the doorstep.

She was human again.

'She doesn't remember anything,' Jonas said after we bandaged her wounds and tucked her up into bed in his spare room.

After we had done that, I stood with Jonas in the doorway of his shop. The air was already starting to clear. The poison from the god-monster in the sewers was being washed away by man's sewage and waste, and the city was returning to a place which was at least inhabitable by humans again.

We sipped whisky from china cups in silence. Sometimes there really was nothing more that could be said.

The Book of the Gods

Lady Arabella Hutchinson lifted the skirt of her wide ball gown and pulled out the gun that was holstered against her thigh. The weapon had been made to her personal specification. Adapted from the old style duelling pistol, the gun now featured a small steam-powered engine linked to several copper tubes, which wrapped around the long thin barrel and connected with the bullet chamber. It was semi-automatic; meaning that the mere squeeze of the trigger instantly loaded a new shot and powered it from the muzzle, saving time, and Arabella's neck, on many occasions.

Arabella shrank back against a large crate as the first mate, closely followed by the Captain came into the gloomy warehouse. The situation had deteriorated far faster than she had expected.

'What's all the commotion about?' demanded the Captain, pulling the first mate up short.

'The crew say the woman cheated at cards and stole their money,' he replied, casting his eyes around the storage area.

'A *woman*?' asked the Captain.

'Yes, sir.'

'Where is she now?'

'I don't know Captain,' said the first mate. 'I left her on deck for just a second, then she was gone.'

Arabella edged forward. She would have been long gone before the obvious dawned on one of the men but she had stayed behind to finalise the documents while the cargo was loaded on the carriage, and her partner in crime, Joseph, spirited it away. The Captain had been detained, which meant that Arabella had been left to her own devices for too long. While she waited she had explored the dock warehouse, hoping to find something of value that she might add to the haul, when she came across a small group of sailors playing poker. She couldn't resist the opportunity to fleece the unsuspecting men. A mistake, she realised, she may not live to regret.

It was their own fault. They shouldn't have assumed I was just 'a girl'. she thought. She knew this excuse wouldn't wash if the crew found her stash of money and papers; some of which she had won, others she had taken. When the row started, she had slipped away, hiding right under their noses, even as the sailors scurried around shouting 'thief'. It was not long before she realised that the cry had nothing to do with the small haul she had taken but rather with something else entirely: something large and more valuable.

'Must be the girl,' the boatswain had said to the first mate. 'She's taken my wallet.'

'And mine,' cried another man. After that they all realised they had lost something and so Arabella was also being accused for these other things too. The thought annoyed and intrigued her. She didn't mind being accused for thefts she had committed but was somewhat outraged when the accusations were unfounded.

Why didn't I just leave with Joseph? she thought. *My damn arrogance will be the death of me.* She knew perfectly well why she had stayed. She had secretly been hoping to be discovered. The excitement of escape made the effort of deception so much more thrilling.

The Captain and the first mate moved away from the crate and Arabella sighed softly. She glanced down at the ball gown. Crinoline wasn't the quietest fabric to sneak around in and the large skirt made it difficult to run. Fortunately she had come prepared. She placed the gun down on the floor and, reaching behind her back, she began to unlace the tight corset.

A rustling sound whispered across the warehouse; Arabella paused and listened. She heard the sound of feet running towards her and so she pressed back against the crate and reached for her gun. It would be unfortunate if she had to kill over some stolen cargo and a few pounds, but Arabella would do just that if it meant getting away in one piece. She felt the familiar rush of adrenaline coursing through her veins.

A small group of crewmen ran past her hiding place, and Arabella held her breath a moment longer. She knew she was too well hidden and they could not know where she was. The space she had squeezed through was tiny, even though behind the crate there was lots of room.

'Captain!'

The Captain reappeared and the first mate ran back to meet him. The two men stopped close to the crate that Arabella was hiding behind.

'The book is missing too, sir,' said the first mate.

'That damned woman!' the Captain hissed. 'Don't let our passenger know until after we find her.'

Interesting, thought Arabella. *What book? And if they think I shouldn't have it, then do I want it?*

Once the men had moved away, Arabella finished her transformation. She pushed the corset, dress and bustle back into the far corner behind one of the other crates. Then she rolled down the legs of the dinner suit trousers she had been wearing under the dress. She opened her carpet bag and pulled out a dinner jacket and shirt and shrugged herself into them. Next she placed a wig and hat on her head and glued on a fake moustache. Finally, she pulled free a bottle of gin, sloshing some of it on her clothes, and took a large swig directly from the bottle. Once the disguise was in place, Arabella squeezed back out from behind the crate and slipped away. She tucked the gun away in the inside pocket of the dinner jacket. She left the carpet bag behind with her dress, neither of these items contained anything that could lead the sailors back to her, and she walked out onto the dock and into the chaos.

Sailors were running back and forth between the ship and the warehouses and few of them noticed the thin, drunken, aristocratic boy who stumbled around, holding a bottle of gin and singing bawdy songs rather badly. As the Captain walked down the gangplank, the boy fell across his path, breathing a blast of gin right into his face. The Captain was a member of the Temperance Society and active supporter of Lyman Beecher, God rest his soul, and he pushed the boy away in disgust.

'Filthy rich,' he muttered as the boy staggered on and away from the port.

Arabella kept up the pretence until she was out of the dock and back onto the main road. She hailed a Hansom cab and made her way to the rendezvous point.

Her partner, Joseph, resided in the rough part of town. He had a semi-respectable cover as the landlord of 'The Sailor's Rest' and so Arabella arrived there with her disguise still firmly intact because a young man entering the premises would be less noticeable than a woman.

The carriage pulled up, and Arabella paid the driver before making her way around the back of the Inn to the rear entrance. She gave the secret knock, three slow raps, and the heavy lock slid back from the door.

'You took your time,' Joseph said. 'Poker game was it?'

'You know me so well.'

'You'll be the death o' me one day lass,' Joseph laughed.

He sat down at the fire and picked up his pipe. Arabella smiled at his grumpy bearded face and sat down opposite.

'The strangest thing happened,' she said.

'They figured out you cheated, huh?' Joseph grunted.

'That's what I thought at first, but something else went missing. It seems they had also lost a book, and they believed I'd taken it. I hadn't. This does mean another thief was working the docks tonight.'

'A book? Not really your style,' Joseph commented.

'Not unless it's valuable,' Arabella agreed. 'That is the point I think. This book they wanted must be valuable. There was an awful amount of activity. The whole crew was out looking for me and it. They didn't even realise that they had handed their cargo over to the wrong people. Or at least cared less about that than this book.'

'I see you escaped despite it all,' Joseph said. 'Right

enough. No one would believe that disguise hid a lady underneath.'

Arabella smiled and preened. 'That's because they cannot conceive of a woman getting the better of them.'

Joseph took a swig of ale and puffed his pipe. 'Crate's stowed in the usual place,' he said finally. 'Want to open it and have a look?'

'Of course.'

They went down into the tavern basement. Barrels of ale and wine were stowed under the feet of the clients, and so too was an underground escape tunnel into a storage area that smugglers had hollowed out some years before. Arabella led the way by first opening the doorway that was hidden in the front of one of the huge barrels. She and Joseph passed through the crawlspace and out into the tunnel.

The torches were already lit, and so they traversed the narrow passage to the storage room without difficulty. After a few moments Arabella came face to face with her haul for the first time.

The crate dwarfed the small room. It stood taller than Arabella and she had not recalled it looking quite that big on the cart as it was loaded; but then she had been distracted. In fact it looked like the same crate she had hidden behind in the warehouse, although she knew this couldn't be the case.

'We brought it in through the sewers,' Joseph said. 'It was heavy. Damned thing. Took three men to pull it through.'

'I can imagine,' Arabella said.

She walked around the crate, excitement colouring her cheeks. She noted the lettering that covered the box was in a language that she had never seen before. There were several customs' stamps too. This crate had been as far as Tasmania, and had passed through several European ports before finally reaching its destination in London.

'Let's open it then,' Arabella said removing the masculine dinner jacket, which she threw casually onto the floor.

Joseph came forward with a crowbar and they eased the front off the crate. Straw and sawdust tumbled out and

Arabella reached inside to brush the packing away from the statue. As she did so, her hand caught on a protruding nail and she yelped. The nail had torn a deep cut across the palm of her hand and blood already tarnished the straw. She took out a handkerchief and wrapped it around the wound and then, taking more care, she pulled back the straw to reveal the face of the statue.

It was hideous. Joseph took a sharp breath behind her, 'What is that thing?'

'An ancient god,' Arabella said. 'Worshipped by the Aztecs I believe. The statue was found when it washed up in Australia. Luckily for us a Colonel in the British Army thought it would make a good trophy for the Queen.'

'But how did you know about it?' asked Joseph.

Arabella laughed. 'The way that I know about anything. I have sources. In this instance it was a rather helpful sailor, who was very, very put out that his Captain wouldn't let the crew drink on their shore leave.'

Joseph eyed the statue suspiciously and Arabella reached her bandaged hand forward to examine the demon figure's carved fangs. It had the face of a wolf, and yet the body was that of a naked man.

'What does this say?' asked Joseph pointing to the writing on the side of the crate.

'I don't know,' Arabella said.

'It doesn't look like a god to me. It looks more like a devil,' Joseph said.

Arabella pulled back her hand and realised she had smeared the wolf-like snout with blood. It gave the statue a sinister sneer and the blood streaked its fangs as though it had just made a kill.

'I agree it is grotesque. But this, my dear friend, might just be our ticket out of the city,' Arabella said.

'I'll make some discrete enquiries with our sailor friend tomorrow,' Arabella said, after they re-nailed the front onto the crate. 'I have to meet up with him to complete the payment now that we have the goods. Maybe he'll know about this book they were so keen to find. Perhaps it is connected to the statue.'

Athos crept along the gangplank and off the ship. By midnight the search had been called off and the sailor was free to retrieve the book from its hiding place. Everyone had assumed that Arabella had taken it. Athos had set her up well. After all, who needed an old and cumbersome statue, when an ancient grimoire would pay so much more and was easier to steal?

Athos recalled how often he had seen the book left out on the writing desk. The Captain had been so casual about its safety, never suspecting that members of his crew might understand what the book was.

The most interesting thing of all though, was the civilian passenger, a Mrs Constance Stirling, who owned the book; even though the Captain kept it in his cabin. Stirling slept in the cabin above Athos, and the sailor had soon learnt that the woman talked in her sleep. The narrow space between him and the ceiling had always felt confined and claustrophobic, but unlike the other sailors who shared his small room, he was in a prime position to make out the words behind the passenger's mumblings. Athos was for once pleased that he slept in the top bunk.

Athos discovered that Stirling was distressed and fearful; her dreams filled with unmentionable horrors. And gradually Athos began to understand how some of that was because of the book. She feared its content. In her sleep she often cried out, 'Don't read it! Never read from the grimoire!'

Athos realised that an equally susceptible collector might perhaps be led to believe that the book really did contain some power, and part with good money to own it. Athos himself did not believe in such things, even though he knew people who claimed to have witnessed supernatural happenings. Ghost stories were common among the sailors, and so were tales of beautiful seductive sirens. Athos had never seen anything on land or sea that couldn't be easily explained by some natural cause. He only believed in what he could see with his own eyes and Athos knew that words could not hold magic. They were just words, even when people set such store in them.

Athos slithered along the dock to a heap of empty barrels that were stacked high against the warehouse building. He reached behind them and retrieved the book. It was wrapped in an old sack and Athos hugged it to his chest and slipped away from the docks, never to return.

The next morning, Arabella ate breakfast with her parents. She was the model daughter, dressed neatly in a brown velvet skirt, jacket, a white ruffle blouse and a subtle bustle. Her hair was tied up and she looked like someone who would make the ideal governess, except that a lady in her position didn't have to work.

'Good heavens!' said Lord Hutchinson. 'Sailor found dead in house of ill-repute! How the devil can they justify putting that story into a respectable newspaper?'

Arabella said nothing. She was used to her father's outbursts and she didn't agree that the newspaper was respectable at all. She knew far too much about the editor's other line of work and the backhanders he took to write stories that suited the sensibilities of the empire. It was all propaganda. The story did interest her however because of her recent scrape at the docks. It seemed an unlikely coincidence. She wondered if she knew the sailor in question. She waited for her father to discard the paper before subtly retrieving it and went back to her room to read the piece.

A sailor had indeed died in a brothel and Arabella knew the place well. She had arranged to meet Athos there later that day. From the description of the dead sailor she strongly suspected that her useful contact would be of no further use.

'I'm just going out to the Mission to visit the sick, Mother,' Arabella said as she walked into the drawing room. She was carrying a wicker basket and a jar of cook's homemade damson jam peeked out from under a piece of muslin.

'You're such a kind girl, Arabella,' her mother said but she didn't look up from her embroidery. Arabella left the room and headed out.

In the family carriage, Arabella pushed aside the jars of jam, block of cheese and the small jug of sloe gin. She was already wearing her thigh holster and gun; her automatic crossbow and spare arrows, bullets and gunpowder cartridges were hidden in the bottom of the basket. She covered the weapons just as the carriage pulled in at the Saint Christopher's mission building.

'Come back for me at five,' Arabella instructed her driver and she turned and walked up the steps of the mission.

Inside, Arabella passed the sick, disabled and helpless that the mission helped every day. She felt no remorse. Her money helped these people, especially the extra revenue she and Joseph brought in from their nightly excursions. Helping the mission was her justification for being involved with Joseph's band of thieves, though Arabella would have done what she did regardless. She was addicted to the adventure. It made her feel strong and powerful. She resented how women, with the exception of the Queen, were considered to be so fragile and weak. The money she earned paid for her gadgets and gave her the life she wished to live: albeit secret.

Through the back door another carriage waited. This one was driven by one of Joseph's men. Arabella climbed inside and found Joseph waiting for her.

'I think my contact is dead,' she said. 'The sailor found at The Red Room?'

'Nasty stuff. The word is he died badly.'

'Get me into the morgue. I need to see the body.'

A few greased palms later and Arabella and Joseph were looking down at the dead body of Athos. His face was twisted and distorted with the agony of his death.

'What killed him?' Arabella asked. She could barely keep her face and voice bland.

'Animal attack,' the mortuary assistant said. He was a man in his late forties, with greased back hair. There were several splashes on the front of his apron, which Arabella took delight in observing to be blood in varying stages of freshness. Some of the stains were a dark brown, others still vibrant red.

'Animal? But how?'

The assistant pulled back the cloth covering the body and Arabella and Joseph saw the victim's naked, ripped stomach. He looked as though something had tried to eat him from the inside out.

'Innards, what's left of 'em, are over there,' the assistant said.

Arabella placed her handkerchief over her mouth and nose and feigned disgust while really it hid her smile. Her eyes followed the assistant's hand and she saw a bowl containing the remains of Athos' guts resting on a weighing scale. The blood and gore intrigued her. Death was, after all, the ultimate adventure.

'Most of his intestines were eaten,' said the assistant and his cruel eyes scrutinised Arabella for signs of nausea. She pretended to find his words distasteful.

'Oh my! How dreadful. I do feel terribly ill at such a horrid thought,' she said.

'Didn't anyone hear or see anything?' Joseph asked the assistant, pressing a pound note into his hand.

'I overheard the police inspector say that the doxy's there said they heard nuffin'. You'd fink someone would have though. Apparently the room was covered in 'is blood.'

Joseph released the note and the assistant hurriedly placed it in his pocket.

'There's more for you if you hear anything else,' said Joseph.

The assistant nodded. Arabella and Joseph left but they weren't sure what to make of the death.

'Perhaps one of the whores has a dog,' Arabella suggested. 'Maybe Athos stepped out of line with one of the girls, the dog attacked and they are covering it up.'

Joseph shook his head. 'Never heard of a dog being at The Red Room, but then I'm not in the habit of visiting the place.'

'Well it was just a thought,' said Arabella.

They returned to the mission and as Arabella let herself back in the rear entrance, Peter, one of the helpers, greeted her.

'This arrived for you a few hours ago,' Peter said holding out a parcel made up of brown paper and string.

Arabella took the package. It wasn't unusual for one of her contacts to send things to the mission even though she hadn't been expecting anything. Her eyes narrowed as she looked at the package.

'Who brought it?'

'Street urchin.'

Arabella took the parcel into the mission office. The old nun who worked there nodded but said nothing as Arabella headed towards the back room. The nun was used to the lady being around. Arabella closed the door and sat down at the desk. This was technically her office. She paid rent for the space, and gave the mission so much money that her use of the room was never questioned.

She placed the parcel on her desk and reached into the top drawer to retrieve the letter opener. Arabella then carefully cut the string and the paper slipped away to reveal a large, thick leather bound book. Arabella stared at the book cover. She couldn't understand the writing at all that covered the front. It was just like the scrawled letters that had been on the outside of the crate containing the wolf god statue. That was enough to make her realise that they were indeed connected.

'The book,' she murmured. 'But who sent you to me?'

Her mind flew back to the planned meeting with Athos. Had he taken this from the ship and sent it to her before his death? It seemed likely. She turned the book over, checking the back. There were symbols carved into the animal skin.

'What's so special about you then?'

On the spine she discovered a faded word. It was too difficult to decipher. Whereas on the opposite side, the pages were held together by a strap that wrapped around from the back to the front keeping the book closed. It held some kind of spring lock. Arabella examined the mechanism. It looked like a glass fronted pocket watch had been submerged into the cover. She turned what she thought to be the winder but nothing happened. The device seemed to be broken or jammed. She picked up the letter opener and probed the lock with the silver knife point. At that moment the watch cover sprang open.

'Ouch,' Arabella remembered the sharp gash she had received from the night before as a hard piece of metal scraped against the cut, reopening the wound. A drop of blood fell on the lock. The cogs began to turn and instead of the ticking she might have expected, the sound of music box notes playing an unfamiliar melody echoed through the room. The lock sprang open.

The book fell open and Arabella looked at a page of illustrations and words, none of which were familiar. The shapes began to move and form into English words and she realised she could read it. The picture formed into a half man, half beast: a direct facsimile of the statue.

It's a poem, she thought. 'No. A spell.'

The words formed on her tongue, her mouth opened and the language, strange and ancient poured from her lips. It burnt like liquid flame. Sharp and yet still intangible, she read the words but their meaning and sound dissipated as each one was spoken.

Arabella felt a dark horror eating away at her soul. In her mind's eye she saw an ancient resting place, a sarcophagus surrounded by hideous statues. Malformed humans, monstrous insects, creatures from the sea, and there was the wolf: a large animal head on a human male body. She found herself lying at the statue's feet, felt its claw-like hand stroke her hair. Then, Arabella did something she had never done: she screamed. A terror-filled cry that released her very soul from the cage of its human form.

Arabella woke. Her cheek was pressed against the animal skin cover of the book. She raised her head and looked around the room. For the first time she noticed how decayed the office was. A dark green mould grew around the window frame and up over the ceiling. Arabella blinked. The lamps were lit yet her eyes felt dull and sluggish. It was as though she had brought the darkness from her dream out into her world. She tried to retain some remnants of what she had been dreaming but could only conjure up the image of a room and the vague shapes of statues.

It's this book! She thought. *The words inside made me ...* Her mind stumbled and she glanced down at the desk trying to remember the thread her thoughts refused to find.

The book was closed again and no matter how much she fiddled with the lock it refused to budge. She didn't remember feeling tired, or settling to sleep, but when she looked outside she saw that the day had rapidly passed into evening and she realised she must have just drifted off and imagined opening the book.

Even now the images and words evaded her. If only she could remember! In the dream, she was sure, they must have had clarity, but despite every effort to recall them her mind wouldn't obey.

She felt tired and drained. As though she had been doing anything else other than sleep. *That will serve me right for not getting home early last night.*

Her driver should have come for her hours ago. Arabella pulled her watch out of her waistcoat pocket but it had stopped. She rewound it and saw the second hand start its sweep.

She picked up the book and re-wrapped it in the paper, then, holding it against her chest, she opened the office door.

'Sister Mary?' Arabella said. 'Do you know what time ...?'

Her voice trailed off as the outer office was strangely dark and quiet. Sister Mary wasn't there. Arabella frowned and walked out into the mission looking for the staff and nuns.

The lamps were lit but the building seemed empty. Maybe there had been some emergency and everyone had left, forgetting that she was still in the office. This scenario seemed more and more likely as Arabella wandered from room to room, finding them all empty. Even the sick were missing, the covers thrown back as though they had left their beds in a great hurry.

As she drew closer to one of the sick beds she saw the stain of a body, left to rot in one place until the flesh had disintegrated, becoming a vile sludge of fluids. For a moment she couldn't understand what she was seeing. She hurried from bed to bed seeing similar stains: evidence that people had been there and had died in a hideous manner. It all seemed too horrible. The mission now appeared to be a charnel house allowing the patients to die and rot away for years. Arabella backed out of the ward then turned and ran from the mission.

Outside, the world was unfamiliar. The city seemed to have fallen into decay. She looked up at the mission and watched as the roof began to slowly cave in, the building walls sagged and the heavy marble steps melted like snow in the sun.

I'm still sleeping, she thought. It was the only explanation for her bizarre surroundings. She pinched her arm but the pain was real and so was the hunger she felt deep inside the pit of her stomach. It was the appetite of the impoverished and it burnt into her like the flames of hell. Arabella had never known such pain. She doubled up, holding her stomach, and retched bile onto the cobbles. This was one adventure she could not enjoy. The ending seemed far too uncertain.

An hour later she stumbled down the empty streets fighting her way back to her home, and possible safety. The houses on either side of the road began to disintegrate as she passed by. The street pooled into muddy water and Arabella waded through it until she reached the steps of her parents' home. The house looked as desolate as the streets, but she ran up the steps – they remained sturdy beneath her feet – and as she reached the top the door opened for her.

'Miss Arabella,' said the butler. 'Your parents are waiting for you in the drawing room.'

She stumbled inside; her muddy velvet skirt clung to her legs, tripping her as she fell forward.

'Miss Arabella!' said the butler. He helped her to her feet and stared down at her dishevelled clothing. 'What happened, Miss?'

Arabella looked around the hallway. All appeared to be normal. She looked back towards the door and the butler hurriedly closed it.

'Can I help you Miss?' he asked.

Arabella narrowed her eyes. Through the stained glass panel beside the door, the world was colourful and light again. The streets were normal and the murky night had changed back to the afternoon daylight that she had expected to see when she woke in the mission.

'Please tell my parents that I don't feel well,' Arabella said, and hurried up the stairs to her room.

In her bedroom Arabella hid the strange book under her pillow before stripping off her clothes and wrapping herself in a robe. Her mother entered the room without knocking, and by then Arabella was sitting in the armchair by the window. She watched the street for signs of change but the world moved on as it always had. For the first time she felt truly afraid and it was not enjoyable.

'My dear, are you are ill? Do you wish me to send for the doctor?'

'No mother,' Arabella said. 'I'd prefer to rest first. I'm sure I will feel much better tomorrow.'

Her mother didn't appear to notice the muddy clothes piled on the carpet beside Arabella's bed.

'Very well, rest up and I'll have some food sent up to you.'

A few moments later a tray of food was brought up. Arabella devoured the soup and bread and asked for more. She drank a pitcher full of water and afterwards she felt the liquid squeezing through her body, watering down her veins with the coldness of death. The emptiness and pain remained like a dull ache. She felt no joy in the world.

Through the window she observed that the street outside remained the same. After some hours the night slowly drew in and eventually Arabella climbed into bed and slept.

Her dreams were haunted by statues. A squid-like monster reached out its tentacle arm and stroked her face, while a ghost-like blur dissolved into a foggy mass of poisonous gas. She choked on the fumes as the creature passed through and around her. Then there was the wolf, rearing and twitching as it contorted and turned. The creature ended up as a despicable half human, half animal and it sniffed around her until she crawled away, hiding behind crooked tombstones.

In the morning Arabella felt the darkness gathering around her eyes. If she closed one eye she could see her home rapidly turning into the decayed and rotted shell of the crypt in her dream. If she closed the other eye then all seemed well. With both eyes open she felt the coldness of one world fighting against the warmth of the other. It was a battle that raged whether she was awake or asleep.

She refused to join her parents for breakfast or lunch, accepting the tray of food which was sent up for her, and by afternoon she had demolished a full cooked breakfast, a ham and cheese platter with pickles and bread and she was settling down to afternoon tea of cucumber sandwiches, spotted dick, jam and clotted cream when a messenger arrived with an urgent note from Joseph.

Miss Arabella,
  I urgently write to tell you the statue is gone!
  Yours
  Joseph

'Tell him I'll be over as soon as I can be. I haven't been feeling myself today,' Arabella explained.

When the messenger had gone, Arabella dressed carefully, ensuring that all her weapons were in place. She had a feeling she might need them. Part of her didn't want to go out, but she knew she must.

Maybe I have lost my nerve? she thought. The idea seemed absurd yet entirely possible.

'Arabella, you are not to go out today,' her mother said when she saw her in the hallway with the wicker basket. 'You've done quite enough for the poor this week. What if you've caught some dreadful disease?'

'I'm fine mother. There are many starving children relying on me.'

It took some time but she finally persuaded her mother to let her leave and outside Arabella told the coach driver to take her straight to The Sailor's Rest. The man said nothing, and she couldn't tell if he was curious because he was bundled up in his heavy coat, a huge scarf wrapped around his neck and face and his hat was pulled down over his eyes.

Joseph was down in the basement when she arrived. Arabella felt nervous as she crawled through the secret passageway into the storage room. Though her hallucinations had stopped after her third meal she still felt strange. She did not want to feel that cold wind, or see the beams of the building cave in around her. The crawl space filled her with unnameable dread but still she forced herself onwards.

'What happened?' she asked as she reached the storage room.

'One minute the thing was there, then it was gone. I've had the men search every inch of the cellars and sewers but they found nothing. I don't know how the thief got in so quietly and took the statue,' Joseph explained.

'This is very odd indeed. When did you notice it gone?'

'This morning. But it could have been taken at any time after yesterday afternoon.'

Arabella climbed back into her waiting carriage, giving instruction to return home. Then she opened the wicker basket. Her weapons were there, but so too was the book. Arabella didn't recall placing it inside the basket. She rubbed her eyes and sat back while the carriage drove through the streets.

She felt ill again. It was as though someone had placed a curse on her. She thought back to her lucid and terrible dreams, and how these had all occurred after they had acquired the statue, and, more tellingly, the book. Even since it had come into her possession, Arabella had felt wrong.

The carriage came to an abrupt halt. Arabella looked out and discovered that they had stopped at the docklands.

'Driver! What are we doing here? I said you were to take me

home.'

When she got no response, Arabella opened the door and looked out. The driver's seat was empty, but for the coachman's scarf and hat. She looked around. The dock was unusually quiet. Several cargo ships were tied up along the massive harbour, but no sign of life.

She retrieved her crossbow and patted her leg to reassure herself that the gun was still attached to her thigh. Then she prepped the crossbow. It was small and easy to fire, with a trigger mechanism. She draped the basket, still containing the book, over her free arm and walked down the dock to look for her driver. He would be reprimanded for this.

She saw the ship that had brought the crate, with none of the activity she might have expected on board. There was no one on the deck at all. The ship appeared to be as deserted as the rest of the port.

This is like the dream I had in the mission. Only, Arabella was sure now that it had been no dream.

At the warehouse Arabella placed the crossbow down and removed the book from the basket. She unwrapped it and held the leather skin against her chest. Things had gone wrong since she had opened and read from it but how could she reverse that? She left the basket on the floor, retrieving her crossbow as she clutched the book against her chest with the other arm.

The warehouse was cold and deserted and smelt of fish. There was no group of sailors enjoying their game. There was no Captain screaming of theft. Only a circle of crates stood in the middle of the otherwise empty space. Arabella noted a coffin at the centre. She walked around it, looking suspiciously at the peculiar markings on its surface and at the daunting and varied shapes of the others that surrounded it.

Then she noted the obvious gap; a space in the circle of the same shape and size as the crate she and Joseph had taken.

'You have the book,' said a voice behind her.

Arabella turned, bringing the crossbow up on instinct while she firmly clasped the book against her chest.

It was a woman she had not seen before, wearing the heavy

coat of her driver. She removed the coat and threw it aside to reveal a red velvet dress. She shook her hair free of the driver's hat and it fell long, silver over her shoulders. She was striking to look at but not young. Perhaps in her fifties but was full of all of the vitality of the young.

'Who are you?' Arabella asked.

'A guardian,' she said. 'I keep the Ancient Ones safely in their own realm.'

'You talk in riddles ....'

'You opened the book and now one of them is free,' said the woman.

Arabella shook her head. 'No. I couldn't open it.'

The woman smiled. 'My dear Lady Arabella the book opened for you, and you read from it, and it brought you to me.'

Arabella felt fear then. A real terror that what the woman said was true. She recalled the sarcophagus and glanced at the central crate.

'It's just a book,' she denied shaking her head. 'I had a dream, that's all.'

'It's a grimoire and it holds the secrets to a universe that you couldn't possibly imagine. You didn't dream it. The *Fenrir* is free and he terrorises your city even as we speak.'

'If that is true ... then what can be done?'

The woman's smile widened. 'The only solution is sacrifice. The Ancient One will not return until he can take a soul back with him.'

The woman entered the circle and Arabella stepped back.

'Sacrifice? Look— who are you?'

'My name is Constance Stirling. I am the keeper of the book. I didn't realise that the ship I travelled on was also carrying a certain crate. In a way I should have seen the signs. I was suffering from disturbed sleep, I foolishly allowed the Captain to examine the exterior of the book. It was as though I had lost my judgement.'

'I don't know what you're talking about. But this book ... I suppose it is valuable?' Arabella said.

'What price can be put on the life of humanity?' Stirling replied.

Outside, a cold wind picked up. Arabella felt its icy tendrils slipping along her spine. She was afraid, but unwilling to give the book to Stirling. Even though she now really believed it had brought her bad luck.

Stirling had been slowly edging forward and was now at the other end of the centre crate.

'Tell me something?' Arabella said. 'Is this—a sarcophagus?'

Stirling smiled. 'You dreamed of a temple, the statues positioned around you, this shape in the centre?'

Arabella nodded but her mouth was so dry she suddenly couldn't answer. How could Stirling know this if she didn't speak the truth?

'And the buildings around you decayed, did they not?'

'Yes,' she gasped.

'People disintegrated into vile puddles?'

It was as though Stirling could read her thoughts.

'This will happen if the Wolf is not returned to his cage. The Ancient Ones will rule the Earth and the people will die to satisfy their sick lusts.'

Stirling's eyes gleamed and Arabella saw again the dead and empty streets. She felt the world turning to mud and filth around her and she knew that Stirling told the truth.

'Already they convene,' Stirling said. 'Look around you. You have brought the others here.'

'I didn't,' Arabella protested. Never before had she been so out of her depth. She believed Stirling but still had to deny her part in the madness. 'I didn't take the book. It was sent to me. How was I to know what it was?'

Stirling smiled again and it was not a kind expression. 'My dear, do you know how many souls there are in Hell who cry out their innocence? Crimes against humanity, be they by accident or by intent, still bear the same punishment. The only way to salvage this is to sacrifice yourself for the good of all.'

It slowly began to dawn on Arabella that Stirling was suggesting that she die for her mistake.

'You're insane,' she said, raising the crossbow to point at Stirling. 'I'm leaving. Don't try to stop me. I'm not above using this on you. You wouldn't be the first person I've killed.'

Arabella backed away from Stirling and circled the sarcophagus as she made her way back to the warehouse door.

She turned around only when she thought Stirling wasn't following her, but found herself not in the warehouse at all, but back in the temple of her dream.

'Set us free,' a voice hissed. 'Open the book and read.'

She turned back to the room. The crates were gone; in their place she saw the monsters. They surrounded her, touching, tasting and stroking her skin and hair with their vile appendages.

'I can't …' Arabella said backing away until she was pressed against the hard wall.

'You freed our brother,' murmured another of the creatures, this one, a huge and monstrous snake with a female head and pendulous breasts. It reminded her of the mythological Medusa except that her hair wasn't composed of snakes but glistening tentacles and they reached for her like loving arms. Another creature, the most monstrous of all, had the sex organs of both man and woman. The penis writhed and twisted as though alive, and the vagina opened and closed like some horrendous greedy mouth. Another of the creatures was mist, formless and yet suggestive of the most terrifying nightmares, while one was nothing more than a vile ichor, dripping greenish black all over the marble slabs of the tomb, and then pooling and collecting, driven by some hellish intelligence.

Arabella was suddenly pulled back. The temple fell away as her crossbow was yanked from her fingers and she found herself lying Stirling's feet. She was back in the warehouse; the crates had moved and were closer now to the one standing in the centre. She shuddered as the vision hung in the air between them.

'They are drawing you into their realm,' Stirling explained. 'It is only a matter of time before they persuade you to set them free.'

'They are horrible. Vile. I could never let them into this world.'

'Don't you understand? They have a direct pathway to you now and they will torture you until you give in. Arabella, these things know our deepest and darkest fears. They will use that against you. You won't be able to resist. No one can.' Stirling said.

'But you ...?'

'I have never opened the book,' she explained. 'And I never would.'

Stirling's steady gaze met hers. 'I'm so sorry,' she said.

'What for?'

'This.'

Stirling lifted the crossbow but Arabella dived out of its path just seconds before the arrow fired. She was on her feet, grabbing for the weapon with her right hand; the fingers of her free hand clawed at Stirling. She scratched at the other woman's face, leaving bloody furrows on her cheek below the eye. Her desperate fight was useless. As the second bolt loaded automatically Stirling pulled the trigger and the arrow fired between them straight into the book still clasped against Arabella's heart.

The arrow pierced the cover, penetrated the sheets beneath and buried itself deep into Arabella's chest. She sank to the floor, a look of astonishment on her face.

Her blood and bone began to dissolve into the book. She shuddered as her body twisted, her skin merging with the dried leather cover. Stirling watched as the markings faded from the book and then return as Arabella's twisted body warped, becoming part of the book, as so many sacrifices had before her.

Arabella tried to scream, but her breath was taken from her and. with the sound of snapping bone and tearing sinew, she ceased to exist, being absorbed totally into the grimoire.

Stirling looked at the book on the floor. It seemed so innocuous, so harmless. She then retrieved a pair of leather gloves from her pocket. Her hair was no longer silver, but had become a deep chestnut. Her face no longer had the aspect of a mature woman, but appeared to be no older than mid-twenties. The youthful spring was well and truly back into her step. She turned and looked at the crates.

The Wolf God was back in its place and Stirling smiled sadly.

Behind the central crate, Stirling picked up the carpet bag that Arabella had left behind on her previous visit. She placed the book inside then turned and walked out of the building.

Now that she had the grimoire, Stirling knew that she had to travel once more, far away from the crates and their monstrous contents. They would follow her; perhaps once again, one of them would catch her in a moment of weakness. Stirling was only human after all and the Captain of the ship had been most attractive and persuasive. But then, at least there could always be more sacrifices to undo the lapse. And to give her back her youth whenever she needed it.

In an ancient tomb in an unknown place Lady Arabella Hutchinson lay at the feet of the Wolf. His claw-like hand stroked her hair as the tentacled arm of another monstrosity burned furrows into the pale skin of her legs. She screamed. It was the deep terror-filled cry of someone who had finally lost her soul and her mind.

The Gold of Roatán

'I'm looking for a room,' Daniel Meriwether said as he placed his heavy trunk down on the floor and took a seat at the bar.

'You've come to der right place,' said the barmaid in English with a distinct Creole twang.

She was wearing a purple dress, off the shoulder and cinched in at the waist with a flared skirt. The dress was old fashioned, faded, but clean. It was reminiscent of the garb of a Spanish dancer. Gypsyish. With her long black hair tied up on the top of her head, she was a woman out of her time: unlike the women of England with their fashionably short hair cuts and flapper dresses. In fact she would not have been out of place 100 years ago.

The girl poured rum into a tin schooner from a large glass bottle, then placed the drink down in front of him. She had beautiful hands. But her face was even more youthful.

'I'm Skylar. How long you plannin' on stayin'?' she said.

Taking off his hat, Meriwether introduced himself. 'You're name is unusual,' he said.

'It's Dutch.'

Meriwether's eyes ran over her tanned skin, and wondered which of her parents had come from Holland and which was from the African settlers, formerly from the Cayman Islands. This island was full of mixed breeds, none of whom were native.

Following the arrival of Christopher Columbus, the indigenous population of the island was rapidly made extinct. Innocent fishermen and farm folk were enslaved but the invaders also brought with them infectious diseases that wiped out the remaining population: leaving Roatán free for the Conquistadors to use as they pleased. Later, when the island was discovered to offer nothing to the invaders, barren of everything but plant life, they abandoned it.

'How long I stay depends on if my business concludes sooner or later,' Meriwether said.

He used his hat as a fan. It was afternoon and it was as hot inside as it was out, but Skylar didn't appear to be affected by it at all.

'What business you in?'

Meriwether didn't speak. He cast his eyes around the inn, noting that no locals were in earshot. Yet, he suspected that Skylar knew everything there was to know about the locals and perhaps even the person he was looking for. After all, he hadn't come to The Coxon Inn on a whim. Nor had he travelled all the way from England, to Roatán's capital, Coxon Hole, without valid reason.

The war had ended two years earlier, but the waters were still not that safe to travel. Meriwether was an ex soldier, out of the army officially for medical grounds. Unofficially, he had been thrown out for running a black market ring, but his senior officer, a friend of his father's, managed to smother the scandal and get him an honourable discharge instead.

It was 1920 and Meriwether had found himself out of the army, a promising career as an officer, completely ruined, and his father had cut him off without a penny. But Meriwether had made many contacts during his smuggling and fencing days and soon found work as an investigator of sorts. Hence why he was now in the Caribbean.

'You'll feel right at home there,' Simon Ratcliffe, the lawyer who had sent him, had said. 'It was the home to over 500 pirates once. Right up your alley.'

Ratcliffe had sniffed as he said it, then dabbed at his nose with an embroidered handkerchief. Meriwether hadn't taken any notice of Ratcliffe's slight. Pirate or smuggler, what was the difference really? Ratcliffe had paid him well, in gold coin, and there would be more of it on his return.

'I'm looking for someone,' Meriwether said to Skylar now. 'Someone I expect to find here.'

'Oh?' Skylar's expression showed little interest as she

polished a tankard with a dirty cloth.

'Maybe you would even know this person?' Meriwether said.

'I know *everyone*.'

She smirked and it was a pretty smile that Meriwether warmed to. He wasn't the sort to pander to silly prejudices, anyway: especially when a deal could be done. Meriwether had always had an eye for the ladies, young, older, pale skin or other. It didn't matter to him.

While he toyed with the idea of seducing the girl her eyes sparkled with intelligence and knowing. It occurred to Meriwether that she could read him. What was it he had heard about Skylar? She was his client's contact after all and the person he was supposed to touch base with. But Ratcliffe had also said she was a 'seer'?

Meriwether picked up the rum and sipped it. The drink warmed his throat but didn't burn. It was the finest he had ever tasted.

'Locally made?'

'Yes,' said Skylar.

Meriwether wondered if she spoke the truth – Roatán was not known for its rum – but he detected no deceit in her. Perhaps it was never exported and something only the locals knew about and drank? Either way, it didn't really matter to Meriwether. What did matter was finding the descendant of Captain John Coxon.

But formalities first: he needed a safe place to stow his things and then the investigation would begin.

'So? About that room?'

Skylar rang a bell behind the bar, and a young African boy appeared from a room off to the side.

'Help Mr Meriwether get his trunk upstairs,' Skylar said. 'Here's dee room key. It be on dee first floor. Room tree.'

'Thank you,' said Meriwether and then he downed the rum and left two gold coins on the bar which Skylar spirited away before anyone saw them.

'Dat will cover a week,' she told him. 'And all food and

drink.'

Meriwether nodded and turned to follow the boy who had lifted his weighty trunk with barely a shrug and was trotting up the stairs with it. By the time he caught up the boy had already unlocked the door and was waiting for Meriwether to go in first, which he did.

The room was nothing special but Meriwether wasn't looking for home comforts. The bed was firm, the pillows soft enough. It was certainly better than the ship's cabin he had spent weeks in on his journey from England.

The boy placed his trunk at the foot of the bed and Meriwether gave him some money for his trouble. The boy bit the silver coin, grinned, then bounced out of the room without saying a word. Meriwether wondered at his energy in this cloying heat. It must have been over 100 degrees.

There was a chair placed by the bed and Meriwether sank down into it. He removed his shoes. Sweat poured down his brow and stained the armpits of his shirt underneath his jacket.

He saw a bell pull at the side of the bed and rang it. A short time later Skylar appeared.

'You need someting Mr Meriwether?'

'A bath tub, some water – warm not hot.'

Skylar's smirk was quick to her face, 'Sure.'

Meriwether watched her sashay back down the corridor but within minutes a tub was brought in followed by a team of local women, who, dressed similar to Skylar, carried buckets of water, as though they had been waiting for the order all along.

Later, wearing a thin cotton shirt, and white cotton trousers, he ventured down to the bar again. Skylar wasn't there, but another girl, this one full bloodied African, served him with a jug of cold wine, and a platter of fish, salad and fruit. Meriwether ate it all; it was fresh and delicious, better than the ship's food had been by the end of the journey.

Afterwards he cast his eyes around the inn, but it was almost deserted and there was no one of interest that he wanted to talk to. He retired early. He was tired anyway; the heat was hard for his British constitution.

In the room he opened the bedroom window, but made sure to lie underneath the mosquito net that draped over the bed. A weak breeze wafted into the room and Meriwether, despite the heat, slowly slipped into a deep sleep.

There's a mosquito under the net, he thought. He turned over, pulling his leg under the thin sheet. His calf stung as though a thousand needles had pierced him. He struggled to wake put despite himself, the tendrils of sleep clung to him.

Then he was floating above his own body. Something squirmed under the covers and a figure moved closer to the bed, cloaked in darkness, but Meriwether could see wizened hands holding a box, a miniature treasure chest. One of those hands reached underneath the net and lifted the cover.

A small wormlike creature suckled on his calf, Meriwether felt nothing but his mind screamed.

A light knock on his door woke him in the early hours. He jumped awake. It was as though he had just plummeted back into his body from a great height. There was a rush of sound in his ears, and cramp in his calf. He tried to move his leg but the intense pain almost made him cry out. He sat up and rubbed the tender spot. The pain receded.

Someone knocked at the door again.

Meriwether stumbled out of bed favouring his leg. He reached for his robe, pulling it on quickly before approaching the door.

'I know why you come,' she said Skylar when he opened the door. 'You aint the first, and you won't be the last, but dere aint no Coxon gold here. If dere ever was, it was taken when der pirates left the island.'

'I'm not looking for gold,' Meriwether said. 'I'm looking for the descendents of John Coxon.'

'What makes you think any of dem would be still here? I told you all the pirates left.'

'This island was home to some many pirates. It was a safe harbour, a place they hid plunder. I have it on good authority that they also brought family here, that they also had wives, lovers, offspring.'

113

'You got anymore of dem gold coins?'

'I can pay you to help me, but you'll have to give me information that I can verify first,' Meriwether said.

'Okay. Ask me.'

'You said earlier that you know everyone.'

'I see dee wives in dee market, dee husbands in dee bar. I know everyone in Coxon Hole for sure.'

'Then you'll know if there are any descendants of Coxon left here?'

'I know everytin',' Skylar said again.

'Then you could take me to them?' Meriwether said.

'That depend on a lot of things,' Skylar paused. 'Like why you want to meet dem? Dey got no knowledge of Coxon now. He bin gone over tree hundred year. What you gain from it?'

'My client has something *for* them.'

'Now we getting somewhere. You bin paid to come here? To find them?'

'Yes,' Meriwether said. 'And it will be worth your while if you can give me any information or help.'

Skylar was quiet now. She glanced down the corridor as though she half expected someone to find her talking to Meriwether.

'I can help you,' she said. 'But I got to speak to der family first. You need to give me some proof you mean no harm to dem.'

'Then we are at an impasse,' said Meriwether. 'Because all I can do is give my word that this is so.'

Skylar turned and walked away ending the conversation abruptly. Meriwether closed the door, shutting out the dark corridor. Clearly his word was not enough.

He walked over to the window, looked out. The sky was getting lighter and dawn approached. Through the open window he could smell the sea, and could just make out the movement of fishing boats as the hardworking fishermen set out to make their daily catch. The air was already hot and heavy, as though a storm was brewing. Meriwether dreaded the rise in temperature as the sun came further up over the sea.

Rain would be so welcome right then.

Meriwether believed he wouldn't get any more sleep but still he returned to the bed. He had almost forgotten the weird dream that Skylar's arrival had pulled him from, but his calf still ached. Skylar was on his mind though. She was a bold and fearless girl, coming to his room like that. He wondered at her motivation, first implying that he was there to look for some obscure pirate treasure, then telling him she wanted payment to help him find Coxon's family. Skylar had been his first and only contact on the island and his client had been the one to suggest The Coxon Inn and Skylar – as if he already knew that would be his best informant. From that, Meriwether had gathered that Skylar would be expecting him, would know already what he wanted, but her suspicion of him said otherwise. For the first time he began to wonder what situation the lawyer had sent him in to. The occupants of the island, from what he had seen on his brief trip from the ship, didn't seem to be bad. They were, he thought, a very simple people, whose knowledge of the world was far less than anyone living in Europe perhaps. If Skylar was not willing to help he would just have to begin talking randomly to locals and see what he came up with. Why would any of Coxon's family want to hide who they were? As Skylar had said, Coxon had been dead and buried centuries ago. Yet, she behaved as if she, and they, might expect an enemy to appear at any moment.

A rustling sound woke him. Light poured in through the open window. Meriwether could hear the sound of gulls and the soothing swish of the sea as it rolled over against the reef. He had been told by the captain of the ship that Roatán had a natural barrier reef. In his half-waking state he imagined the marine life that a diver might see there but he had no urge to see them for himself. Meriwether had a morbid fear of confined spaces and the thought of wearing a cumbersome diver's suit, and trusting someone to pump air down to him through a tube, terrified him more than the thought of drowning might.

He got out of bed and glanced out of the window. His calf still ached but he ignored it. He was surprised to discover that he had slept on late into the morning. The harbour was bustling and the fishermen were already selling their fresh catch straight from the sides of their boats to the fishmongers stalls set up on the walkway. In the distance, beside one of the stalls he thought he recognised the shape of Skylar but it could have been any woman shopping there. Though his keen eyes noted that the woman turned and stared at the inn as though she knew she was being observed. He turned back to the room and was about to ring for fresh water to make his ablutions when he noticed an envelope. It smelt of musky perfume. Meriwether saw Skylar in his mind's eye. Even before opening the envelope he was certain that it was from her.

> *A carriage and driver will collect you after lunch.*
> *Skylar*

Meriwether looked at his wristwatch and saw that it was gone noon already. He pulled on his clothes, another white cotton shirt and suit that he knew made him stand out as a visitor to the island but he had nothing cooler to wear. Then he placed a straw hat on his head to protect him from the sun.

Sliding open a secret compartment in his trunk, he checked his stash of gold, taking some out for possible bribes. From inside the trunk he pulled out the envelope from his client, placed this in his inside jacket pocket. Then he locked the trunk and put the key inside the same pocket.

For extra safety he locked the bedroom door and took this key with him as well, stowing it in his trouser pocket. Then he headed back downstairs and to the front entrance of the inn.

'Mr Meriwether?' said a man in perfect English. 'I'm your driver ...'

His name was Samuel, he was only 18 years old, and he was the son of an English missionary who lived on the island.

'I've lived here most of my life. My mother tells me that in England people sometimes have bathrooms inside their houses. They have water running through lead pipes direct to their kitchens and bathrooms. Is this true?'

'Yes. Plumbing is a luxury we now enjoy.'

'We live on a house on stilts,' Samuel said. 'Outside privy. I can't even remember England. But you'll see the type of houses I mean as we drive.'

Meriwether climbed up onto Samuel's carriage. It was a basic, old-fashioned Landau, pulled by a sturdy, tall carthorse. As they drove through the town, Meriwether saw for himself that, as with his observation of the dress of the people here, they were years behind England in advancements and luxuries.

'Living here has its benefits. You probably wouldn't enjoy the British weather now,' he said to Samuel.

Samuel laughed, 'You haven't seen our rainy season. Or experienced the hurricanes yet.'

'Where are we going?' Meriwether asked.

'Miss Skylar said I wasn't to tell you anything,' Samuel said. 'But she hoped you'd feel safer with me than perhaps a regular local of the island.'

'She's very astute.'

Samuel clicked his tongue and the horse began to trot as they drove away from the harbour and farther in land. They passed the coloured houses built up on stilts. A hive of activity was in the town as flamboyantly dressed locals went about their business. Meriwether couldn't help comparing this place to his homeland. It was a far cry from England of the 20s where women wore skirts shorter than they had ever done before. He let his mind wander, seeing but not seeing the world around him as if he could layer London over Coxon Hole. But there was no comparison really.

It was only when the more established roads became little more than worn tracks through tropical forest that Meriwether felt concerned. After all he only had Samuel's word that he was the preacher's son. And could he trust Skylar anyway?

'How much further?' Meriwether asked. He was tense and the heat made beads of sweat drip down his spine, soaking his shirt. Could he ever feel clean here? He had a growing sense of dread as any sign of civilisation disappeared as they were swallowed by jungle.

'Almost there,' said Samuel.

Then the forest opened out and they came to a clearing with a peculiar stilted house perched in the centre. Unlike the houses he had seen as they left Coxon Hole, this house was not painted with bright colours, but remained the natural wood colour, which had silvered with age and weather. The house was surrounded by a cultivated garden. On one side grew tropical plant life, on the other were vegetables. Behind the house was a steep waterfall. Meriwether felt that the whole set up would be an artist's dream: he was surrounded by nature's colours. Reds. Greens. Yellows. And the blue of the perfect, clear sky. Yet there was an incredible stillness and a sense of something unnatural about the house. It was as though it were a set on some movie picture studio lot. Not that anyone on this island would have ever seen those. But he almost expected some moustached villain to be waiting inside.

'Where are we?' asked Meriwether as Samuel drew the horse to a halt at the front of the house.

'Go inside. She's waiting for you,' Samuel said. 'I'll be here when you're done.'

'Who is?'

Samuel smiled and it was reassuring though Meriwether shuddered as he stepped down from the carriage.

Anxiety followed him as he found his way up the wooden steps, and walked round a wide veranda. The doors were open and he paused.

'Mr Meriwether?' said a frail female voice from inside the room. 'Do come in.'

Meriwether entered a small sitting room with makeshift bamboo and wooden furniture. It had the rustic feel of a country cottage. In the centre of the room, sitting on a wooden rocking chair, was an old woman.

She was white. Pale as though she hadn't stepped outside for years.

'Please sit down,' she said. 'You must be thirsty. And hungry.'

He sat in a chair opposite. Between them was a platter of

fresh fruit and a jug of lemonade placed on a low table. The old woman leaned forward and picked up the jug. She filled two glasses and handed one to Meriwether. Then she sat back in her chair and watched him as he sipped from the glass. She did not drink from hers and so, naturally suspicious, Meriwether only pretended to drink.

'My name is Amelia Coxon,' she said. 'I believe you have something for me.'

Meriwether was taken aback that the search was concluded so easily. He wasn't sure what to say.

'I … do have something. If you are a true descendent of Captain John Coxon, the infamous pirate.'

Amelia smiled, 'I am indeed and I grew up on this island always knowing this day would come.'

'Forgive me but I need, a little more proof …'

'Of course you do dear boy. Open that chest. You'll find all the evidence you need.'

Meriwether turned to the indicated chest, stood and opened it. Inside were papers, deeds, birth and death certificates, and a detailed document that explained the lineage from John Coxon to Amelia Coxon.

'As you see from the letter left to Coxon's wife and children, Coxon was going on a raid that he thought he might not return from,' Amelia said. 'She never did find out what happened to him. He vanished. Just like that. Coxon and all of his crew, and the ship they had sailed on. They were never heard from again. But then, in the twilight years of every descendent, comes a note. A gift from a law firm in England. That law firm sent you didn't they, Mr Meriwether?'

Meriwether was taken aback. The proof was there and he saw no reason to delay in handing over the envelope he had. All he wanted was to return to the cool on the British Isles and hope never to return to the island. Though his experience had not been as difficult or tiresome as other searches might have been, he felt a growing sense of unease. He was struck again at how simple and easy it was. Too easy? Or just fortunate?

'I suppose the lawyer told you to go to the Coxon Inn too. To find Skylar?'

Meriwether nodded. He took a sip of the lemonade. It was surprisingly cold and fresh. 'Yes. I'm wondering how he knew. I had thought this would prove to be more challenging.'

'There is always a Skylar working at the inn,' Amelia said. 'Please eat something. I'm sure you are keen to finish with this business and be on your way.'

Meriwether could see no reason to doubt the old woman when all of the evidence appeared to be in order. He removed the envelope from his pocket and held it out to Amelia. For the first time since he had taken the job he began to wonder what was inside.

Amelia squinted at the envelope, and then opened it. Meriwether said nothing, but he watched her scan the words with cataract scarred eyes while he picked at the bits of fruit and sipped the lemonade.

'Good!' said Amelia.

'May I?' asked Meriwether.

Amelia smiled kindly. 'I'm afraid it won't mean anything to you. You see what we Coxon's receive every generation is a new piece of the puzzle that we have been trying to solve.'

'What puzzle?'

'What happened to Coxon of course. And why he made this strange provision for his future descendants. Why he left us a clue every generation. But I hope this one will bring about a final conclusion.'

Amelia placed the paper down on the tray and stood.

'And now I must give you a reward for your trouble,' she said.

She turned away and with slow steps left the room.

Meriwether reached for the paper, scanned it, and placed it down exactly where Amelia had left it.

Then the old woman returned and she held out a pouch of gold that Meriwether took, despite the fact that he had already been amply paid for his trouble, and would receive more on his return when he confirmed delivery of the letter.

'I now need to return with proof that we have met,'

Meriwether said, realising that he wouldn't get his fee if he didn't have evidence.

'Of course,' said Amelia and she handed him a pre-written and sealed letter with the name of the law firm written on the front.

Meriwether took it. *Too easy,* he thought. *You had this all ready for me didn't you?* He glanced once more at the letter Amelia had left face down on the table.

He took Amelia's sealed letter and placed it his jacket pocket.

'Good day, Mr Meriwether,' Amelia said.

Meriwether nodded and then left the house, and returned to Samuel and the carriage but he already had the details of the letter that the law firm had sent to Amelia and he knew now, without a shadow of doubt, that Amelia Coxon had just received a treasure map.

He spoke very little to Samuel on the return journey, but he knew who might be interested, even curious, about what he had given Amelia, and he knew he had plenty of gold to pay for any help needed.

Back at the inn, Skylar was behind the bar again. He took the same seat that he had taken on his previous day.

'Der be a ship leaving for England tomorrow,' Skylar told him as she placed a tin schooner of rum down in front of him. 'I can give you a refund, now your work is done.'

'No refund necessary, I plan to stay a little longer. Take in some of the local sights,' he said.

'You done here. Best you go.'

'Aren't you even a little curious about this?'

Skylar met his eyes, 'Yes. But curiosity can be no good ting around here. Everyone knows what you tink. All the time.'

'You deserve a reward for your help though, and I said I would pay you,' he said.

'Yes. But not here. I come to your room again. Later.'

Meriwether drank the rum, then left the bar and went back upstairs to his room. When he closed the door behind him, he reached into his pocket and removed the money pouch that

Amelia had given him. As he opened the pouch, tipping out a handful of gold coins, he realised with some shock that he had been given Spanish Doubloons. This was gold lost, or stolen, centuries ago and yet Amelia had used it to reward him. On this bag of gold alone, Meriwether could probably live handsomely for many years.

A knock on the door signified that Skylar had found the time to come for her reward. Meriwether pushed the pouch and gold back into his pocket and then he removed two pieces of his own gold coins from his other pocket. When he opened the door, Skylar was there as predicted. He took her arm and pulled her inside. The girl didn't even protest which Meriwether found curious.

'A reward,' pressing the gold into her palm. 'But there will be more if you can help me.'

'What more help can you need?' said Skylar. 'You did what you came to do. Why not let it alone now?'

Meriwether knew the girl would take some convincing. Maybe she did not know that Amelia held the map of a great treasure in a note sent from the past by John Coxon. He reached into the pocket with the money pouch and retrieved one of the doubloons.

'I need your help with this,' he said.

Skylar looked at the coin with round eyes. 'Dat is old …'

'Yes,' Meriwether waited for the idea to take shape in Skylar's mind. She was a bright girl.

'Der's more of dis?' Skylar said.

'Yes. If you help me we can split the plunder.'

Skylar's eyes narrowed. 'What you found out?'

'I saw the note that my law firm sent to Amelia Coxon. It was the final piece of a treasure map, and I suspect that Amelia has all of the other pieces now.'

Skylar was silent while she continued to examine the doubloon. Meriwether had the suspicion that she knew on sight it was genuine – just as he had.

'Okay. But if I help you. You have to promise no harm would come to Amelia. And dat we don't take it all, just some, and leave der rest for Coxon's family.'

'I'm not into hurting innocent people,' Meriwether said then he agreed to her terms because he wanted her help, though he didn't know why she inspired so much trust in him. Around her he felt safe, confident.

Meriwether told Skylar some of what the final letter had said, but held back on the detail that would identify the hiding place.

'I understand it,' said Skylar. 'I know der place it mentions. It sounds like a complete map to me, too, not a part of one.'

'My thoughts exactly.'

'Well, maybe Amelia's ancestors were all sent some of the treasure to pass on to the next generation. It would explain why she already had some of the gold. Does she have a child to pass wealth on to?'

'A granddaughter ...'

'The picture is shaping up. I bet this island is full of buried Coxon treasure. And I bet Amelia has enough to see her through anyway.'

'I come back for you with help soon,' Skylar said.

True to her word, Skylar returned with Samuel and two other men. She gave Meriwether some local clothing to put on. The style was old fashioned, the fabric worn. A long colourful shirt, with three quarter trousers. Skylar had changed out of her flowing Spanish influenced dress and wore the same clothing as the other men.

Samuel smeared a brown paste on Meriwether's exposed legs, arms, face and chest. Then they wrapped a bright red turban around his head.

'You won't stand out so much like dis,' Skylar said.

They left the inn via a back door that Meriwether had been previously unaware of. Behind the building a large cart waited for them and Samuel climbed into the front and took up the reins for two sturdy ponies this time instead of one.

'Does Samuel know what we are doing?' Meriwether asked Skylar as she climbed into the back of the cart with him.

'Yes. He and dease men are trustworthy and we will reward

them for dair trouble.'

Meriwether wasn't used to trusting others, although having dealt so closely with smugglers when he was running the black market, he had grown an appreciation for the unspoken code of honour that these people had. They had to trust each other. On an island that once housed over 500 pirates, Meriwether wondered what kind of code the criminal sector here would follow.

'So will you trust me with this location you recognised now?' Meriwether said.

'The riddle in the letter was referring to Old Port Royal. Dey are ruins. An old pirate fort. Gold has been found der before,' Skylar said.

'Maybe this gold? Perhaps we are too late?'

'Coxon was clever,' Skylar said. 'It won't be somewhere obvious. What did you not tell me about the letter?'

'I'll tell you when we get there,' Meriwether said.

The light was almost gone when they reached Old Port Royal and Meriwether, Skylar and the two men, began to walk up to the ruins, while Samuel tied up the cart. The men had oil burning torches with them and they lit several of these and carried them. Two in each hand, which Meriwether thought peculiar, but didn't comment on.

'There's an old burial ground here,' said Meriwether.

'I know it,' said Skylar. 'Dis way.'

There Meriwether told them the last piece of information. The treasure was buried in the grave of a child. The name on the grave was Thomas Everridge.

They found the grave quickly as the graveyard was only small. And the two men that Samuel brought began to dig. They unearthed a chest just two feet down, and as they heaved it forth, found another one. Several more followed as they widened the digging area.

'Incredible!' Meriwether said. 'I wouldn't have believed it possible.'

The opening of the first chest confirmed that the map

Meriwether had seen was indeed authentic. The chest was filled with gold and jewels and treasures of all kinds. They didn't open the others until all the digging was complete. Then they loaded them all onto the cart. It was heavy work, but all of them, including Skylar and Meriwether, put their backs into it.

'You can't mean to share this with Amelia now,' Meriwether said when Skylar did not object to the removal of all of the chests.

'You've done well, Granddaughter,' a voice said behind them as the last of the treasure was heaved from the ground.

Meriwether turned to find Amelia Coxon dressed in pirate garb with an old man, sitting on an open topped Sedan chair with four men stood around him.

Skylar bowed to the old man in the chair. 'Everyting is ready.'

Meriwether knew he had been tricked long before the two men that had been with Samuel caught hold of him. They dragged him before the old man and forced him down on his knees.

'Don't feel too bad,' Amelia said. 'This was always meant to happen. Otherwise I would never have left the letter for you to see.'

'You've got your treasure, just let me go and I'll be on that boat back home tomorrow.'

'I'm afraid I can't let you do that ...' said Amelia. 'We still have need of you ...'

Meriwether looked up at the old woman. She was holding a small chest in her old, wizened hands. A memory stirred of having seen this box before, though he couldn't recall where. He looked for pity and found only a cold blankness in her wrinkled face.

Skylar approached. She was now wearing a long robe and a crown made of exotic flowers. Her hair was loose and wild about her shoulders and he thought then that the girl had never looked more beautiful or bold, but her eyes – and why hadn't he seen that familial similarity in them before – were exactly like her grandmother's: cold, sure and somewhat terrifying as they danced with an evil light which was emphasised by the oil lamps that Samuel and his men were placing around them in a wide circle.

'What do you plan to do with me?' asked Meriwether, even though he was afraid of the answer.

Skylar nodded her head towards the men holding him and they pulled him back to his feet.

'Reclaimed Coxon gold comes with a price,' Skylar said.

The men dragged him towards the large hole in the ground. Lighting pierced the sky, illuminating the opening. Then the tropical storm, that Samuel had mentioned earlier, began. The heavens opened and poured warm rain down. Meriweather was soaked in seconds, but the pirates, for Meriwether recognised them now for what they were, all remained dry. Even when the pirate graveyard turned to mud, the rain was unwilling to hit them.

They dangled him over the hole: it was larger than it had been. Meriwether stared down and a shift of earth revealed something completely new. A burst of dark light lit up Meriweather's face. He was terrified. The fear that they would bury him alive surged up into his head, resulting in panic. He was unable to think, unable to move, paralysed completely with fear as he was.

There was an angry roar from below: something resented being disturbed. The men holding him gasped with their own fright, and then Skylar was chanting. Odd words that sounded like no language he had ever heard before.

'Show the mark!' said the old man from the safety of his sedan.

Samuel stepped forward and using a dagger, cut away the borrowed trousers from one leg. The browning gloop washed away, Meriwether, glanced downwards and saw a burning brand on his calf. Why had he forgotten the dream?

The hole widened and now Meriwether could see something moving below. His mind told him it was a snake filled pit, and then beastly, tentacled limbs reached for him.

He screamed.

The two men let go of him. Arms flailing, Meriwether fell forward unable to prevent it.

The thing below caught him and Meriwether barely had an opportunity to draw breath back into his winded lungs before the creature, quite literally, ripped him apart.

Blood sprinkled over the hole. And out into the air, joining with the rain. Skylar wiped a splash of blood away from her cheek. She turned to look at her grandparents – both had been showered in Meriwether's blood. Now, her frail grandfather, former pirate, Captain John Coxon, stood up from the Sedan and took the hand of his wife Amelia. Both of them were changing, age was replaced by youth. Amelia looked fresh, a woman of no older than 30 and Coxon became a youthful middle-aged man. The very age he was when he 'disappeared'. That was when he made a deal with the Old Ones.

Their granddaughter, Skylar, whose name meant 'One who seeks shelter', had never aged from that day either. She was the lure. And as for Coxon's crew, they too remained how they had been. Ever the slaves to Coxon and his corrupt family.

'Take the gold to the usual place,' Coxon said.

The crew hurried to do their master's bidding, knowing that a fair share of the plunder always came their way. They did not mind their enforced immortality, especially when it guaranteed them wealth as well.

Skylar glanced at the churned earth which now refilled the hole in the graveyard: she had always known where the gold was. Had merely been playing the part given her so long again as the conduit to the old ones and the bringer of the sacrifice. She knew that beneath the earth more gold chests would replace the ones they had removed, and they would be there, waiting, when the family next needed to renew.

'He was quite a pleasant young man,' Amelia said.

'Yes. A perfect sacrifice. The right measure of greed and naivety. His blood the perfect blend.'

She glanced at the chest Amelia still held. 'The right taste,' Amelia said. He fingers moved over the top of the box as though she were stroking a favourite pet.

'Don't forget to send one chest of gold to the law firm,' Coxon said.

'Shipping has already been arranged, Grandfather,' Skylar said.

'Good girl! You never forget any detail do you?'

'You taught me well,' she said.

As the warm rain continued to pour down, they turned and their way back to town.

The Rift

For the poet Cardinal Cox

The clock was ticking. Cardinal could feel the time he had left running out, dripping from his veins like sand in an hour glass.

'Remember, you'll only have twelve hours,' Professor Curtis had said and then he injected Cardinal with the serum. 'Any longer and we won't be able to bring you back.'

He had wanted to ask what would happen if he stayed, but the question was pointless, no one knew what had happened to those who failed to return. Cardinal's logical mind thought that they probably just lived out their lifespan in the past.

Certainly there had been some evidence that time-travellers had been at some of the major historical events: archive photo snaps taken in the eras long before digital enhancements were possible. Even in Cardinal's timeline, people still bought into the idea of 'being there' when the big things had happened. The fall of the Roman Empire had been one of the top choices. Cardinal however, didn't do this for pleasure. It was his job.

'The breach will occur sometime after midnight,' Curtis had said. 'So you'll have plenty of time to acclimatise and find the rift.'

But now that Cardinal had arrived, he wasn't at all convinced there was enough time for him to find the wormhole, or stop it from opening up, letting through the evil from the other side.

It was odd that Cardinal had all of these key moments in his genetic code. Even odder that he, unlike others, was meant to go back and fix the anomalies before they changed the world that they lived in. It was almost as if there was no way to fail. After all, the rift had happened, but the scenario hadn't unfolded, and so he, or someone like him, had stopped the fall out in time to make sure that this continued to be the case.

A lot of the things that Cardinal was supposed to fix, or prevent, were events that history said were fictional. Curtis however knew the truth. This was because he, using his father's discovery, devised a serum that unlocked inherited memory. Curtis knew when and where all of the anomalies were going to happen, and which of his team would arrive to save the day. All he had to do was make that happen when the time in the present was right.

And the time had been right to send Cardinal back, just a short three hundred years this time. It wouldn't be a hard journey physically or mentally. For that at least Cardinal was grateful.

The fun part of the trip was that he would, for once, be involved in an actual historical event. It was March 20th, and Jesse James and his gang would have robbed the Russelville Bank in Kentucky, getting away with a cool $14,000. *Nothing by the standards of cyber-thieves,* Cardinal thought. But the crimes of his present in 2168 were not important to him. It was the ones committed in the past that counted now.

But it wasn't the theft that Cardinal was interested in, it was what had followed. And that happened somewhere in or around Russelville.

'You ain't from around these parts, are ya?' said a voice behind him. Cardinal turned to see the sheriff and a posse of men walking out of the salon.

'Hi there Sheriff,' Cardinal said and he touched his hand to his wide brimmed hat. 'I've been sent to investigate the robbery.'

Cardinal produced a badge that said US MARSHAL. It was all the ID that the sheriff required.

'You got word of this quickly,' said the Sheriff.

'I was in the next town when I heard,' Cardinal said.

The sheriff didn't ask any more. These were somewhat naive and trusting times, a badge was a badge. You didn't question its wearer.

'I need to see the vault,' said Cardinal. 'Take me to the bank.'

'Vault is empty,' said the sheriff.

Cardinal stared him down for a moment.

'This way,' said the sheriff turning back toward the main street.

Cardinal followed, and a look from him ensured that the posse remained. The less eyes to see this the better, and time was running out.

They walked along the horse-trampled street, Cardinal avoided a pile of steaming horse shit as he followed the sheriff and soon they were at the doors of the bank. The front door had been blown off its hinges, and out back the wall leading into the vault had been decimated by an intense blast of explosives. Or so it seemed.

Cardinal studied the ridge of damaged brick. To the naked eye the scorched remains were an indication of explosives, but Cardinal was looking for other signs in the gunpowder smuts. He waited until the sheriff was distracted before he removed a small phial from his pocket. He unscrewed the lid and removed a long thin swab, which he used to smear the edge of one of the bricks. Then he placed the swab back inside the tube. As he sealed it the swab inside began to change colour. Cardinal had his answer before he buried the phial back into the deep pit of his pocket.

This was as they had expected.

A Few Hours Earlier

'You wait here,' John Jarrette said. 'Anyone follows us outta town, cut 'em down.'

Jesse James glanced over at his brother Frank before nodding. They hadn't known Jarrette long and this was the first job they had agreed to do with him. They knew and trusted George and Oll Sheperd, not Jarrette, who bragged of his leadership and fighting skills in the war. Jesse didn't know how true it was. He only had the man's own word to be the testament to his bravery, and he never took anyone's word.

He cleaned and loaded his gun as Jarrette talked. Arthur McCoy hung on his every word, as did the Sheperds. Jesse and Frank said nothing. Later, when Jarrette and the others left, Jesse stepped up to show his real leadership skills. He was young, but already he knew he had more intelligence than Jarrette and his gang.

'We ain't waitin' out here like nobodies,' said Jesse.

'What you wanna do?' said Frank. 'This is gonna be an easy pay day. No risk. No one will even know we're involved.'

'I don't trust Jarrette,' said Jesse. 'And Cole is a blabber mouth.'

'This ain't our raid,' said Frank. 'We follow orders.'

'Come on,' said Jesse. 'I'm heading into town to watch it go down.'

Frank reluctantly climbed on his horse and followed Jesse. The trail of the other gang members was easy to follow.

'That could lead right back to us,' Jesse said. 'We are gonna head 'em off when they come outta town. Send them north instead.'

'I see no issue with that,' Frank said. 'And it shows initiative. The trail in, being different from the one outwards.'

They reached the edge of town just as the robbery started. From a safe distance, the James brothers watched as Cole Younger and Oll Sheperd fired bullets up and down the street to keep at bay any brave, or foolish, men who thought they could take on the gang. Soon Jarrette, McCoy, Younger, and Oll and George Sheperd where pounding the dirt street with horses fired up to ride hard out of town.

Jesse and Frank waited on the edge until the men were in sight then they let their presence be known. The gang followed them away from town via Gallatin Pike and five miles away, Jesse and Frank led them all safely in and through the woods. Their pursuers all left behind.

'Why'd you change the plan?' Jarrette asked.

'The rail was two obvious,' Jesse said.

'Well it worked. Well done. You earned your cut,' said George. 'See, I told you these two were worth bringin' in.'

Jarrette took a swig from a bottle of rye whiskey. 'I don't like my men to change things but … you did the right thing boys. This time.'

Jesse double-checked the money he'd been given before they said goodbye to the others.

'See that?' Jarrette said. 'He don't trust us.'

'I don't trust anyone,' Jesse said.

Jesse, Frank, Oll and George took their cut, leaving the others in the forest. As they rode away, Oll pulled his horse alongside Jesse's.

'Somethin' on your mind Oll?' Jesse asked.

'Somethin' strange happened in the town yesterday.'

'All looked like it went to plan to me,' said Jesse.

'What d'you mean?' asked Oll.

'Frank and me were watching.'

Oll was silent, taking in the implications of Jesse's confession. Jesse knew he probably wasn't sure if this meant Jesse and Frank didn't trust them, or just Jarrette.

'We didn't like Jarrette's attitude,' Jesse said.

Oll nodded, he looked relieved. At the end of the day he knew what a good shot Jesse was and he didn't want to ever have to go up against him.

'This thing. I wanted to tell you about it … last night,' Oll said, 'but George said I was seeing things. Too much moonshine.'

'That shit can send you crazy for sure …' Jesse nodded.

'I'm staying off it. From now on. But …'

'Go on.'

'I don't think I imagined what I saw.'

Oll began to tell Jesse the strange tale. Of how, as the others filled their saddle bags with money, he glanced towards the outside wall. They had thought of blowing it, but figured it was easier to come inside and hold the cashier at gunpoint. And it had proved easier. But Oll had seen something and he knew it was real. Just as sure as the money in his saddle bag.

'It was a light. Growing in the centre of the wall. I was gonna point it out to George but he had the cashier pinned down and couldn't take his eyes away and Jarrette, Arthur and Cole were busy grabbing the money.'

'Oll, I think George is right. You were seeing things,' Jesse said.

Oll let his horse drop back behind Jesse's and he never mentioned it again.

Two hours to go to the anomaly.

'What I don't get,' said the sheriff, 'was why they blew the wall out. Even after they got what they came for. It was just destruction for the sake of it. It made no sense.'

Cardinal accepted a tot of whisky from one of the deputies, but he didn't drink, merely placed it on the table before him. They were in the salon. Loud music was coming from the corner of the room, where a piano player pounded the ivories with skilful aggression, and one of the whores sang a rude ditty, slightly off key. Those gathered around the piano had been drinking for hours and so they cheered and clapped as the girl sang as loud as she could.

'When did the wall blow?' asked Cardinal over the din.

'Soon after they rode outta town,' the sheriff said.

'It was a distraction. To stop you all following,' Cardinal said.

The sheriff knocked back his shot, slammed the glass down and reached for the bottle of whisky placed in the centre of the table. Cardinal knew that the man was in it for the long haul.

'Goddam outlaws,' the sheriff said. 'Stealing from decent hard working folk.'

Cardinal said nothing. But when the sheriff downed his next drink, he switched his full shot for the empty one.

'I'll bid you gentlemen goodnight,' he said.

He stood and left the salon. Neither the sheriff nor the deputy noticed.

Cardinal walked down the street, back to the bank and around the back to gaze at the gaping hole in the wall. They hadn't attempted to secure it, just moved any remaining valuables that the thieves hadn't taken. Cardinal stared at the space. It was glowing when it should, at this time, be a gaping black hole.

'Okay. This is happening,' he said.

He unholstered the gun at his left hip. From his right hip he removed another weapon. They looked like any normal weapons of the period. A chemical reaction joined the two guns as Cardinal pressed the barrels together. The guns became one piece, elongated and thickened. Anyone seeing this would not even recognise it as a weapon at all, but just an object of unusual proportions.

The glow from the wall intensified, and Cardinal reached inside his waistcoat to retrieve an eyeshield. This was going to be easy. As soon as the creature stepped out of the wormhole, Cardinal would blast it back to where it came.

'What's goin' on here?' said a voice.

Cardinal glanced over his shoulder. He saw a tall, dark haired man wearing a coat, shabby with road dust, standing at the corner of the bank looking at him. Cardinal recognised him from his photographs. It was Jesse James, and he realised then that he had just witnessed James' true involvement in the crime. He had always 'believed' him to be involved, but the varying historical accounts offered insubstantial evidence.

The distraction was enough to throw Cardinal's aim off. The wormhole opened, Cardinal fired, but he hit the wall of the bank instead.

Brick and plaster burst out into the back street, Cardinal threw himself aside to avoid being injured by the debris. Jesse James propelled himself forward.

'That gun ...' he said.

He towered over Cardinal and then the time traveller noticed. James only vaguely resembled the tired old photographs that had been archived in the historical museum. Jesse James was somehow an ancestor, and Cardinal looked just like him. This was why he had the inherited memory in the first place. He *had* to explain to Professor Curtis.

'Out of the way!' cried Cardinal.

Jesse turned and looked at the growing hole that seemed to be taking over the entire side of the bank now. Jesse stared into the vortex, mesmerised by the swirling of what looked like a star-filled night sky.

'I said get outta the way!' yelled Cardinal. He hurried to his feet toward Jesse and then – the creature he'd been expecting from beyond burst forth in a toxic mist. Jesse breathed in the fumes: it was poison to his lungs. His insides erupted in agony and he fell forward rendered insensible with shock and pain.

He was caught by the swollen, blistered appendage of the creature. Its gaping mouth flapped wider, and the outlaw was lifted towards the thing. Sharp teeth bit down into the neck of its prey, and as Jesse came out of his poison-induced stupor he screamed.

Blood spurted like an unchecked fountain, spraying the wormhole, the remains of the wall and Cardinal as he propelled himself forward.

The creature stuffed Jesse into its awful mouth. The thing chewed and the crunch of bones would haunt Cardinal's dreams for years to come.

Cardinal raised his weapon and fired.

Cardinal had ridden away from the bank, his face covered with a scarf as Frank James fired bullets behind them to stop the posse from pursuing. They had been riding for years now and the James gang was infamous. A large bounty lay on both his and Frank's head.

There was no way back for Cardinal once Jesse had died. The paradox would have wiped out his entire future. The only way forward was to *become* his ancestor. Frank hadn't even noticed, though Cardinal knew that he and Jesse had many differences. The colour of their eyes for one. But if Frank noticed anything at all about the change in his brother it was the cold and knowing expression that Jesse now wore, as though the burden of the world was on his shoulders.

And it was true too. Cardinal knew the very day that Jesse James would die in history and so he spent his days preparing for that moment. He knew he could change the course of his destiny with just one false move and so he played out Jesse's life, and love, to perfection. Even feigning surprise when, on that fateful day, his once trusted friend shot him in the back.

Tell Me No Lies

New Orleans, 1926

'My manservant, Henry, tells me you can help me, Mister Bajolière,' Adrienne said.

Andre Bajolière was a private investigator, a fixer. He was tall, with dark wavy hair and hazel eyes. His mother was mulatto but there was only a hint of it in the man's light skin. Adrienne didn't care about his heritage; only what he could do for her.

Bajolière dressed well. Like a gentleman of the time, though slightly more garish: the sort of man she had seen playing poker in the speakeasy club where they had chosen to meet. Yes, Bajolière was a handsome man: Adrienne knew that many a woman had fallen foul of those dark mysterious looks. If she had been interested in men, Adrienne thought it likely that he also had a dangerous spark that she would have found attractive too.

'How can I help?' he said. His voice was deep with a subtle Creole drawl, as though Bajolière was used to mixing with all types of people and he had become adept at softening his tones. Indeed, even in Ricky's – a white only club – no one had challenged the man's right to be there.

They sat in a private booth facing the stage. In any other place Bajolière would stand out, but no one was paying attention to them at Ricky's. It was, after all, a speakeasy, and sold intoxicating liquors totally against the Volstead Act that had been enforcing Prohibition for the last six years. A new breed of gangster had risen up since then, and an underworld network of people ran clubs and bars that defied the law. These were once rough and ready street types, but now they provided a service that meant they could rub shoulders with the rich and famous. It gave the mobsters airs and graces that they had previously had no need for. They enforced their own rules, and adapted others to their needs.

Adrienne pulled a cigarette and a long onyx holder out of her purse. She fitted them together, leaned forward, lit the cigarette on the candle in the centre of the table and took a long pull before blowing out the smoke towards the stage. Bajolière waited patiently until she was ready to speak while he observed his new client. She had fair hair, green eyes, Attractive – striking even, but not conventionally beautiful. She had too little curve for his tastes but her androgynous figure suited the long straight dress, favoured by flappers.

'I need to find someone who can ...'

The words wouldn't come for a moment. How could she really be asking this ridiculous question?

'Don't be afraid to ask, whatever it is,' said Bajolière. 'There's nothing that can shock me. Nothing I haven't heard.'

Sarah's loss had hit Adrienne hard. While trying to maintain public decorum she had spent months in mourning. It hadn't been easy to hide her utter devastation. Even from the police when she chased some of her contacts at the local station to find out what they were doing to catch Sarah's murderer.

'A friend of mine was murdered,' she said. 'Other than her killer I was the last person to see her alive.' Her voice trembled despite her promise to herself to keep all emotion in check and the tale poured out in an unpractised rush.

'This friend,' Bajolière asked. 'How did she die?'

Adrienne was plummeted back to that night.

Sarah arrived at the smoke-filled club, wearing a gold dress, with cream fringe that just covered her rouged knees. Sarah had such beautiful legs ... accentuated by the rolled down stockings. Unlike Adrienne she had dark hair, deep brown eyes. She was shorter than and curvier. Sarah was pure Creole: her Spanish settler family was strict Catholic. No one could ever know about her being in this place, or her relationship with Adrienne.

'Strangled. With one of her own stockings.'

She expected the usual well meaning expressions of

apology, but Bajolière did not say that he was sorry for her loss. He said nothing at all and his face remained blank. That's when Adrienne knew she could trust him with the truth. Bajolière was someone on the periphery of society, of the underworld. Perhaps he even worked for the mob. He would make no judgment because, as he had said, he had seen it all.

'She was my lover.' Adrienne put her head in her hands. 'She was supposed to meet me the next day. When she didn't arrive I rang her house and …'

'Miss Carter is dead …'

It was the day the bottom fell out of her almost perfect world.

'The police have done nothing at all and the trail is going colder every day. I believe there are people among *your* contacts that can speak to the dead. I want you to find me one. Not someone who does parlour tricks to make an aging widow feel less alone. I want to find someone who can *really* contact Sarah.'

'Why? What do you hope to learn?' Bajolière said.

'Who killed her … ?'

'But what use would this knowledge be? The police aren't going to believe what a medium says, no matter how accurate the information.'

'I know.'

'Then what will be the point of learning who the killer is?' Bajolière said but his voice held no criticism, it was a factual query.

'Revenge. I'm going to kill him,' Adrienne said.

'Killers of women deserve no less.'

Adrienne was surprised, but pleased, by his reaction.

'I can help. But … the realms I move in can be dangerous and you have to be prepared for any outcome. You may not get exactly the answer you seek.'

'I am prepared for anything.'

Dressed modestly, in something one of her servants would wear to church – a calf length skirt in brown and a white blouse, covered by a short brown jacket – Adrienne met Bajolière in the French Quarter the next day. The detective appeared to be completely at home and she even noticed, as they walked through the streets like any ordinary couple might, how the shop keepers nodded to him. She didn't know if this formal acknowledgment was a good or a bad thing. Bajolière was definitely known in the area, respected perhaps, but Adrienne couldn't help wondering what he had done to earn such esteem and familiarity.

It was afternoon and Adrienne had spent the morning worrying whether she was doing the right thing in trusting Bajolière. The sheer nature of their somewhat clandestine arrangement made her feel nervous, and excited. Never normally shying from new things, Adrienne shouldn't have experienced quite the level of apprehension that she did but so much was riding on the meeting. She had to get in contact with Sarah. She couldn't move on with her life until she did.

'Here we are,' Bajolière said as they turned into a quiet street.

Then he took an immediate right and led her down an alley around the back of the houses. 'Don't be nervous.'

'What do I pay?' she asked.

'Whatever you think the knowledge she gives you is worth.'

Adrienne prided herself on always being a good tipper – the bigger the tip the better the service – and this concept of paying what something was worth (after you have the service, and not before – like she usually did to ensure the best table at a restaurant) was odd to her and left her feeling vulnerable. Would the medium give her the best without knowing what was in it for her?

'Things are done differently round here,' Bajolière said. 'Some things money can't buy.'

They approached through a small yard. A white painted door had been left open and Bajolière appeared to be all too familiar with the route.

He walked into the dimly lit kitchen. Adrienne followed.

'Welcome,' said a voice from the corner of the room.

141

Adrienne's eyes took some time to adjust to the gloom after the bright day outside.

'We are here to see Elgenor,' Bajolière said.

'She's expecting you.'

Adrienne could see the owner of the androgynous voice; it was an old man with wizened coffee coloured skin. His body, probably once robust, was shrunken and bowed with age. He was impossibly old – close to a hundred. Or at least looked it. Even so, he surprised Adrienne by moving quicker than she would have thought him capable as he hurried across the room to open another door.

'Go through,' he said.

Bajolière and Adrienne entered the next room. This one was even darker than the kitchen but almost as soon as the old man closed the door behind them, a match was struck and a candle glow spread from a table in the centre of the room.

The flame flared and sputtered and the face of a beautiful young woman was illuminated in the glow.

Elgenor was white. *Not even a trace of colour*, Adrienne noted as she walked towards the table. Her hair was the palest blonde, eyes deep blue. If heritage was anything to go by, Elgenor was a throwback from the Saxons. What was she doing living here?

'Sit,' Elgenor said.

Bajolière stepped back and took a seat by the door as Adrienne moved forward and took the one opposite Elgenor.

'You're younger than I thought you would be,' said Adrienne.

Elgenor smiled slowly, she had black painted lips, charcoal around her eyes. 'Appearances can be deceptive,' she said. 'You wish to contact someone newly crossed over.'

Adrienne nodded but she was taken aback by how the woman went straight into the formal discussion with no warm up: making no attempt to leech information from her only to feed it back later.

'A lover. A woman. Murdered.' Elgenor said.

Adrienne glanced at Bajolière. He sat with his eyes closed as though he had fallen asleep.

'He can't hear any of this,' Elgenor said. 'What happens here is between us, no secrets will be shared with those who do not need to hear it. And so, you must tell me no lies. The spirits detest liars, and will not help you if you do.'

Adrienne nodded. The woman was impressive but so far everything she had said could have been fed to her via Bajolière.

'You'll know the truth when it presents itself,' said Elgenor. 'Who to trust is always a big part of it. *He* means you know harm, I've known of him for some time. People around here trust Bajolière. He's a good man and always does the best he can for his clients.'

Adrienne met the girl's eyes. 'How did you know what I was thinking?'

'That's why you're here.'

The candle flickered and dimmed, like a gaslight being turned down, and Adrienne was plummeted into Elgenor's world as she fell into a calm trance.

Elgenor closed her eyes; she looked as though she were sleeping. Adrienne waited to see what would happen, half expecting the table to move, noises to float around the room, strange smells to waft from nowhere, but all was silent. Then Elgenor opened her eyes.

'Sarah has passed beyond,' she said.

'What do you mean?' asked Adrienne.

'She went on to the other plane. Only those who refuse to move on can reach me.'

'Bajolière said you could do this, that you're genuine.'

'I'm sorry, I can't talk to her. I would if I could.'

'I need answers …'

'Sarah cannot give them. She was truly ready to go when she did,' Elgenor said.

'How could she be ready? She was murdered! She died so young!'

'Such mysteries are the way of the other world,' Elgenor said. 'But only those with unfinished business remain. Or the stubborn. She was neither of these things. In fact I would take heart from this. It means that her life was happy and complete. You helped to make it so.'

'There must be a way to reach her …' Adrienne said, ignoring the words that were meant to comfort her.

'You must accept this as a good thing. She is in the best realm now.'

'I can't. I *need* the answer.'

Elgenor sighed.

'I need to know who did this. *Who murdered my lover?'*

Elgenor glanced over at Bajolière, who slept on oblivious of the torment that Adrienne was experiencing.

'Very well. There is another way,' Elgenor said. 'But it is dangerous.'

'I didn't come into this with concerns for my own safety.'

'We could summon the Keeper of Secrets …' Elgenor said.

Adrienne did not understand the implications of what Elgenor offered – even the clause that once the 'summoning' began there would be no going back until the spell was ended. The smell of the perfumed candle lulled her, making her more receptive to Elgenor's low whispered explanation of the process. It was surreal, dreamlike. There was no question. No doubt. She had to take any risk to learn the truth.

'Do you agree?' Elgenor asked when her description of the ritual ended.

'Yes.'

'Come with me.'

They stood up from the table. Behind her chair Elgenor pulled aside a curtain that covered another doorway. Beyond was a set of steps leading downwards, into what Adrienne thought was a cellar. But as she followed the woman, the stone steps changed, becoming narrower and they began to curve around a central pillar of stone. Adrienne grew tired as she followed, and then she remembered that they had left Bajolière behind. She briefly felt some concern about being alone with Elgenor and taking part in this ritual, but she was unable to change her mind: she had made a promise to see this through. She had to know who had killed Sarah didn't she? No matter what the cost?

They reached a wide cavern cut into the solid rock. Adrienne had no concept of how far below the ground they were but she speculated that the cavern must be buried beneath the other houses on the street.

'The Keeper of Secrets does not *give* away his knowledge. A price must be paid,' Elgenor said.

'What price?' Adrienne asked.

'I don't know what he will demand. But it will be a payment for the future, not for today.'

Adrienne thought about her life, and how it would be now that Sarah was gone from it. Love, even a secret one, had made her life richer. Without the knowledge that Elgenor offered, she didn't feel she would ever be able to put her life back on track. She may never meet anyone like Sarah again but perhaps by finding out what happened she would be able to move on.

'Let's do this,' Adrienne said.

Elgenor nodded, and then, turning her back to Adrienne she raised her arms. A thousand candles sparked and lit and the cavern became illuminated with a flickering yellow glow. Now Adrienne could see the weird, rough shape of it. It really did look as though someone had carved this secret place out of the rock, one chip of a miner's pick at a time.

In the centre was a stone slab altar, and on it rested the trappings, Adrienne assumed, of Elgenor's craft. A bowl, a dagger, more candles. Some kind of book bound together in what looked like blackened pigskin. Around the slab was a ring of candles in large ornate holders. These too had sparked into life and created an additional circle of light around the altar. Adrienne followed Elgenor into the centre and looked at the book. She tried to read the words on the front but they swirled and swayed in the flickering light and it made her head swim and eyes sting. She gave up trying to read and returned her attention to Elgenor instead.

Elgenor took up the dagger and held out the bowl to Adrienne. Adrienne accepted the bowl and then, before she could react, Elgenor pricked her hand with the tip of the knife.

Blood bubbled from the tiny wound and Elgenor gathered it in the bowl. Then the girl pricked her own finger and merged her blood with Adrienne's in the bottom of the bowl.

'To guarantee our safety this day,' Elgenor explained.

She placed the bloodied bowl on the altar, and picked up the book.

Taking Adrienne with her, Elgenor backed out of the circle of candles.

The circle closed up as they passed through the small gap: the candles had a life of their own and the flame from them rose higher merging into a wall of fire.

No heat came from the flame.

Adrienne remained by Elgenor's side as the girl opened the book and began to chant in a language that Adrienne didn't recognise. There were words that sounded a little like Creole but mostly it was a guttural combination of sounds that made no sense to her at all.

The blood in the bowl began to sizzle and burn, it was as though all of the heat from the candles was focused into the circle.

'Volgna-Gath: Keeper of Secrets. Appear to us, your servants, and share with us the secret of the death of Sarah,' Elgenor said now in French, a language that Adrienne did understand.

The flames rose higher, and Adrienne took an involuntary step back towards the stone steps, fearing that any moment the cavern would be consumed. But the flames, though growing, became colder, not hotter. Adrienne shivered with the increasing cold, and anticipation of what would happen.

The fire lapped around Elgenor but left her skin and clothing undamaged even though she stood so close to the ring that she was almost part of it. Even the book remained intact, though Adrienne was certain that any normal paper would have caught fire instantly.

In the centre, flame burst up in the bowl as the blood caught fire, smoke poured from the flames and formed into a shape that stood beside the altar. It was a brutish form. Heavy – ugly as a gargoyle – with charcoal skin that smouldered in the flames.

'The first toll has been paid with our blood,' Elgenor said. 'Now quickly, ask your question.'

Adrienne stepped forward. 'Who killed my lover Sarah?'

The creature turned to face Adrienne and Elgenor. Its mouth opened and the flame in the circle seemed to be sucked inside. Blackened razor sharp teeth chomped on the flames. A rush of sound assaulted Adrienne's ears at it spoke in a garbled tongue.

'What does it say?' Adrienne asked.

'It said … *you* did!' Elgenor answered.

The creature began to fade and with it the flames died down until the circle was nothing more that candles surrounding the altar.

Adrienne stood in shock as Elgenor finished the ritual ensuring that the creature could not break through from whatever hell dimension it had come from.

'It lied!' Adrienne said when the last of the candles dimmed.

'The Keeper of Secrets may have his own agenda, but he never lies.'

'It said *I* killed Sarah … I didn't. Why would I look to find the truth if I knew all along?'

'Come,' said Elgenor. 'We must seek to expand on this truth.'

'I swear to you …' Adrienne said.

Elgenor picked up one of the lit candles and led the way back up the steps. Once they were back in the room she placed the candle on the table and dropped the curtain back down over the door to the cavern beneath the house. Then she offered Adrienne a seat once more.

'Where have you been?' asked Bajolière who, having left the room in search of Adrienne when he woke from the trance that Elgenor had induced, now returned.

'All is well,' Elgenor said. 'But we are still on a journey to find the whole truth.'

'I don't understand why that thing would lie …' Adrienne

said.

Elgenor said nothing. In the centre of the table Adrienne now noticed a red velvet cloth which draped over something round. Elgenor uncovered a crystal ball and gazed into it.

'Look deep here,' she said and Adrienne leaned forward. 'This will reveal the truth of that night.'

Adrienne was sitting in her usual booth at Ricky's when Sarah arrived. Sarah was wearing a gold dress, a shiny fringe barely covered her rouged knees. She had her stockings rolled down in typical flapper fashion – a style that suited Sarah so much but one that Adrienne had never adopted.

Adrienne made a gesture with her hand to draw Sarah's attention but there was no need as the girl knew exactly where she would be sitting. She made her way across the smoke-filled room towards the booth nearest the stage. Louis Armstrong was going to be playing later … Adrienne had always thought it ironic that a whites only club cared nothing for segregation when it came down to real talent. She was glad of it. Armstrong was a wonder to behold.

Sarah slid into the booth beside Adrienne. She was so close that their thighs touched. Adrienne was wearing a cream silk dress and a silver fox fur stole, which she removed and placed on the seat on the other side of her. Sarah leaned close and placed a furtive kiss on Adrienne's lips, then ran her hand over Adrienne's thigh. She slipped her fingers underneath the soft fabric, finding the bare skin above the stockings. She probed further, running her fingertips over the front of Adrienne's silk underwear. Adrienne gasped.

'When can we be alone?' Sarah asked.

Adrienne kissed Sarah full on the mouth, pressing her tongue between her rouged lips. She released Sarah when she became aware of the approaching waiter.

'Something on account,' she murmured as the waiter placed a silver bucket down in the centre of the table along with two champagne saucers. 'Oh the good stuff,' said Sarah.

The waiter poured champagne into the saucers and Adrienne and Sarah raised their glasses to each other.

'Nothing but the best for my lover,' said Adrienne as the waiter

walked out of earshot. 'Tomorrow I have the house all to myself.'

Sarah smiled, 'I can't wait!'

Adrienne placed a key down on the table. 'For the servant's entrance. Let yourself in, I'll have a surprise for you.'

Ricky's was buzzing with excitement that night, and so Adrienne and Sarah did not risk another transgression. There were other places they could go to, clubs that catered for women and men who were attracted to the same sex, but these were far more likely to be raided. Ricky's was their safest bet, as long as they weren't too indiscrete. After all, most of the senior police force attended this club, along with many local judges and politicians. It made the place untouchable. But that didn't mean that Sarah and Adrienne's relationship would be tolerated by some of the less tolerant religious types. The bible-belt had been the driving force behind Prohibition as it was, and the women did not underestimate the power these people had. The last thing either of them needed was a scandal that might result in some form of witch hunt. For this reason their passion must always remain a secret.

The image faded and Adrienne found herself back in Elgenor's room looking into the glass. She had tears on her face at the sight of Sarah looking so beautiful. She had never forgotten the detail of that night, but to see it – in glorious images like a 'talking' colour picture; a technology that was rumoured to be available even now – was like reliving the night all over again.

'Why did it fade?' she asked as fresh tears leaked from her eyes.

'We are at the moment of truth now,' Elgenor said. 'You need to prepare yourself.'

Adrienne wiped her face and then Bajolière pulled up a chair beside her. The Creole detective took her hand.

'Are you sure you want to know der truth, Cher?' he asked.

Adrienne could see more colour in him now, as though some form of disguise had hidden it during their meeting at Ricky's. But of course, he wouldn't have even gotten over the threshold if anyone had noticed his heritage, would he? Adrienne felt confused, duped, even though she had known who and what Bajolière was from the beginning. But his skin and his accent had changed in the last few moments, and the façade had dropped. Was he a witch too?

'He wore glamour,' Elgenor said. 'It is a gift I gave him for helping me some time back.'

'Glamour?'

'A mask you might say. It makes his work easier,' Elgenor said. 'Are you ready for the truth?'

Adrienne glanced back at the crystal ball. Fear sat like cold sludge inside her stomach. She wanted to see Sarah again, and remember those happy moments they spent together but she was afraid of what she would learn. Even so, she leaned forward and looked down into the glass once more.

It was dark outside Ricky's as they left. Adrienne's driver picked her up and she left Sarah alone, standing on the sidewalk waiting for a cab. Adrienne waved and now she saw herself through Sarah's eyes as her car pulled away.

The street was quiet, it was around 3am and the heat was oppressive. Sweat broke out on Sarah's brow as she waited for a cab to turn up. She wasn't afraid, as she had done this many times before. Even so, Sarah decided to go back inside.

'Will you look out for a cab for me?' she asked the doorman. 'It's cooler inside.'

'Yes, ma'am,' said the man. He was tall, wearing a lightweight summer uniform of white, yet the sweat still pooled around his armpits – there was no avoiding the summer heat.

Sarah took a seat in the reception, near the cloakroom, and she fanned herself with her purse.

'Cab here now, ma'am,' called the doorman a few moments later.

A black Ferris Sedan waited for her outside. The back door was open but she couldn't see the driver. She climbed inside and pulled the door closed. She saw the dark shape of the driver in the front seat and told him her address. Then the car began to move.

The cab turned. It was going in the wrong direction.

'No. Not that way!' Sarah said but the driver ignored her.

She banged on the glass panel that separated her from the driver – but to no avail.

They drove for a while before the cab pulled over. As the vehicle came to a halt Sarah yanked on the door handle and pushed the door open.

'What the hell are you playing at?' she said walking to the driver's door. 'I said down town, now we're in the middle of nowhere!'

The driver's window slowly slid down but all Sarah could see was a black void.

Then, the car set off leaving her stranded.

Sarah stared after the cab: for the first time she began to feel afraid. She looked around. She was on the main road out of New Orleans and it was deserted, dark and lonely. She turned back towards the town, trying to work out just how far she had come in the cab. It had to be at least three or four miles. It was annoying but she would just have to walk back, hail another cab and then, tomorrow, she would complain about the driver's behaviour.

The temperature rose as Sarah walked. Sweat dampened the silk dress until it clung to her back. Her stockings began to slip and she halted frequently to neaten them until in the end she bent down and pulled them both off. Carrying them in her hand with her clutch bag she began to walk faster.

The New Orleans sign was in her sight when she heard a car approaching. She stepped into the side of the road and looked back. The car pulled in beside her. The back door opened and Sarah looked inside, realising that this was the same Ferris Sedan that had abandoned her earlier.

'You don't honestly expect me to get back in do you?' she said.

She was trembling but she tried to appear brave.

'I just don't know what your game is. But I'm going to report this to the police and to the company you work for tomorrow.'

A wave of heat washed over her and the back seat illuminated as though it were lit by a thousand candles.

Sarah could see something then. She stepped forward, enthralled by the sight of a cavern lit up in a bright circle. On the other side of the flame she saw Adrienne. She called to her. But the sound was swallowed in a whoosh of flame.

A blackened hand reached out to Sarah. It snagged one of the stockings from her loosening fingers and then, wrapped it around her throat.

Another whoosh of flame burst up within the circle. Sarah saw a small bowl set on fire, she smelt burning and she heard an unfamiliar voice speak.

'The first toll has been paid with our blood,' said the woman. 'Now quickly, ask your question.'

It was a beautiful young woman who spoke, she stood beside Adrienne. Adrienne who didn't look as vibrant as she had a few hours earlier. She looked older somehow, more fragile and she bore the expression of one who had suffered great loss.

Adrienne stepped forward. 'Who killed my lover, Sarah?'

The creature turned to face Adrienne and Elgenor. Its mouth opened and the flame in the circle seemed to be sucked inside. Blackened razor sharp teeth chomped on the flames. A rush of sound assaulted Adrienne's ears at it spoke in a garbled tongue.

'What does it say?' Adrienne asked.

'It said ... you did!' Elgenor answered.

The stocking tightened on Sarah's throat as the dark creature chuckled from the burning flame. She heard Adrienne's distant denial, but she knew it was the truth. Her search to find Sarah's killer in the future, was the cause of Sarah's death in the past.

Adrienne stood up and backed away from the table. Her chair fell with a crash down onto the floor. *Oh the horror of it!* Her love, her selfish desire for answers had been the cause all along.

'Some magic requires a human sacrifice,' Elgenor said.

Adrienne couldn't bear to look at the woman as she ran back out of the room, into the kitchen and out into the daylight.

Bajolière caught up with her outside. She was leaning against the back fence, stomach retching into the gutter.

'What did you see?' Bajolière asked.

'It's all my fault!'

'Things aren't always what they seem ...' Bajolière said.

'I saw it. I caused it.'

Adrienne glanced back at the house. The withered old man stood in the doorway just shy of the bright sunshine. He was smiling. His teeth appeared to be sharp, blackened points.

'I should pay her something,' Adrienne said remembering

herself.

'No need,' said the old man and then he closed the door on both of them.

'What was that all about?' Bajolière said. 'They've never refused payment before.'

He frowned, staring at the doorway. Then he took Adrienne's arm and led her away from the house and back onto the main road.

'You need a drink. My place is nearby,' he said.

'You need to tell me what you saw. What happened? I don't remember anything beyond sitting down, then finding you were gone.'

Adrienne stared at Bajolière. Could what he said be true? Did he really have no idea what Elgenor had shown her? Could he even be trusted?

She felt betrayed, like a lamb led to the slaughter. If she had never met Bajolière then she would never have gone to see Elgenor, never made the deal that had, effectively, killed Sarah.

Despite her reservations she poured out all that she had seen and experienced through Sarah's eyes to Bajolière as he placed a glass of whiskey in front of her.

'It was as though I were her. And she knew, right at the end, that the deal I'd made killed her. She was the payment I agreed to make, but I didn't know what I was agreeing to.'

'You dealt with one of the Old Ones. And there is always a dark price to pay. They only deal when it benefits themselves.'

'Elgenor said that her soul has gone on. What would they gain from her death?'

Bajolière shook his head. 'I don't know.'

'You said you could trust Elgenor.'

'I've used her many times. This has never happened. Something bad has gotten into her. Maybe she has dealt with the Old Ones too long.'

Bajolière's skin was still darker and there was no doubt of his origin: the spell that Elgenor had cast was broken. She saw the confusion on the detective's face as he glanced down at his hands. He too was betrayed and she knew then that he would do everything he could to find out why.

Adrienne sipped the sour mash and grimaced. It was not something her cultured palate would normally enjoy, but it was warming and soothing, and so she soon finished it.

Bajolière lived in a one level shack in the French Quarter, clean but very modest. Adrienne was in his small kitchen, sitting on a rickety wooden chair at a roughly carved table. There was no tablecloth. She surmised that Bajolière did not have a woman in his life that might think to do these things.

He placed the bottle of bootleg whiskey down on the table, after splashing some more into both of their glasses.

'I feel like a trap was placed. My love for Sarah would be frowned upon by most ...'

'The Old Ones don't care about who we love, only how to manipulate us. Look, stay here, I'm going back to talk to Elgenor. I need to get to the bottom of this.'

'I'm coming with you,' she said.

'Okay. But let me do the talking.'

'The door ...' Adrienne said.

They had reached the rear of Elgenor's house and had just passed into the yard. Bajolière looked up to see that the back door was not only still closed, but had changed colour. Instead of the whitewash paint it was now a dark blue.

'They've painted it ...' Adrienne said.

'No. This isn't Elgenor's house.'

Bajolière took stock of the back alley. It was the right place and the house sported the same fence that Adrienne had held onto while she was sick – less than two hours earlier. Bajolière noted the stain, though the mess had been cleared up. He re-entered the yard and went up to the door.

The paintwork was old, not new, with a few blue sundried flakes peeling off. Bajolière knocked and a middle-aged Creole woman answered the door. She was wearing a flour-covered apron and Adrienne could smell spicy fried chicken and pie.

'We need to see Elgenor,' Bajolière said.

'Nobody live here by dat name.'

'Of course she does,' Adrienne said. 'We were just in there a few hours ago.'

The woman looked Adrienne up and down.

'What you doing round here? We don't need no trouble ...'

'Sorry to have bothered you,' Bajolière said and he took Adrienne's arm and pulled her away and back out of the yard.

'What are you doing? She's lying. We need to get back inside there.'

'I just realised somethin'. Whenever I've been here, it's always been the same time of day ...' Bajolière said. 'We need to come back tomorrow afternoon. Then, I reckon, Elgenor will be here, doing business as usual.'

Bajolière talked about portals. Other worlds and dimensions. Adrienne thought that Bajolière was losing his mind, or just trying to stop her pursuing Elgenor. No magic could relocate a medium from one place to another. Could it? It was all too insane for words.

Adrienne was tired. Reluctantly she let Bajolière put her into a cab and she returned to her beautiful house in the Garden District.

As she walked through her front garden and up the steps to the front door she couldn't help noticing the stark contrast between her own home and where she had been that afternoon. Bajolière's simple abode and Elgenor's mysterious cavern: her own place felt alien in comparison now.

She went inside and was greeted by Henry, her manservant. She was in shock, horrified by the revelation the day had brought, but she didn't reproach Henry about it, despite the fact that he had been the one to find Bajolière for her.

'*Bon apremidi* ...' Henry said.

It had always amused Adrienne to converse solely in Creole with the elderly servant. Now she couldn't find the words, and so she went straight to her room, drawing the curtains to shut out the remaining daylight.

She stripped off her dress and lay on the bed. The room was too hot and Adrienne was reminded of the burning heat that Sarah had felt coming from the cab. She pushed the image away, closed her eyes and drifted to sleep.

The horror of Sarah's death followed her.

She woke in the early hours shuddering as the nightmare replay of Sarah's death lingered. The large house was quiet with all the serving and house-keeping staff retired. Adrienne was still stretched out on the bed. She stood up, went into her private bathroom and ran cold water into the washbowl. Then she splashed it on her face, arms and chest.

She wasn't happy to wait to return to Elgenor's house. A deep, dark suspicion pressed against her. Who could she trust now if not Bajolière who knew everything about her? But she didn't trust him, or anyone else. There had to be other times when Elgenor returned to use that house as her … what could she refer to it as? Lair? Was the cavern still underneath, even when that witch wasn't there?

Lions and tigers have lairs. Somehow, in the darkness, Adrienne could imagine predatory qualities in Elgenor.

She dressed again in the clothes she had worn that day. She had to return to the French Quarter, and she didn't want anyone to know she was doing it. She went downstairs, pulled on a hat over her ruffled hair, and then left the house via the servant's entrance.

She walked along the road for a few blocks until she came to a local hotel. There she paid the doorman to hail her a cab.

A black Ferris Sedan drew up and the hotel doorman held open the rear door. Adrienne experienced a feeling of *déjà vu*. The driver turned around, opening the glass panel and spoke to her in a friendly jovial manner. He was not some burnt-black demon.

'Out late tonight, ma'am? Where can I take you?'

She could see his smiling face and felt herself relax. Then she gave the address and the driver frowned.

'You sure you want to go there?'

Adrienne nodded. 'I'd like you to wait for me while I check

something out too. Can you do that? It will be worth your while.'

'Well I wouldn't want to leave you over there, ma'am.'

The house was in darkness as the driver pulled up in the alley. He asked Adrienne if she was sure again, and he looked around, concerned that thieves or some other ruffians might leap out on them at any time.

'I'll drive around in a circle until you're ready to go,' he said.

Adrienne didn't answer as she climbed from the cab and entered the yard. The back door was open once more and she saw a dull light shining inside. As she entered the house, the old man appeared from the gloom.

'She's expecting you ...'

Adrienne approached the other door and went inside.

Elgenor struck a match and the room lit up.

'I have sympathy for your plight,' she said. 'Sit.'

Adrienne was confused but she approached and sat once more at the table.

'What has been done can be undone,' Elgenor said.

'My lover is dead. How can that be altered?'

'The Keeper of Secrets only requires one soul for payment,' Elgenor said. 'Look into the glass. See what could be, instead of what was.'

Adrienne gazed down into the glass and was once again sucked into the world of that night, so long ago now, when she lost the only person she had ever really cared about. This time the story ended differently.

Adrienne saw herself wearing her silver fox fur stole as she waited at the front of Ricky's. Then, a black Sedan approached.

The temperature around her rose as the cab pulled in beside her. She didn't glance at the driver, nor did she give him instructions, she merely opened the back door and climbed inside. The heat seared her body.

Adrienne realised then that she had a choice. She could die in the past, instead of Sarah: taking her place to save the woman she loved from this awful fate. She looked at Elgenor.

'Is there no other way?'

Elgenor shook her head. The pain on her face was visible.

Adrienne let her eyes fall to the crystal ball. 'Then I accept.'

At once she remembered the pain of the fire as the demon consumed her. Her mind became shattered as time re-wrote itself around her, events and memories changing and shifting as the Universe repaired the paradoxes as they were created. There was a moment of intense pain as her flesh was consumed by the Old Ones. A replay of that evening flashed before her eyes. She was the one left behind at the club. She stepped into the black Sedan. And then nothing.

Sarah stood up and backed away from the table. Her chair fell with a crash down onto the floor. *Oh the horror of it!* Her love, her selfish desire for answers had been the cause all along.

'Some magic requires a human sacrifice,' Elgenor said.

Sarah couldn't bear to look at the woman as she ran back out of the room, into the kitchen and out into the daylight.

She leant against the back fence, stomach retching into the gutter.

'What did you see?' Bajolière asked.

Sarah pushed her dark hair back from her face and met Bajolière's eyes. Her dark brown eyes were pools of intense pain. It jolted Bajolière and an intense sympathy for the woman made him want to help her even more.

'It's all my fault!'

'Things aren't always what they seem ...' he said.

'I saw it. I caused it.'

Sarah glanced back at the house. The withered old man stood in the doorway just shy of the bright sunshine. He was smiling. His teeth appeared to be sharp, blackened points.

'Let me take you home,' said Bajolière, leading Sarah away.

But Bajolière was confused for a moment. Hadn't the

woman he sent inside to meet with Elgenor been tall? Blonde? Slender? He recalled them walking side by side – had though she was almost the same height as himself. Now she had withered – shrunk somehow – to stand below his shoulder, not level with it.

A feeling of *déjà vu* made him feel light headed as he took Sarah's arm and led her away. He glanced back as they left the yard. The door was closed. It was also blue. Hadn't it been white only moments ago?

A rush of memory rewrote itself as time caught up with Bajolière. He shook his head. Then seeing the distressed state that his client was in he said, 'I think you could use a drink. My place is near.'

Other Monsters

The Jealous Sea

'The signs are so cute,' Angela said.

Garrick laughed; she had said this about every sign they had seen since crossing the border into Wales.

The promenade was deserted as they reached Rhyl. It was six in the evening, in the middle of summer, yet the sky was overcast and the sea wild. It was as though it knew a storm was on its way. They passed a huge theatre with the Welsh name of *Theatr Y Pafiliwn*. Thankfully the signs were also in English and so Angela immediately translated this to *Pavilion Theatre*.

As they approached a small roundabout Angela could see there was a cluster of colourful structures, which housed children's rides, farther up on the left. The area resembled a fairytale village but was still tacky nonetheless. To the right was a White Rose Shopping Centre,

And, as they crossed the roundabout, a long row of arcades lined the promenade. It was all so dreary that Angela felt her mood plummet at the thought of staying there – even if it was only for one night.

'Why?' she murmured.

'I told you, everywhere else was booked at this time of year. It's only a pit-stop,' Garrick said.

'It's seedy.'

Garrick sighed but said nothing more as the SatNav told him to take the next left. He turned the car into a small side-street, and a bright neon sign illuminated the way to their bed-and-breakfast.

'There,' said Angela.

Garrick took a right turn just after the hotel and they found a very small but underused car park.

He pulled up near to the rear entrance and both he and Angela climbed out. It had been a long drive and they were happy to stretch their legs.

Garrick took their overnight bag from the boot. He ignored the frown on Angela's face as she glanced around at the broken bottles, empty cans and litter that was scattered on the ground.

'This looks okay,' he said as they passed through a back corridor into a large reception. To Angela the place looked anything but okay. It was dirty, old and lacklustre. It reminded her of some bad comedy sketch she had once seen, but couldn't fully remember.

'As long as the sheets are clean ...' she said.

They approached the old wooden desk. Angela thought it was corny that there was a bell ring, but she said nothing as Garrick hit the top with his palm and the loud *ring* echoed through the hollow emptiness of the hotel reception and out into the obscure back room.

Angela looked around while they waited and noticed a cabinet full of stuffed animals at the other side of the room. She shivered when she saw the large fish in a glass cabinet hung from the wall. 'That's horrible ...'

'Can I help you?'

The woman was a cliché of bed-and-breakfast landladies the world over. She had silver hair scraped back into a bun and a scowl that seemed to be etched permanently on her face. Everything about Rhyl screamed mundane, grubby and above all 'chavvy'.

'Mr and Mrs Briant,' Garrick said. 'We have a reservation.'

The woman frowned at an old book that lay open on the desk and then nodded.

'Honeymoon is it?' she asked.

'No. We're travelling to see relatives. Thought we'd take the scenic route.'

The landlady failed to see the irony in Garrick's words, but Angela giggled behind him.

The landlady frowned. 'Only one night then, is it?'

Garrick nodded.

She told him the price and waited as Garrick fished out his credit card to pay for the room. Angela was surprised when the woman dutifully retrieved a wireless card machine from under the desk; she had half expected her to have one of the old imprint machines, or not to be able to take the card at all.

'That will be an extra charge of one percent,' the woman said.

She held out a key with a thick block of wood attached to the end, and after a few vague directions, Angela and Garrick found themselves on the third floor in front of a thick oak door.

'It's like *Fawlty Towers*,' Angela giggled. 'I'm not expecting this bed to be very comfortable.'

'It's just one night,' Garrick reminded her as he opened the door.

The room was unexpectedly clean, with a large four-poster bed in the centre. It was surrounded by matching furniture, and a bright red rug took up the centre. There was even a flat screen television on one of the chest of drawers.

'We hit lucky,' said Garrick as he opened a door beside the free-standing, oak wardrobe.

'*En suite* bathroom. The website said they only had a few. Looks like we got the best room in the place.'

Angela felt a little better. She hadn't relished the idea of tripping out onto the landing to find the nearest bathroom. She sat down on the bed and found it to be comfortable.

'This isn't that bad actually,' she said.

After they freshened up they went back downstairs and wandered out to look for a place to eat. The town centre was quiet and as deserted as the promenade had been.

'Where is everyone?' asked Angela. 'Thought it was the holiday season down here?'

The air was suffocating and the light was starting to fade. Heavy clouds gathered over head and the sound of the sea dominated the empty streets as the waves rose and fell against the promenade. Angela could feel pre-storm tension in the atmosphere. She felt like a diver in a pressure chamber, waiting to hear the bad news that she was suffering from the bends.

They passed by one of the arcades. Above the loud music Angela could make out the sounds of machines working. She saw a group of teenagers gathered around a racing car game. In the back of the shop an old man staggered from one machine to another holding a plastic cup from which he retrieved two pence coins.

They passed a pub and sounds of revelry issued from the door as it opened for a young man with sleeve tattoos on both arms. He lit a cigarette and stared out towards the sea.

'Danny?' said a girl from the doorway. 'Don't stay out too long. You know it's going to be a bad night.'

Garrick took Angela's hand as they weaved inwards towards the main shopping complex. It was now around seven thirty in the evening and so all of the shops were closed for trading. But Angela noted how many had whitened glass and had shut down permanently.

'Here's a pub that serves food. Should we try this?' Garrick asked.

'Yes,' Angela said.

They went inside and despite the outward appearance the pub was cheery and the menu varied. It was also quite busy. There were more people inside than they had seen since they arrived in Rhyl. Even so, they managed to find a small table in the corner by the window.

'You're not from around here, are you?' asked the waitress as she approached.

'No. But then I suppose not many people are in a seaside town,' Garrick said, smiling.

The waitress was young but serious. Her hair was jet black and pulled back severely into a high ponytail. She wore a name badge that said she was 'Aimee'.

'Staying somewhere nearby?' Aimee asked.

Garrick nodded.

Aimee said nothing more but quietly took their order. When she had gone Angela leaned over the table and took Garrick's hand.

'She was a bit chavvy wasn't she? Liverpool face-lift and all.'

Angela's snobbery sometimes grated on him, but this time Garrick laughed. 'This place is a bit ... okay it's seedy. I know.

But it's kind of fun too.'

Angela leaned over and kissed him. 'Anywhere is fun when we're together.'

The food arrived after only a short wait. They ate in silence but Angela couldn't help looking around at the people who were in the pub. There was a family sitting on the next table: husband, wife and two children, one a boy, the other a girl. All of them were wearing football shirts supporting the same team. The son was a clone of the father, even down to the shaved head and the mean expression on his face.

A group of young men were gathered around one of the tables. They talked excessively loud as they swigged from pints of beer, interspersed with shots of pale blue liquid. Angela frowned over at their rowdiness. They were so like groups they had seen before. Even down to the razor-patterned haircuts.

The door opened and a gaggle of girls entered – all wearing ridiculous heels, skirts that were too short and clip-in hair extensions. Angela tried not to stare. They all seemed so stereotypical of this sort of resort, and she couldn't shake the feeling that she was in the middle of some kind of stage play that was being given for their benefit.

As Garrick paid the bill Angela went to the ladies room. As she passed each group of loudly chattering diners she found that they were speaking gobbledegook. At first she thought it was the sheer loudness of the chatter that made it indecipherable, but as she paused beside a family of four she began to believe that they weren't talking at all. It was just noise. Almost like elevated white noise. She tried to listen in again, make sense of the din, but a blast of music from an old juke-box made it impossible.

Angela felt the stirrings of a headache, that gathered behind her eyes just as the brewing storm congregated outside.

'I need to get out of here,' she said as she met Garrick by the door. 'It's too loud.'

Garrick nodded. 'I know.'

'You're not going outside on a night like this, are you?' asked Aimee appearing behind them.

'Of course. A night like this is exactly what we look for,' Angela said.

They passed through the shopping precinct once more and headed for the sea. The wind was pounding the land and the water beat against the promenade as though it were a giant living beast that would consume anyone who dared to confront it.

'It's beautiful,' said Angela. Her eyes reflected the dark storm, turning them from blue to grey.

Garrick frowned.

They walked the promenade, daring the waves to reach for them, but it was a game Garrick disliked. Rain beat down on the flagged pavement and the sky cracked with lightning. Across the road the arcade music grew louder as though it was trying to compete with the storm. The smell of burnt onions wafted towards them. Angela wished there was a pier at this resort. It would have been fun to walk out and tease the sea a little more.

'What are you doing?' asked Garrick as Angela leaned over the rail and stared down at the angry waves.

'It can't get us Garrick. No matter how hard it tries.'

Garrick took her arm and pulled her away from the edge. 'One of these days it will. You shouldn't mess around like this. It's dangerous.'

They walked back across the road. Angela was elated by the storm. The spray from the sea had energised her and her eyes glowed with a green, sub-aqua light.

Garrick's concern deepened. Her eyes always reflected her inner calm or, alternatively, her inner turmoil. Now they showed change.

'Let's go back to the hotel,' Garrick said.

'Not yet,' Angela said.

She was drunk on the storm. It made her presence outside all the more perilous.

'Come,' he insisted.

Back in their room Angela was still glowing as she rubbed her hair dry. Even the blonde looked brighter and her hair appeared to have grown. It was flowing around her like sun bleached seaweed. Her clothes were soaked but she barely noticed.

Garrick was afraid. He felt the chill of the sea. The dark cold beckoned him, but never broke through his resolve to stay on land. Angela was a different story; the sea called to her despite their promise to shun it forever. Part of her wanted its possessive arm to swoop her back. The seaside trips made the torment both wonderful and torturous to them both. But Garrick loved the land more than the water. Angela had left the sea for him. He often feared that one day she would lose the battle and be called back into its jealous embrace, leaving him desperate and alone.

'What?' Angela said as though reading his thoughts.

'This was a bad idea. It was too dangerous. Plus this place ... it's not normal. Not like the other seaside resorts.'

'What are you saying?'

'Back there, in the pub. You noticed it, didn't you? The people were ... different.'

'They looked like the people we find in all of these places,' Angela said.

'Yes. They did. They *looked* exactly like them. That group of girls ... didn't we see them in Newquay? That family wearing football shirts ... I'm sure they were the same people we saw in Blackpool ... They were caricatures, Ang. Don't you see?'

There was rising panic in his voice but Angela said nothing. Instead she stripped away her wet clothes and began to dry her damp skin. Garrick tried not to notice the green scales that patterned her stomach, thighs and legs. He was relieved to see the telltale sign of change disappear as the towel soaked up the last drops of salty water.

'I might take a bath,' she said.

That is a good idea, he thought. The sea's saline poison would be washed away by the clean land water. Angela would be calmed. Garrick went into the bathroom and began to run the warm tap into the large bath.

As he poured in the bubble bath he heard the outer door open and close.

Garrick hurried back into the bedroom. Angela was gone and so were her wet clothes. He pulled on his water-proof coat. His heart burned with fear. Since they had returned to the room the storm had stopped raging. The jealous sea had rapidly forgotten their proximity and Garrick had thought the danger past.

As he reached the reception he saw the old woman standing behind the counter. It was as though she had been waiting there all this time, without moving – just for him.

'Have you seen my wife?' he asked.

The old woman's scowl turned into a smile. Her teeth were razor sharp.

Garrick's terror increased. He hurried out into the storm, ran along the street and crossed the empty road to the promenade. The wind buffeted him as though it were trying to stop his progress. Garrick screamed into the night in frustration.

He saw Angela by the railings. As he crossed the road, she walked away, crossing back towards the arcades.

Garrick felt a momentary relief. At least she had left the shore and was walking back to safety. The rain lashed at him as he crossed the road and followed Angela into the arcade. As he paused at the door the man they had seen earlier was still feeding coins into the machines. His movements were stiff and he moved in rhythm with the overly loud music.

Angela walked passed him and Garrick hurried forward.

'*Ang! Wait!*'

Angela disappeared round the corner as Garrick reached the man. He glanced at the machine – it appeared to be a cardboard cut-out and the man was nothing more than an automaton.

'What's going on here?'

He reached the back of the arcade just in time to see Angela slip out through the back exit.

He found himself in an alley. The emergency exit door closed behind him and the sound of the arcade faded completely. As his eyes adjusted to the darkness, he saw Angela's red coat lying over a dumpster. He picked it up and looked around. Angela was at the end of the alley and turning back onto the strip.

'*Angela? Stop! What are you doing*?'

As he left the alley he found himself back on the row of deserted shops. Angela was nowhere to be seen but he turned towards the strip, just as she had.

He saw the young man with the sleeve tattoos, still standing outside the pub, cigarette in hand. As Garrick approached he remained like a frozen statue, even as the elements beat against his already soaked skin and clothing. The cigarette disintegrated under the onslaught, dropping from his fingers in thick brown tears. 'You shouldn't be outside on a night like this,' said a female voice from the doorway.

Garrick glanced up, half expecting to see yet another fake person. Instead he came face to face with the waitress, Aimee, from the pub.

'Come inside, quickly,' she said.

She grabbed his arm and Garrick felt the will to resist leave him.

'Have you seen my wife?' he said.

Inside, the pub was full of cardboard figures.

'What's happening?' Garrick asked.

Aimee's hair was no longer in the tight ponytail; it flowed around her shoulders, the colour of octopus ink.

'You aren't human?' he said.

'Anyone who can move around here right now is like us,' she said. 'When did you escape?'

'We've been on dry land about five years,' Garrick replied. 'And you?'

'Fifty.'

'That's a long time.'

'Yes. And I plan to stay dry. But every few years it sends something to find us,' Aimee said. 'You are lucky you haven't been caught so far.'

Garrick sat down at a small round table. There were two pints of bitter standing in a sticky mass. The pub smelt of spilled, stale beer. It permeated the carpets and curtains.

'I need to find Angela,' Garrick said.

'I ... I think it's too late for her ... She went too close. The sea got her.'

'No ...' Garrick said.

'I saw her on land. In the arcade.'

'You don't understand. On nights like this ... the sea has power on land too. It got her as soon as you drove up the promenade. I could smell it on her when you came in the restaurant. What do you think has happened to all of these people here?'

Garrick shook his head.

'They are *inbetween*. They won't even remember this ... All they will remember is a bad storm.'

'What do you mean 'inbetween'?'

'It's a place where the sea is on land and the land is in the sea. Both have merged.'

'How?' Garrick asked.

'How did it keep you prisoner in the first place? How did the greedy, jealous sea hold onto us for so long? It has power. But you know that or you wouldn't have woken and left in the first place.'

'The land seduced us ... me first. Then Angela came with me. I was never sure she really wanted to leave.'

The door of the pub rattled as though a hand were trying the handle.

Garrick stood, but Aimee caught his arm.

'It's looking for us.'

A gust of wind huffed against the door but it didn't open.

'As long as we stay inside we will be safe,' Aimee said. 'The storm will pass in a few hours.'

'*Garrick*?' The door rattled again.

'That's Angela! I have to let her in!'

'No!'

Garrick was at the door before Aimee could stop him.

Angela stood in the doorway wet and bedraggled. Seaweed clung to her clothing, and through the outline of her skirt, Garrick detected the faint shape of legs reforming from a tail. It was as though she had pulled herself once more from the bottom of the sea.

'It tried to take me, but I couldn't go back without you,' she gasped.

Garrick pulled her inside. He turned to look at Aimee, but the girl had backed away as far as she could from the door.

'Help me,' he said. 'We need to dry her. Get the salt off.'

Aimee hurried to the ladies toilets and returned with a large wad of paper towels. Garrick began to pat Angela dry. Aimee backed away again, frowning.

'A drink. Get her some brandy. She's freezing cold to the touch.'

Garrick took off his own coat and placed it around Angela's bare legs. The scales were receding again but Angela was shivering.

Aimee placed a drink on the small table as Garrick sat Angela down, and pulled her close to help warm her. He picked up the glass and held it to Angela's lips. He noticed how blue they were and remembered the first time her saw her underwater. Her pale yellow hair was like the sunlight he had glimpsed shimmering on the ocean, and her scales were the palest green.

'We were happy in the ocean then ...' said Angela as though she could read his mind.

She had stopped shivering and was watching him carefully.

'It can be good again,' she continued.

'We made a pact,' Garrick said.

'Put her outside,' Aimee said. 'The storm is almost over, but it won't end until it takes her back.'

'She can't go out there!' Garrick said. 'What is *wrong* with you?'

Garrick hugged Angela to him as he glared at Aimee. He didn't see the smile that spread over his wife's lips, only the terror this expression brought to the other girl's face.

'She's not your wife anymore. Can't you see that?' Aimee said backing away until she was behind the bar.

He felt the splash of salty water on his feet first. He looked down. The bar was filling with the water from outside. He stood, pulling Angela up.

'Come on. Stand on the bench. It's flooding in.'

Aimee was crying as she climbed up onto the bar before the water could reach her. 'I'm not going back. I'm not. I should never have helped you.'

Garrick looked around, confused. He couldn't see where the water was coming from.

'It's not your wife!' Aimee said again. 'You let it in. You let the *inbetween* in!'

Garrick turned to Angela. Water poured from her mouth and out into the room. He stepped away afraid, and tumbled from the bench down into water now waist deep. He could feel the salt sinking through his clothes and into his skin. His legs began to change. It hurt. It hurt a lot.

It was like the first time he had pulled himself out of the sea and lay on the beach. The sun had dried him, soaking up the salty liquid until he wept with pain. The heat was agony after the constant cold of the sea and he felt his blood burn in his veins. That day he was born into humanity and he had lived in their world ever since.

Now, the hurt was reversed. He felt the cold seeping back into him. Destroying the warmth he had learned to enjoy. It was far worse than the burn of the sun had ever been. This was dying, not living. And Garrick screamed, even as the water came above his head and forced its way into his lungs. He choked it in, suffocated on his salty poison.

Then he felt Angela's arms. Her hair wrapped around him when he tried to resist. She pulled him out through the door. They swam through the flooded streets out towards the ocean with the *inbetween* following them as it released its hold on the town and the storm drifted away.

Life fell back into normality. The streets of Rhyl were vibrant and bustling. The arcades were alive with loud music and the sounds of coins falling as the machines paid out. The flat two-dimensional people, filled out, moved, and stretched their tight limbs, unaware of their strange paralysis. The gaggle of girls, the beer swilling youths and the football-shirt wearing family faded back into the distant memory of a merman who once escaped the sea to enjoy time on land.

Aimee stood in the doorway of the pub looking out at the cloud that drifted over the water. The jealous sea was satisfied for now, but it would send the *inbetween* again and again until it snatched back all of its wayward children. Aimee knew it was only a matter of time before it reached her too.

Still, there would be more like Garrick and Angela. Every season brought one or two of them to the seashore. They would look out at the water, daring it to take them back. And as long as there were sacrifices Aimee would be safe. The sea would back away with its prizes like a tourist with an inconsequential toy, never realising it had missed out on the biggest prize of all.

It was several hundred years since Aimee had left the water, not fifty.

'I'm not going back. Not now, not ever,' she murmured.

The cloud huffed, the wind rattled along the promenade, but it was nothing more than posturing. The power had receded. The ocean could do nothing more that day. But it knew she was there and wouldn't be satisfied for long.

The Collector

For Elain Freeman and Chaz Martin

The door burst from its hinges and Chaz threw himself aside, narrowly avoiding being crushed as an army of Snerks marched in.

'Where's the girl?' growled the Snerk leader.

He wore a grey jabber over a green-tinged chest. It was the only thing that distinguished him from the others. Snerks all looked the same to Chaz. Malid or falid, and rank was determined by jabber colour.

Chaz was half-human and if you didn't notice the extra lid that swept over his grey-blue eyes, seconds before his external eyelid, then you would be excused for not realising he had Lathan in him at all. Unfortunately, he hadn't inherited his father's scaly skin – though underneath his grey flesh ran dark green blood, cold in temperature, unlike the human norm. His mother had been a newbie on the planet – it hadn't taken her long to sample the delights of the Lathan: lizard-type men known for their sexual prowess. Chaz's mother had stayed with his Lathan father for several years and he had two sisters who looked more like his father than his mother. It was a disappointment to Chaz, since he would have had more success with the ladies himself if his skin had at least been silver rather than a somewhat ill-looking hue.

'What girl?' he asked and the Snerk leader cuffed him across the head with a casual swipe, a pile of reeking excrement falling to the floor as he did so.

'You know who we mean ...'

'No. I don't,' said Chaz, his eyes stinging from the smell of the Snerk-waste. 'Describe her and I might be able to help.'

'Silver skin. Lathan with human eyes.'

'Nope. Doesn't ring any bells.'

The Snerks searched Chaz's small living space. Then, finding nothing, moved on to the next in line.

'Hey, who's going to pay for this broken door?' Chaz called after them. 'And clean up this shit?'

The Snerks marched on, completely ignoring him, leaving the broken door and their droppings behind.

'Fucking Snerks ...' Chaz said. He retrieved a shovel from the utility cupboard and began to scoop up the Snerk crap, tipping it down the waste shoot. 'Ought to be a law against them.'

'Have they gone?' Elain said, opening the panel that concealed the small room she had been hiding in.

'You know they are as dumb as ... shit,' Chaz said. 'What did you do this time, sis?'

Elain helped Chaz prop the front door back up, then she pulled a bore drill from the tool box, removing and fixing the hinges before helping him re-hang the panel.

'Not a great job but it'll do for now,' she said.

Then she sat down on the relaxer, silver skin glowing in the neon lighting that illuminated the container. Her casual behaviour irritated Chaz.

Container Town was named thus because it was literally made from old containers – once used to ship goods from Earth – that had been converted into housing for the poor. Chaz and his twin sisters Elain and Jalia, had moved into the area when it became fashionable. The containers were durable, though small. If you had money, you could convert the extra long ones, as they had done, dividing it into two spaces. The back half, with the concealed panel, had proved useful since Elain didn't always walk on the right side of the law.

'You didn't tell me why they were after you?' Chaz said.

'Bootleg liquor,' Elain said. 'Brought it across the border.'

Container Town was of course a place of temperance. Usually the occupants just went to other communities to get their alcohol fix. Not risking bringing it back for fear of the Snerks wrecking their homes. They couldn't afford it generally so they opted for cheap drugs instead. Snerks didn't have a problem with narcotics, just booze. Something about alcohol made them a little crazy.

'Where is it?' asked Chaz. 'The booze?'

'Not here. I wouldn't put you at risk like that, but you'll get a share at the party tonight.'

'What party?

'The party of the people I got it for. They are paying well and they said I could join the fun and bring a friend. So you, brother dear, are coming with me.'

The party was on the east side on Container Town. Here the occupants owned large sprawling container mansions, each with gardens that featured a swimming pool. High, electrified fences surrounding their properties. Here lived the governors and judges and police chiefs. Here they were safe from Snerk invasion regardless of the amount of alcohol they consumed. And there were no cheap drugs, only expensive, exclusive blends that gave the rich the perfect high with no down crash.

Elain had changed into a black one-piece leotard which came up high on her silver legs, and dipped low to reveal her scaly silver cleavage. Her hair was like their mother's had been: long, black and wavy. She wore it pulled into a high ponytail, tied with silver thread, as shiny as her skin. Her eyes, unlike Chaz's, were very human. A deep, intense blue, made all the more startling because of her silver skin. On her feet she wore a pair of black boots, which emphasised her slim calves and ankles.

Chaz was playing to his human good looks; he wore a silver unitard which looked good with his skin. The silver reflected against his extra eyelid as it flashed open and closed over his eyes, illuminating the fact that he did indeed have Lathan blood flowing in his veins.

'I have a delivery for Maxwell,' Elain said as the Lathan security guard looked her up and down with interest.

'Yeah. He's expecting you,' the guard said. His lizard tail

twitched up between his legs. 'Come in.'

'Thanks,' she said giving him a wink. 'But keep it in your pants when you're on duty. Okay?'

Duly chastised the guard's tail dropped back behind him and he stepped back to allow Chaz and Elain to enter. Between them they pushed a heavy trolley full of bottles.

They moved under a long arched walkway towards the mansion entrance.

'This way,' said Elain turning right.

'You've been here before,' Chaz said.

'Only once. It was a really great party too.'

At the back of the house, Elain was greeted by a servant who took control of the trolley, and handed the payment over which she stuffed into a hidden pocket sewn into the low cut cleavage of her outfit.

'Come on,' she said.

Chaz followed her back around the house and to a cordoned off piece of garden. They entered through another narrow covered walkway and emerged into the pool area. The booze trolley was already out and the party in full swing. Chaz noted how the bar area around the pool was already fully stocked with every Earth type booze you could want. There was also a counter with containers laid out full of pills, like candy in a sweet shop.

'The pink ones are aphrodisiacs,' Elain said, 'the blue are hallucinogens. You can live out a whole lifetime in one night on those. Imagine you're the king of Oasis or something. So I've heard. It's not my thing ...'

'Not mine either,' Chaz said. 'What's the silver one do?'

'Those, brother dear, are Lathamites.'

'I've never heard of those.'

'Let's put it this way – you always wanted skin my colour didn't you?'

'It turns your skin silver?'

'Not just that. It also gives you other Lathan attributes.'

'That's a DNA changing drug?'

Elain nodded. 'Very dangerous. Keep clear of it. The side

179

effects aren't worth the 24 hours of adorations you'll get as a full Lathan.'

'I didn't think those were possible,' Chaz said.

'Come on,' said Elain. 'Let's test out some of the booze instead.'

Chaz followed her to the bar but his eyes strayed back to the drugs counter. He didn't see anyone approach the pills and so he turned his mind away and back to the party.

The pool area was full of beautiful people. Malid Lathans in full prowess; gorgeous female humans walking in around clear plastic dresses. An Adamine relaxed in the water, her violet tail swished up and down as though she were inviting male attention, but anyone who understood Adamine nature would know this was in fact the signal to indicate that she wanted to be left alone.

Over in the far corner of the patio, a human man lay on a sun lounger as though trying to catch the sun. He wore dark glasses and appeared to be sleeping. He stood out because he was less than perfect.

'Max,' Elain said as she noticed Chaz looking at the man.

'The owner of the house?'

'The owner of Container Town,' Elain said. She poured herself a pint of neat vodka. 'Just a little drink to take the edge off.'

Chaz said nothing; his Lathan blood gave him massive tolerance to most human substances and Elain was no different. She'd need a few bottles of the stuff before she was even tipsy. Chaz took a cocktail mix off the bar without worrying what was in it. He took a swig and immediately felt an impact.

'Take it easy on those,' said a female voice. 'They are Lathan strength …'

Chaz turned to see a pretty blonde woman who appeared, like Max, to be fully human.

He blinked slowly in an attempt to reveal his second eyelid to her but she turned her head and looked across the pool at Max.

'I'm half Lathan,' Chaz said.

'Oh,' said the woman. 'There are a lot of Lathans here. Max likes them.'

'I'm Chaz,' he said.

'Marca,' she replied. 'Max is my brother.'

She looked around as though the whole party bored her, and then walked away without looking back.

Marca reached the patio doors of the main container. Chaz looked around in time to see Elain disappearing into a summer house with two Lathan males. He shrugged trying not to think about what his sister was doing, then he turned and followed Marca.

No one stopped him from entering the main house. From outside it looked like three containers stacked on top of each other, but as he entered Chaz discovered a palatial space. The containers had been upscaled to the degree that they no longer resembled them inside. This looked like a retro-Earth-style mansion with all of the luxuries, including a broad staircase leading up into a circular landing and several wings – former containers – off for bedroom space.

Marca stood on the landing.

Chaz looked up at her and she smiled. 'Why didn't you take the silver pill and complete the job?'

'Would you like me better if I did?'

Marca laughed. 'All of them. Out there. Not one is a real Lathan. You and your sister are the closest Max ever gets.'

Chaz didn't know how to respond.

'Aren't you going to say something? You followed me inside for a reason.'

'You don't seem too happy with the party, or your brother,' Chaz observed.

Marca walked down the stairs towards him.

'It's the same thing every night.'

'How dull for you,' Chaz said.

Marca reached the bottom of the steps. 'Maybe it will be more fun tonight. Come with me.'

She led him through the house, out through the kitchens and into the gardens behind. Then on to an aluminium container that stood at the end of their land as though it were a super-sized garden shed.

'The museum,' she said as she reached the door.

'What kind of museum is it?'

'My brother is a collector of things as well as people.'

She tugged at the old container lock and Chaz realised that the exterior of this one at least had not been changed from its original usage. The door creaked open with difficulty, but Chaz didn't offer to help for fear of Marca's scorn but when she finally opened the door he peered inside.

There were no lights inside the container. Nothing modern or upscaled. It was as it had been, in original form.

Marca produced a torch from somewhere and switched it on. She played the light over the interior. It was powerful enough for Chaz to see the many crates that lined the walls and ran down the centre of the container.

'What's in here?' he asked.

'Would you like to see?' Marca said. The question appeared to be harmless but Chaz had the strange image of the Mallish asking Huwanthan what he could give him for the mere price of his soul.

'Should we be out here?' he asked.

'I thought you would be different,' said Marca and she turned off the torch and began to close the container door.

'Wait …'

Marca paused. They were stood in the shadow of the container and the lights from the garden were obscured.

'Curious?' Marca asked.

'Yes. I want to see what your brother collects.'

Marca turned the torch back on and entered the container. Once again Chaz followed but Marca stopped him just in the doorway.

'You need to sign this first,' she said holding out a crumpled piece of paper and a pen.

'Good trick,' Chaz said. 'What is it?'

'A disclaimer. It says you agree to our terms and conditions.'

Chaz glanced down at the paper. 'Yeah? What conditions?'

'Oh the usual. Things like you won't discuss what you see with anyone else.'

Chaz shrugged and on impulse he scribbled his name down on the paper.

'Good.' Said Marca. She stuffed the paper into her clothing. Chaz didn't see where.

Despite the light from the torch, the space was full of dark shadows and eerie shapes. Nothing moved.

'This is the first one …' Marca said

A glass panel covered the front of a converted crate. In the torch light Chaz could make out straw and a shape.

'A statue,' he said.

'A piece of art,' Marca said. 'Max's first.'

'He's a sculptor then. That explains the wealth.'

'This is his hobby, not his career path,' Marca said.

Chaz looked at the sculpture. He searched his mind for something intelligent to say, even as he took in the distorted lines of the face, the angular and repulsive deformity of the body.

'It's very unusual,' he said. 'Ugly. But I suppose that was his point.'

'Come and see this one,' Marca said. She turned the light away from the makeshift cabinet and it left Chaz feeling oddly vulnerable to be stood in the dark alone beside the awful statue and so he hurried to follow her.

She stopped by a smaller cabinet. This one held a female shape that was even more deformed than the previous figure.

She showed him other twisted and warped things. Half-animal, half-human shapes merged as though in mid transition. And then came a Snerk. An ugly brutish thing with a Lathan tail raised up in prowess between its legs.

'Your brother has a vivid imagination.'

'All failures I'm afraid, which is why they a consigned to the museum. He doesn't even come to look anymore, not since his discovery of the silver pill. With every usage he adapts the dose, alters the transition.'

'What do you mean?' Chaz asked.

'Max is the CEO of Maximillian Pharmaceuticals. The silver is an invention he cooked up and so far it works better than the others.'

Chaz frowned. He wasn't sure he wanted to hear any more of the fantasy story Marca was creating around the statues. It wasn't amusing and he didn't believe for one minute that Max was *the* Maximillian. Perhaps Marca wasn't even the man's sister. This was all some fantastical game that their host was playing. Chaz was starting to believe that he, for some reason, had been picked as the butt of their latest joke. Maybe Elain had set him up? It would be just like her.

'This was the last failure ...'

The last cabinet was the biggest and Chaz didn't want to look in it.

'What's the plan? I walk over there and someone jumps out in a costume?'

Marca looked over her shoulder at Chaz. 'You aren't taking this seriously?'

'No.'

'You don't believe me?'

'Look it's a fun story, and no doubt my sister is in on the joke since she pointed out the silver pills to me earlier. But I don't appreciate it. If you don't mind I'll be leaving now.'

Chaz turned to leave and then his knees gave beneath him.

'Wazz happ'ning ...?'

Chaz couldn't make out where Marca was because the torch light had gone out.

'I'm a bit squeamish about the transformation, so you'll forgive me if I don't watch,' Marca's voice floated to him on a miasma of pain.

Bones cracked. Arms and legs changed position and length. A ripple of nerve-shredding torture ran over his skin. Chaz tried to scream but his vocal chords were restructuring and only a squeak issued from his mouth. He collapsed forward onto all fours and then the darkness swam around him sucking at the bare skin on his arms and legs. The unitard ripped and tore away as a Lathan tail issued from his lower spine.

'You okay?' said Marca. The torch light was shining in his eyes.

'Must have blacked out …' he muttered.

'The transformation is complete,' Marca said. 'Very complete. I've never seen it take so well before.'

Chaz flicked his tail and heaved his bulk upwards to a standing position. He felt heavier, but stronger than he had before.

'Look,' said Marca.

A large mirror reflected the light of Marca's torch and Chaz's inner eyelid closed reflexively to protect him from the glare. He looked down at his arms and naked body, which shone with the radiance and flickered on his silver scales. Down below, his tail had curled up between his legs in prowess.

'Impressive,' Marca said.

Chaz didn't know if she meant his aroused state which was a common thing for Lathan malid or the change she had somehow wrought that had turned him fully into a copy of his father.

'Max would enjoy having you at the party now,' she said.

Then the screams and yells began and Marca ran for the door of the container before Chaz could react. When he reached the doorway he found Marca peering out into the garden.

More cries erupted and Chaz saw now that two Lathans were running riot. They had come around the side of the house, near the container, chasing two women. They grabbed at them, throwing them to the floor and attempted to force their prowess onto them.

'*The insanity*. It must have been a bad batch.'

Marca looked fearfully at Chaz as though she expected him to attack her any moment.

'They had the pills?' Chaz said.

'Yes. So did you …'

'I didn't.'

'You had the cocktail … Nothing else?' Marca asked.

Chaz nodded. His head felt bigger, his jaw and nose had elongated and merged. There was no pain now. It was as though Chaz had achieved his natural state.

'Tell me what the pills do?' Chaz asked.

'So now you believe me?'

'The proof is here …' Chaz held out his arm to show off his scales.

'The pills force a DNA restructure. But you said you didn't take them.'

'I didn't.'

'Then, the drink did this …'

'How?'

'The cocktail was designed to stabilise the changed humans when they became Lathan. It's a top-up to the pill to prevent early reversion.

'The natural DNA usually reasserts itself after 24 hours. Then there is a painful change that sometimes doesn't work out well. The longer the human retains the Lathan shape the better for the reversion. I don't know why.'

Chaz glanced back into the container.

'The failures. They aren't statues at all.'

'No. They were Max's earliest attempts.'

'But the drink. It should have been labelled …'

'It's harmless to human men normally. Just strong. Like a massive dose of alcohol.'

Chaz realised what had happened before Marca explained. He had changed because he already had Lathan DNA. The drink had pushed his body to do what his own cells hadn't achieved.

There was another commotion outside as several security Lathan arrived and subdued the two wild Lathans. The party was plummeted into silence.

Marca took Chaz's paw and led him back around the house to the pool area and towards where her brother Max had been laying, watching the action impassively from behind his dark glasses.

Max's head turned as they approached but his face remained still. Marca explained Chaz's transformation to Max but her brother barely acknowledged her words.

'I refuse to become one of your collection,' Chaz said. 'I'm getting my sister and we are leaving.'

He hurried around the pool and towards the summer house where he had last seen Elain. Calling her name, he hoped she and the two Lathans had finished their fun. He didn't want to walk in on her; he wasn't sure how stable he was in his present condition. How long would the change last? Would he too become over-excited and attack some innocent woman? He had to get away from here and put himself some place where he could do no harm.

Elain was lying naked between the two Lathans. Their private party was over fortunately, but Lathan slime was all over her. Chaz felt a little sick as he grabbed Elain's leotard from where it had been tossed aside, and threw it at her.

'Dress. We're leaving.'

'Look if you're feeling a little frisky there are plenty here who will ...'

'Get. Dressed.'

Chaz waited by the door with his back to Elain and the Lathans. He knew it was one night that the two men would never forget, especially if they were metamorphosed humans. Then Elain joined him and they went back out to the pool area.

The security Lathan were back and waiting. Marca was with them.

'I'm afraid you can't leave,' Marca said. 'We have no idea what damage you may do once you start to change back.'

'It's just a drug,' said Elain. 'I'll lock him down until it wears off. No need to bother yourself Max. And I apologise for my brother. He's a little naïve and didn't know what he was doing.'

Max stood up for the first time and approached.

'Side-effects are different in everyone,' Marca said. 'My brother knows this to his own cost.'

Max's droopy tail skimmed the surface of the pool as he walked in a strange, lop-sided gait towards them. As he reached the summer house he removed his glasses.

His eyes were pure Lathan. As Chaz looked, he saw the inner nictitating membrane snicker across, followed by the outer eyelid. Max grinned.

Marca nodded to the guards.

One Lathan seized Elain's arm. She looked petite but had surprising strength and she threw him aside as if he were a mere human. Two more dived on her and four others restrained Chaz as he tried defend his sister. They struggled. Chaz's tail hit one of the guards full in the face. He fell back, rolled and landed in the pool beside the Adamine. The creature spat venom in his eyes to punish him for his intrusion into her personal space, and her tail lashed decisively.

The screaming from the blinded Lathan was a great distraction and it helped Chaz to free himself from another of the guards. Then Chaz received a hard blow to his thick skull. Right on the Lathan weak spot. His legs crumpled beneath him. He fell forward onto his face. Stunned, he couldn't move.

Held down, tail tied to his back, Chaz felt the strength leak out of him and he could do nothing to prevent the guards from dragging him and Elain down to the container at the bottom of the garden.

His limbs remained frozen as Chaz felt the leather straps of a winch wrapped around his body. He was hoisted up and then lowered into a cage big enough for an Oasis bearlion.

His inner eyelid automatically closed as they shone light into the cage.

'You can't keep him like that!' yelled Elain. 'He's got rights.'

'Not any more,' said Marca. 'He signed them over to me.'

'What are you talking about?' Elain said.

'He should have read the small print,' Marca said. 'He has just become part of my collection.'

'Chaz!' Elain yelled, struggling against the two Lathan guards.

'Show the lady out boys,' said Marca.

In the corner, Max sat down and looked into the cage. Chaz saw the CEO of Maximillian Pharmaceuticals open his mouth and flick his lips dryly with the stubble of his former tongue.

'He makes a nice addition doesn't he Max?' Marca said.

Max grinned. It wasn't pleasant.

The strength began to return to Chaz's limbs. His hands reached for the cage bars and he tugged and struggled against them.

'And very entertaining too.' Marca said.

Max grinned and giggled, Lathan drool dripping from his mouth. He looked like a sad brain-damaged clown who found humour in childish things. Marca reached over and patted him on the head. Her own little pet, and victim of his own drugs.

Still, she was glad he had the foresight to provide for the collection. She would enjoy adding to it ...

Urban Wolf

Tall, ungainly high rises loomed up before his blood reddened gaze as he padded through the streets. His fury burned brighter than the search light from the helicopter flying overhead. He looked up: the urban landscape of New York City daunted the half moon as he squinted at the sky. Despite the helicopter it was a quiet night but something important was on his mind: dark, blood, torturous death. He wanted out of the rat race, away from the clawing, screaming jealously that followed his daily routine.

To his left Jake passed the expensive shops, frequented in the day by the likes of his boss: Lorna, always putting him down, was never satisfied with anything he gave her. He fought to keep his self-esteem but was a total failure in her eyes and she made him suffer for it, forcing his gratitude from him as he grovelled continuously to keep his job. That bitch with her diamonds and her designer clothes and shoes. One of the girls in the office, Tiffany he thought it was, commented once on how much Lorna's handbag had cost. The amount she mentioned would have paid Jake's rent for three months. The memory brought red rage bubbling up to the surface and the anger grew.

Initially Jake had been so grateful to even have the job. The interview had been awful. Lorna's obvious dislike for him oozed out during his presentation. She criticised all of his ideas, put down the slogans as being 'predictable' or 'unoriginal'. Jake had been surprised when he received the letter offering him the position. He had thought that maybe there had been something good he had come up with after all, but soon learnt Lorna's real motive. Lorna wanted him in more ways than as an advertising assistant.

She began to work on him the very first day. Every piece of

work he turned in wasn't good enough. By the end of the day, Jake had been closed to quitting. He wasn't the sort of man who easily lost his temper but Lorna pushed all the right buttons. At 5.35pm he was at screaming point, then Lorna had changed her tactics. She called him into the office, offered him coffee, and within the space of a few minutes, she was down on her knees giving him a blow-job. Jake was shocked and surprised but went along with it like any full bloodied male would. She was after all a very attractive woman and she smelt great. After that, sex with Lorna became the conclusion of every work day.

Jake had never had a class act like that before and so the affair – if you could call it that – was fun to begin with until he realised that the whole thing only gave Lorna more power over him. What was worse was that Jake had been stupid enough to trust her with all of his ideas, good or bad. Jake had learnt the hard way that she was using his ideas, passing them off as her own.

The latest ad campaign for example: Jake had suggested the slogan at their weekly meeting. Lorna had dismissed him saying the proposal was 'clichéd', but today there wasn't any escape from the fact that she had used his proposal anyway. The new deodorant, *Urban Wolf,* had been launched with the tagline 'It turns Man into Beast': and Jake had been the person to come up with it.

That day he'd sat by, watching the cronies congratulate Lorna. The MD had even come in and called her 'insightful'. Jake knew Lorna didn't have a creative bone in her body, all she did was use the talent of those around her, and then she manipulated herself into being the star. Jake hated her. She was less than human.

Of course he knew all of this was his own fault. He could have gone over her head, made sure the MD knew that the idea had been his, but how would that have looked? Besides, who would believe him? He was nothing. He was just Lorna's assistant and bosses hated colleagues who couldn't be team players.

After every one had gone, Lorna called him in to her office

and her games started again. She didn't even try to explain herself. She was so confident that Jake wouldn't make a fuss about her plagiarism.

'Take your shirt off,' she had said and Jake found himself obeying her. He wished he could resist her, but Jake found it too difficult to so 'No'. There was something about the way she ordered him around that he just found irresistible.

Lorna liked it rough: dishing out pain with her clawing nails while he fucked her on the office floor. Though she was odd about body fluids and Jake always had to use protection. During the sex games, he felt as though he had no will of his own. He obeyed her every command, even when it meant physical pain.

Afterwards, Jake wondered why he went along with her dominatrix games, the bitching during office hours and the threats of dismissal if he didn't do everything she asked. But he knew the answer: Lorna had turned him into the worst kind of pussy. And he was certainly whipped.

Bitch! Jake thought as he hurried back to his car. His back was sore and scarred from her sharp nails and he could feel his shirt sticking to his skin where she had drawn blood. He had never seen himself in this role before, always preferring to be in control. His last girlfriend had even called him a 'control freak', not that Jake really thought he had been that bad. He knew that it was just something women said sometimes to make you feel bad, even though *they* were dumping *you*. But even if he had been controlling, Lorna was more than making him suffer for it.

Shit! What did I even do to deserve this?

Jake reached his car, an old and battered Jeep, and pressed the key fob to unlock the door. He climbed in, wincing as his back rubbed against the seam of the leather seat. He put the key in the ignition and started the engine.

At the gym he worked out for an hour, pushing himself hard. It made him feel stronger and somehow in control but he didn't take his usual swim: the marks on his back were too obvious. After his work out he showered and dressed, keeping his back to the wall to avoid the usual jokes the other guys might make. Before pulling on his shirt he pulled out the roller deodorant: *Urban Wolf*. It was ironic and Jake sneered cynically as he used the product under his arms. *So much for turning 'Man into Beast'*, he thought as he threw the plastic container back into his sports bag. *Fuck you, Urban Wolf and fuck Lorna.*

Jake parked his car near his apartment block and walked to his favourite bar. Then he perched himself on a stool and spent the evening drinking bottled beer for the rest of the evening. He knew he looked pathetic but he just couldn't bring himself to talk to anyone.

'I think you've had enough,' said the bartender.

'I'm just so stressed,' he said. Then he poured out his vitriol for Lorna while the man mopped up spilled beer with a tea towel.

'It sounds like you need a new job, man. Nothing should make you feel that bad,' said the bartender.

Jake left a hefty tip. He had appreciated the small amount of sympathy the man had given him, even though it didn't help.

Back at his apartment, Jake found that the lift was broken again. His body ached. A strange lethargy filled his limbs. He felt so tired he wondered if he could possibly make it up the stairs. Even so, he dragged his weary bones up one flight and then the next, until he staggered down the hallway to his sparse accommodation.

Jake fell asleep in front of the TV with a bottle of beer on the table beside him and a day stale pizza still in the box.

He felt his body shifting. A strange, but painless transition, though his cheek bones ached, as his chin fell down onto his chest. His face grew numb, teeth felt peculiar and large in his mouth. *Grandma, what big teeth you have.*

I'm dreaming, he thought as he stretched out, falling from the chair to land on all fours. Then he saw himself as a wolf running through the streets. The city looked different through colour blind eyes. It was a blur of noise and smells that were difficult to separate one from the other.

He ran and ran, his heart rattling in his chest. He felt wildly excited at the thought of the chase. He would find a strong enemy to battle. Jake knew then that he was hunting his prey.

Jake saw an old man pushing a supermarket trolley full of junk through the dark streets. He stopped about ten feet away and sniffed the air. The man smelt of shit and decay. Filth caked the grooves in his neck and the bare fingers tips that peaked out from fingerless gloves. The man's blood pumped slowly through a haltering heart. He noticed the pronounced limb last: there would be no sport in killing this quarry. This meal was unworthy. Jake backed away, hiding among the trash cans in a stinking alley. The old man passed and the Jake watched him, hungry, but not enough to want to eat a lesser meal.

Jake felt strangely distant from the wolf that he was sure he was dreaming he had turned into, yet still connected. He glanced down at his front paw. The wolf's pelt was the same black as his own hair and he could still smell the faint perfume of the *Urban Wolf* deodorant.

Behind him, in the alley, he heard the beating of warm, hot, young heart. He turned, following the smell and he came across his food unconscious among the trash cans of the local bar. Jake sniffed the young man's body. He was clean, but he smelt of alcohol. The kid oozed it from every pore. Even so, *this*, thought the wolf, *was an easy meal*. He debated waking his victim. A part of him knew that it wouldn't be as much fun if he didn't give chase.

'Pete? Petey?' called a voice from the other end of the alley. Jake noticed a back door open, and heard the pulsing beat of music coming from inside. This was the back door of a club he didn't know and he backed away into the shadows as two other men came outside.

'Shit! What's he doing out here like that?' one of the men said.

The other man knelt down beside the sleeping drunk, 'Come on Buddy, let's get you outta here. Silvia won't thank us for leaving you in an alley the night before your wedding.'

Jake stayed in the shadows and watched as the drunk was lifted by his two friends. He was suddenly glad he hadn't given into the urges of the wolf.

He slipped away, roaming the streets until he found himself outside his own apartment once more. He looked up. The moon was still half full and it burnt down over his apartment block. Jake lay down as he felt the change rippling through his pelt. He was becoming human once again.

The next day Jake dressed in a clean shirt and suit. He didn't think about the strange dream he'd had the night before as he picked up the roll-on of *Urban Wolf*, sniffed it, used it and placed it back inside his bathroom cabinet. By the time he left his apartment, he felt less tired and emotionally drained than usual. In fact he even had a spring in his step as he walked down the corridor to the elevator. The 'Out of Order' sign was gone and Jake took this as a good sign. Today was going to be better. He just *knew* it.

On the street he passed by his usual haunts. The local bar was closed this early but he saw the delivery of beer bottles being lowered into the basement and he waved at the bartender that had been listening to his sorrows the night before.

There goes that freak who doesn't know how to deal with a female boss.

Jake stopped. He looked back at the man and saw he was talking to the truck driver. Had he just heard him tell the driver that he had problems with his boss? Jake stared at the bartender's back. The man's arms were folded casually and he was laughing with the driver. They both glanced over at him. Jake saw the bartender's lips move but couldn't hear the words but he thought that the barman said he was a '*Complete weirdo ...*'

'Hey! Dude! How's it going today?' called the barman. His smile was friendly and casual.

Jake waved again and turned away, hurrying towards his car. *Jesus. I'm imagining things,* he thought. He opened his car door, climbed in and started the engine. He didn't glance back at the bartender and the driver. He had the irrational thought that he would hear more of the man's thoughts.

As he reached the office, Jake thought he heard the security guard call his name. When he looked up he saw the man staring at him, smiling. *You won't be here long. I've seen better than you come and go.*

Jake paused and stared back at the man until the guard became embarrassed and returned his gaze to the security monitors. Jake walked over the polished marble floors and entered the lift. He hoped that no one else would join him in there.

'Ah Jake,' said Lorna. 'Just the person I wanted to see.'

Jake looked up from his office desk and met Lorna's gaze. She was wearing a pinstriped skirt and matching jacket. The jacket was fastened up to her breasts but Jake could tell that she wasn't wearing anything else underneath it.

'Yes, Lorna?' he said.

'I'd like to go over the proposal you sent me yesterday for the yoghurt campaign. I need you to explain what you were thinking.'

'What I was thinking?' asked Jake.

'Yes. If I'm to take this to the board I need to justify why you think this string of adverts would work better than the current ones. We have to validate the cost of re-doing them.'

Jake stared at Lorna. 'You're taking my proposal to the board?'

'That's what I said didn't I?' Lorna snapped. 'But. Credit where it's due. It's good work Jake.' Lorna said and smiled, at him slyly.

Jake was taken aback. He stared at Lorna for a moment before answering. 'I ... I'm free this afternoon.'

'Well I have meetings all day,' Lorna said. 'Come to my office at six and we'll discuss it then.'

After she left Jake stared at the closed door. It wasn't like Lorna to come to his office, nor was it normal for her to meet him to 'discuss' his proposals. He felt there must be some trick. Some scam. She wanted to know how he came up with his ideas so that when she claimed them for herself she would be equipped with the knowledge and links behind them.

Jake felt sick. He couldn't do this anymore. He had to look for another job. Lorna was eating his soul and he felt as though his own creativity was dying. He felt restless and so he stood up and prowled his office, pausing by the glass window to look out over the typing pool. At that moment, Tiffany, one of the young secretaries, looked up and met his eyes.

Loser! We all know you're Lorna's lust puppy.

Jake blinked and then blushed. Tiffany looked back at her screen and continued to work. Jake shook his head. What was wrong with him? He couldn't really be hearing people's thoughts, could he?

He wanted to know what was going on, and so he opened the office door with every intention of talking to the girl. A rush of captured noise came into his room. Snippets of conversation. '...sugar in that coffee?', 'He's ...you', 'I want a raise but just *can't* ask'. Someone had brought in a hot deli sandwich and the smell lingered tantalisingly in the air. Jake half-remembered the hunger he'd felt in his dream the night before. He looked around the room as all of the detail came rushing back. His senses were overwhelmed with it, even though he knew the experience hadn't been real.

He wished he *was* a wolf: outside he could see and smell many a tasty meal. A pretty secretary walked by and smiled. Jake looked at her thin arms and legs and turned away. There wasn't enough meat on her to feed a bird, let alone a wolf.

At that moment, Karen and John, two of his fellow assistants, walked towards him on the way to the coffee machine. He met John's eyes. *You gotta know how to treat bitches.*

Jake quickly looked away but found himself looking at Karen instead. *She does this to all of her assistants. Wish I could offer advice, but I doubt you'd listen.'*

'Jake? You okay?' asked Karen.

Jake nodded but he could barely hear her over the sudden rush of voices in his head. He was afraid to speak in case he gave himself away. Jake was convinced that he was losing his mind.

'Want a coffee?' Karen asked kindly.

Jake sniffed. Karen smelt good like warm pastries and hot chocolate. He breathed in deeply, and then nodded again to hide the fact that he was snuffling around her a dog. But he couldn't shake the feeling that he wanted to *taste* Karen. It occurred to him how perverse this was, after all he saw her as food, not in a sexual light. Even so the thought aroused him more than pornographic visions of her might have done.

'Yes. I could use a drink,' Jake said to cover his thoughts.

Lorna's office was the only one on the floor that had no glass panels. Once the door was closed, you couldn't see what was happening inside which Jake had thought was just as well since they had their liaisons in there. Jake paused outside the door as they passed and Karen and John exchanged a look. *Poor Jerk. He's got it bad.* Then, Jake began to laugh. This was too much. It really was insane. No way could he possibly be hearing all of their thoughts like this. He looked up from the coffee machine to find Karen, John and three of the secretary's looking at him. He turned and walked away from the machine, rapidly seeking the comfort and peace of his office.

At 6pm, like a good, well-trained puppy, Jake went into Lorna's office. She was sat behind her huge desk, her skinny frame dwarfed by the masculine wood and the MD, Kirk Weiss, was sitting on the leather sofa at the other side of the room.

'Jake. Glad you could make it,' Lorna said. 'Kirk would like to hear your ideas.'

Jake had planned to tell Lorna some vague concept of where his ideas came from, but on finding Kirk there, he knew this was his one chance to impress the boss. Jake began to tell Kirk and Lorna all about his thoughts for the yoghurt campaign. It was based on health and fitness. He recommended that the product be sold as if it had health benefits, but without actually saying that.

'But how would we do that?' probed Kirk.

'By implying it, rather than saying it,' Jake explained. 'For example the expression "tests show", or "99% of people found this beneficial". Of course we put on the usual disclaimer to cover the client's back.

Kirk Weiss nodded as Jake spoke and by the end of the meeting Jake felt more like his old self and his confidence was soaring.

'That's good stuff, son,' said Kirk. 'Where did you find this talent, Lorna?'

'Jake has been working very closely with me for the past several months. Recently he's been showing a great deal of promise,' Lorna said.

Jake felt her eyes on him and he glanced up. *I'm grooming you for bigger things.*

Afterwards, Lorna did not demand her usual sexual privileges and Jake went home, for once, to a relatively pain free, early night. He felt elated. He was finally getting some recognition for all of his hard work. So what if he hadn't received the acknowledgment he deserved for the deodorant? The yoghurt campaign was big. This could be his ticket to an executive position in the firm.

He showered and used the *Urban Wolf* roll-on with glee. Tonight, Jake planned to celebrate.

Later he passed by one of the exclusive shops. There was a shirt in the window that he had admired from time to time. It was blue, smart, but expensive. The store was open late and so Jake decided to go in and buy it. Why not? He rarely treated himself and he had been saving all of his spare salary because he had felt so insecure in the job.

He tried on the shirt, and for good measure bought two more work shirts. They were expensive but they made Jake feel like he was an executive already. The dream of success that he had held so closely to his chest now no longer seemed impossible.

When he finally stumbled home, he collapsed fully clothed onto his bed. He's had a very good night and his self-esteem was as high as it could be.

Then, Jake felt the change as he became the urban wolf again. This time he felt every bone break, every sinew restructure. The pain in his face as his chin, mouth and nose, merged and elongated, becoming a dog-like muzzle, was almost unbearable. His joints bent backwards at agonising angles and blood poured from his mouth and his teeth grew down, from swollen, bloody gums. He tasted the blood on his lips and it made the fury and hunger rise inside him.

He found himself outside, slinking in and out of dark corners, around houses, and bars and alleys. The smell of human and animal flesh scorched his nostrils and perpetual hunger twisted his guts, until he could stand it no longer. Jake had never felt so empty. His part human mind railed against it. He had eaten well, was happy. There was no need for this empty feeling.

He found himself hiding at the back of his local haunt staring at the closed door. Even though it was late he could hear the movement of someone still working inside. There was the sharp chink of bottles in crates being stacked up and the smell of food, some slightly rotted, wafted through the small gap under the door. Jake sniffed, taking in the smells and enjoying the nicest aroma of them all: human flesh.

He backed away as he heard the door unlock, slipping behind one of the dumpsters and then he saw the bartender come out carrying to large black refuse sacks. The bartender lifted the lid of the nearest dumpster and casually threw the refuse bags inside. Jake gagged on the overpowering odour of decayed food. He staggered back, knocking over a garbage can. The can fell with a loud clang spilling its vile contents over the alley floor. He felt liquid tacky dampen his paws and he howled in frustration.

'What the fuck ...? Who's there?' said the Bartender. 'Hey! Buddy! What *you* doing there?'

Jake turned, running on all fours, away from the alley, though the hunger screamed louder than his beating heart. He couldn't shake the thought that the bartender had recognised him despite the transformation. The thought terrified him as he ran all the way home.

Jake woke in a fugue, head hurting, teeth and jaw aching as though had been grinding his teeth all night. He shook away the weird wolf dream but it lingered in the corners of his subconscious along with the sick feeling that followed a hangover.

It was Saturday and Jake was relieved when he realised that he wouldn't have to drag himself to work that day. He threw back the covers and slipped gingerly from the bed. He walked groggily into the bathroom and looked at himself in the mirror. He looked awful. His eyes were bloodshot, his skin sallow and his hands trembled as he reached for his toothbrush. He showered and applied the *Urban Wolf* deodorant: it made him feel fresh and vibrant. As he placed the roll-on down on his bathroom shelf, his eyes fell on the slogan. 'It turns man into beast'. It gave him a jolt. It was as though he had only just noticed this on the label, even though he had personally invented the line.

What if that's true? he thought. *What if I'm turning into a wolf?*

The idea was insane, but Jake did feel different. Since the first time he had used the product he had been having strange dreams. Even now, the hangover was rapidly receding as though his powers of recovery had become keener. As he shaved he scrutinised his face in the mirror. Could it be that last night his jaw had grown into the large maw of a wolf? He glanced down at his fingers nails; they were definitely longer and sharper than usual and, it seemed impossible, but had his hair grown too? It had been such a short time since his last hair cut, but Jake felt the style had already grown out. It looked nicer though, somewhat longer and he pushed it back from his face, slicking it with gel.

Then, Jake turned and looked over his shoulder at his bare back. The scars from Lorna's nails were no longer there and the skin was smooth and bare as it had always been. What could this all mean?

On Monday, Jake walked into work with more confidence than he had ever had. He wasn't going to be anyone's whipping boy anymore and he wouldn't take any more crap from Lorna. Instead of quietly slipping past her office, Jake walked boldly in and found Lorna already on the phone in the middle of the negotiations for the yoghurt adverts.

'What's happening?' he asked.

'The client likes the ideas. We've been given the go ahead,'

Lorna said. 'But don't let it go to your head. You're still just *my* assistant.'

Jake gave Lorna his best predatory smile. 'As if I could ever forget that Lorna.'

Lorna blinked. She looked uncomfortable as he towered over her desk and then she stood up. Jake knew this trick: it was how she changed the power in the room, next she would be asking him to take a seat and then, she would tower over him in her six inch killer heels.

'Jake. Why don't you take a seat?'

'No thanks. I'll stand.'

Lorna looked perplexed but didn't push the issue. Instead she perched sexily on the edge of her desk as she surveyed him. This was another tactic and she turned her eyes up to him provocatively.

'After our meeting on Friday, Kirk suggested that you are to attend the board meeting today.'

'Why?' Jake asked.

'You are crucial to our plans.'

Jake left the office. His walk had gone from the downtrodden man, believing he was on the verge of losing his job, to the confident stride of someone who knows he is important. As he passed the typing pool, Jake no longer feared the curious looks of the secretaries, or the pitying gaze of the other advertising assistants. He knew he was on the up and it was all because he had great ideas. Even Lorna couldn't ignore that.

In his office, he added more of the roll-on. The *Urban Wolf* deodorant made him feel strong and confident. It gave him something that nothing else ever had. He glanced out at the secretaries working outside. He wondered if anyone else had learnt the secret inside the product. Somehow he thought they hadn't. He was beginning to believe that the deodorant only had this effect on him.

Karen passed by his window. She turned and waved. *You look good today. Maybe Lorna won't eat you like all the rest of her assistants after all.*

Jake smiled. He *had* changed. Lorna had finally met her match, and Jake would make her pay after the working day. He still wanted her; only from now on he was going to call all the shots and her sharp nails would have to stay sheaved in future.

He worked through the day, efficiently, but slightly distracted and then, when the time came. Laptop under his arm, ready to make the presentation for the string of commercials he had proposed, Jake made his way to the board room on the floor above. Under normal circumstances, he would have been nervous, but he used the roll-on once more and it helped him feel calmer.

'Come in Jake,' Kirk Weiss said as he rapped on the door. 'We're all ready for you.'

Jake had hoped he would find the room empty and have time to set up his laptop before the board members came in. It threw him a little that they were already waiting. The board consisted of three women and seven men. Jake knew some, but not all of them, as the directors kept themselves very much to themselves. He wished that they all had name tags: he feared that he would make some stupid mistake and address the wrong person.

I have to tell them everything and then there won't be any need for them to question me, he thought.

'Take all the time you need,' Lorna said.

Jake quickly hooked up his laptop, and tested it on the smart screen. Finally, when he was ready, he began to tell them all about his ideas and how they would benefit the client. As the presentation started Jake felt like a performer: keeping his audience captivated was paramount and they all watched him intently as he spoke. But following the presentation the board members were quiet. Jake looked around at their blank faces and wondered, as the silence fell on the room, if he had somehow failed their test.

'Well,' said one of the women that Jake didn't know. 'Isn't he just marvellous?'

'Absolutely delightful,' said another.

'A testament to your tutoring,' Kirk said addressing Lorna.

Lorna nodded. 'I had high hopes for Jake and the experiment has proved to be very effective.'

Jake looked around at the now eager faces.

'Experiment?'

'Why yes, Jake. We've been trying a new product out on you,' Kirk explained.

'A new product? Do you mean Urban Wolf?'

Lorna smiled and for the first time Jake noticed the excess of teeth in her broad smile. It made him feel nervous and brought back memories from his half recalled dreams. 'Sort of.'

'I knew it! It's changing me!'

'Not really the product,' Kirk explained. 'But rather the *idea* of it. You see, even a sheep can think it's a wolf if it is in the right environment.'

'What do you mean?' asked Jake. His cheeks flared red with embarrassment. Somehow he had been duped, used. 'Are you saying you don't like my campaign idea? That this is all a joke?'

'Oh no,' said Lorna. 'There's nothing amusing about this and if it makes you feel any better we do love the campaign and will be using your ideas.'

Lorna's face, already long and thin, appeared to be longer, the smile wider and she wore the same hungry expression that she had worn every time she had abused him. Jake looked around him. The board members where changing too.

'I don't understand!' he said backing away towards the door. 'You've changed me. I'm one of you!'

'Sheep need to be fattened up before they make the best food,' Kirk said. 'The roll-on contains a hallucinogenic. You've imagined you were one of us, because deep down you've always recognised what we were.'

Jake turned and ran towards the door. He pulled at the handle but it wouldn't open. *This can't be happening!*

He heard howling, cracking and twisting bones and he believed he could smell blood too. There was a sickened roar, half way between a human cry and a dog howling. It sent a chill through his limbs. He felt paralysed with fear and his fingers lost their grip on the door handle.

SAM STONE

Lorna was the first to reach him, rapidly followed by Kirk. They turned him around and that was when Jake saw the full horror of what was behind him. Lorna was naked, but Jake couldn't reconcile the sight of this monstrous, twisted half-beast thing that confronted him with the beautiful, but cold, woman he had had sex with. Kirk was had removed his shirt and Jake saw that he was deformed, with a hunched back that arched up and showing the warped points of his misshapen spine. His face was long, but not quite wolf, certainly no longer human, and his eyes were misplaced in his head as though he had been dissembled by the artist Picasso. Tufts of hair grew with bald patches all over his naked torso and arms.

'What are you?' Jake screamed. Kirk's laugh was like the chuckle of a demon from hell.

Lorna leered, thick gloop dripped from her serrated teeth as she lay back on the board table, legs open to reveal a greenish-mucus filled vagina. It pulsed, opening and closing like a gaping mouth filled with bile. She had several nipples, all of which were erect, as though she were cold or hugely excited, and they secreted some equally vile substance. She smelt of rot, like the epitome of a sexually transmitted disease, and Jake screamed as she turned her hair covered face towards him.

'Come to me lover?' she sneered her voice distorted by the awful canines.

Jake had never seen anything so hideous in his life. He slid down to the floor, legs giving way beneath him as he blacked out.

The deformed wolves pulled Jake's prone body onto the board table. It was time for their monthly feast, and then they would all once more be able to shift into their full change. They ripped away the new and expensive clothing that Jake had invested in and one by one they began to tear at the soft flesh on his thighs and stomach.

'For you,' growled Kirk as his claws tore away Jake's flaccid penis and scrotum. He tossed the tasty morsel to Lorna and she ate with relish. She deserved it. She had groomed Jake well and the taste of his over confident, adrenaline-filled blood was just the tonic she needed. She didn't even mind when Kirk fell upon her, his huge wolf cock forcing its way inside her as he rutted. The excitement of feeding did strange things to them all.

Afterwards, they mopped up the remains, eating everything bar Jake's white, perfect teeth. These the women shared amongst them like precious trophies.

No longer deformed, the wolves waited until it was full dark and then they slunk away from the board room, into their private elevator and out into the urban jungle that they had made their home.

The Promise

'I've come to take you home.'

Tom looked up from his bowl of porridge to find his cousin Patty standing by the table. For a moment he felt confused. He was in a drug-induced haze; the days had passed in the hospital in a blur of bewilderment.

Patty was a few years older than Tom. They had been close growing up, but he hadn't seen her since Stacie's funeral. He had to force his mind to remember that this was some months before. He didn't even know who had contacted her.

'Come on,' said Patty. 'I'll help you dress.'

They walked slowly to Tom's room. Tom was walking like an old man and knew it had to be the drugs. His mouth felt as though it was filled with fur and his fingers and toes were suffering from a chemical numbness. It was as if his limbs belonged to someone else: somehow he managed to control them, but only just.

When they went inside his room, Patty burst into sudden tears.

'Jesus, Tom. What have they done to you? How did this happen? Why didn't you call me?'

She hugged him awkwardly.

'I'm taking you back to my place until you're better. They reckon the meds will help stabilise you.'

'I'm …n …not sure what happened,' he said. 'Jus' remember the doctor bringing me in for tests …' The more he spoke the more his cracked voice began to work again. He couldn't remember the last time he had even tried to speak.

Patty helped him dress and by the time Tom had his tee-shirt, jeans, shoes and socks back on the fugue was lifting. She left him for a few moments while she went to sort out 'the paperwork', and Tom looked around the small one-bedded room and wondered again how he had come to be here, and when.

When Patty returned, Tom went with her willingly. He needed to be outside; felt as though he had truly forgotten what fresh air was like.

'What …was …how …long?' he asked as they left the ward and walked towards the hospital exit.

'Not surprised you lost time,' Patty said. 'I believe you've been there for about a month.'

She linked his arm. 'It was by sheer luck I found out. I called round to the cottage, saw the pile of post left in the porch, knew something was wrong and so I went to see the farmer next door. He told me the doctor had admitted you to hospital. It didn't take long to find out where you were then.'

'I can't remember anything,' Tom said.

'I came a few days ago. You were so drugged you couldn't even stand. I had to get my lawyer on it to get you out of here. That doctor, the bitch, had you committed. We forced her to release your records – she said you were a danger to yourself and not fit to live alone. It's how we won. I told them I'd look after you. Since then they've been weaning you off the drugs.'

'I'm not a danger …' Tom groaned. 'How ridiculous …'

Patty paused and turned him to face her. 'I know that Tom. I can't believe that hack country doctor could do something like this to you. With everything you've been through.'

Patty's eyes watered up again.

'Why didn't you call me?'

Tom shook his head. He couldn't explain, he was even having difficulty remembering why the doctor had taken him to the hospital in the first place.

'We'll call back at the cottage,' Patty said as they climbed into the car. 'Collect some things for you. Bring that mail across to sort through too.'

As they drove up the gravel path to his cottage Tom began to recall the events before the hospital. Some strange terror that had taken over his life. A fear of something … but his confused brain couldn't remember what.

He wandered through the cottage looking at the old photographs on the walls, the chair with a dog-eared magazine still placed on it, the favourite ornaments on the mantelpiece. So many memories and they all came flooding back.

When they had bought this house and the surrounding land, it had felt like a dream come true. Then Stacie had become sick, cancer was diagnosed and her early death had quickly followed. Tom had found himself alone, surrounded by everything that reminded him of his wife. It had been so sudden that he didn't have time to adjust.

After the funeral he had returned home; grave soil still staining his fingers. Darkness seemed to have descended far earlier than it should have. As he approached the cottage he found himself stumbling around like a sightless man who had lost his cane. Then, when he reached the door he struggled to fit the front door key in the lock without success. It was as though he had been struck blind. The first echoes of panic began to rise in his chest. He couldn't see at all in the dark!

When he finally managed to get inside and scrabbled for the main light-switch he was feeling sick and something akin to total panic made him feel as though he was on the brink of collapse. The light sent the anxiety scurrying away.

In the kitchen, he found the box the hospice had given him. It was full of Stacie's possessions. He couldn't face sorting through them and so he picked the box up, carried it upstairs and placed it on the desk in Stacie's study. Then he turned off the light and closed the door. After that he couldn't bring himself to go into that room again.

After that the night blindness had gotten worse. He couldn't bear to be in a dark room. In the night when he opened his bedroom door and stared out onto the black landing an unreasonable panic would overwhelm him.

'Clearly stress,' Dr Stevens had said when he called in at the surgery a few weeks later. She was a female doctor and always seemed sympathetic.

By then Tom couldn't bear to have the lights off at all at night. The blindness was so complete he was convinced he would fall and hurt himself.

'Not surprising really,' the doctor had added. 'But don't worry: it will pass. You just have to sensitise your vision again. Return to sleeping in the dark. All will soon improve.'

Turning off the bedside lamp once he was in bed he had tried to do what the doctor suggested, but the dark-blindness made him feel as though he were in that box with his wife, buried deep in the ground. He felt suffocated, and grabbed for the lamp, plunging the room back into light to which his eyes adjusted immediately.

After that, the dark became something to fear: something that would make him vulnerable. It couldn't be tolerated, no matter how ridiculous it seemed.

As the months went on the panic became worse. Tom had found that he couldn't even risk going out at night. Driving in the dark was impossible and he didn't want to find himself caught outside in an unlit area.

Once, the bulb in his bedside lamp blew sometime during the night. Tom jolted awake. He found himself in pitch darkness. Fear pinned him to the bed even though his rational mind knew that all he had to do was stumble towards the door and turn on the main light. In the dark he thought he heard something. A vague, imperceptible breathing.

Icy sweat burst out on his forehead. The smell of soil and death had filled his nostrils. Blood pumped loudly in his ears, as his heart beat sped up, his breathing became ragged and he felt utter terror threatening to consume his mind.

I'm losing it! He had thought at the time. But no amount of rationalisation could shake away the fear. Finally, sliding back up on his pillows, he had forced himself to sit. He had the feeling that something was up above him, pressing down like some monstrous torture chamber whose spike-covered ceiling was slowly sinking.

He swung his legs over the side of the bed, then almost pulled them back when he was sure he felt movement.

Something cold had wafted around his ankles, as though a freezing fog was lurking, ready to consume him.

Somehow he had staggered forward. Crouching low to avoid the imagined crushing ceiling, Tom stumbled towards what he hoped was the door and the blessed light.

He tripped and fell hard against the wall as he pulled himself along. There appeared to be no door, no light switch. Overwhelming panic surged again. He had been sure he could feel the ceiling just above his head even though this made no sense at all. And then his hand touched something …

With relief he had snapped the switch down and turned on the light. The night terrors were sent scurrying back into whatever hell they came from. Shaking he had slumped on the floor near the door.

Tom remembered how his eyes had fallen on the bed. He had been certain that there was still darkness underneath it: small enough to be considered claustrophobic and big enough to hide something malignant.

He had been unable to move back to the bed for fear that the light would go out again. And so Tom had remained on the floor until the dawn peeked through his curtains and pushed away the last of the horror the night had given him.

After that he had descended into complete insanity which had led him to not only have lights on day and night inside and outside of the cottage, but he had also had a generator installed as a backup. Now he wandered through the house as though it were a place he had only visited in a dream and not the home he and Stacie had loved so much. It was no wonder Dr Stevens had thought him unfit to be alone.

'You okay?' asked Patty.

Tom nodded. They went upstairs; Patty found an old suitcase under the bed and began to fill it with Tom's clothing. The house smelt musty, as though he'd been away longer than the month that Patty had mentioned.

He looked around the bedroom with disassociation. None of these items filled him with comfort or familiarity in the way they should have. They were things of fear and dread. They were chains in the prison his life had become. They all seemed so dreary and depressing.

He sank down on the bed, remembering a tight-chested anxiety. He glanced up at the ceiling. No spikes and it wasn't closing in on him now.

'Will I ever be back to normal?' he asked.

Patty stopped packing and looked at him. She frowned a little, as though she was concerned about him.

'Do you *want* to be?'

Tom looked down at his hands. They trembled like a Parkinson's sufferer.

'It's the drugs,' Patty explained. 'The doctor's told me they would take some time to get out of your system properly. You'll still have to take a small dose for a while too.'

It was getting dark out. Tom noticed the sun drooping over the field through the bedroom window.

'This will do now,' Patty said closing the case.

'Can we turn on a light?' Tom asked.

Patty tried the switch near the door but to no effect. 'Looks like your electricity is out.'

'Oh no!' said Tom. 'I've been away so long, maybe the bill wasn't paid?'

'More than likely.'

Patty picked up the suitcase and took Tom's hand. 'Come on. Let's get you out of here. We can come back in a few days if there's anything you remember you'd like.'

Tom nodded and let her lead him like an invalid out of the bedroom. At the top of the stairs he glanced back at the three open doors. One the bathroom, the other his bedroom, the third was Stacie's study.

'She wrote books ...' he said suddenly.

'That's right, Tom. Stacie was a novelist. A very successful novelist.'

Something was nagging at the back of his mind as Patty led him down the narrow staircase and into the living room, but he just couldn't remember what it was.

At the front door he paused. 'I need to get something ...from the study …'

He stared back at the staircase. The dark had reached it now; it meant that Tom couldn't walk back.

'Tom?' Patty said.

'It's okay. We can come back, can't we?'

Patty put his case in the boot of the car as Tom climbed into the passenger seat. It was important – something Stacie wanted him to do. Something she said would help when she was gone.

Patty slammed the boot down and got into the car beside him. She turned the key in the ignition. The car spluttered and the starter motor screeched in protest. The engine turned over, then stalled.

'Damn thing is always plaguing me,' Patty said. She turned the key again.

Nothing. The battery was completely dead.

'Bugger,' she slammed her hands against the steering wheel.

'My car?' suggested Tom.

The sun was sinking lower; the field opposite the cottage was now entering that dark and gloomy period known as twilight. Tom became edgy and afraid.

'Dark …' he said.

'Tom. You're all right. You aren't alone. Where are the keys to your car?'

Tom described the location of the drawer in the kitchen. Patty opened the glove box and pulled out a torch.

'I'll be right back.'

She took Tom's house keys, quickly climbed out of the car, then hurried to the front door. As she opened the door, Tom remembered the generator in the barn. All he needed to do was get to the barn, switch it on and the house and grounds would be flooded with light.

The sun was gone now, swallowed whole by the landscape. There wasn't even a moon to illuminate the path to the barn.

Tom stared desperately at the dark house. The open door was a gaping maw waiting to swallow him. But he could see the flicker of torchlight moving across one of the windows upstairs.

'The kitchen …' he whispered as though Patty might hear

his reminder.

What was she doing upstairs? Had she remembered what it was he wanted? But Tom couldn't even recall what it was himself.

He stared at the door but his eyes went blind from the lack of any light and the fear and chaos that had controlled his life before came flooding back in a horrible, cold rush.

He felt her breath on his neck again. The stark, dank stink of death and rot.

Tomas …Only Stacie had ever called him that. Could this horror, this thing that plagued him be her? No, he couldn't believe that. He loved her. He would do anything for her …

Tomas.

He shrank into his seat, afraid to remain locked up tight inside the car, alone with *it*.

You promised, Tomas.

'I don't remember,' he said denial once more on his lips.

Icy air filled the car. Tom felt a freezing hand touch his shoulder. The sensation was familiar. Horrified, he pulled away.

'Don't touch me. You're dead!'

You said you'd love me forever. You said you'd love me beyond the grave.

'No!' Tom screamed.

His hand pulled and tugged at the door handle. He had to escape. The only place he could go was the barn.

'Light. I need light …'

The lock was down. He didn't remember pressing it …He pulled it up, then yanked the handle once more. The door sprung open and Tom tumbled out onto the dirt track.

He crawled to his feet with the support of the car door. Stacie was still inside the car …he could feel her presence and so he slammed the door shut to delay her, even though the thought was irrational: Stacie could follow him anywhere when it was dark. She wanted to pull him back into the grave, down into the dark, to stay with her forever.

He staggered blindly around the front of the car, cursing the dead battery, the faulty alternator and the fact that Patty had left him alone in the dark.

'Patty?' he shouted. 'Help me! Come out. Get me to the barn …'

Patty didn't reply. The house remained a block of blackness before him. He stumbled to the wall, followed it around towards the side of the house, and stumbled towards the barn.

The night was complete. The dark – a suffocating fog – surrounded him like ink in water. The air thickened and grew chill. Stacie wasn't going to let him escape her that easily.

He pushed forward, even as tendrils of icy air grabbed at his ankles and wrists, trying to tie him up in their paralysing cold.

White condensation blew from his lips as he staggered forward into a no man's land, hands waving furiously before him as he pushed aside the cloying phantom. It seemed an eternity before his knuckles hit painfully against the side of the barn.

Nearly there!

His fingers grappled with the wooden walls as he dragged himself closer to the door. His hands fell on the doorway. He tugged, then remembered that the barn was locked.

Blindly he searched until they found the combination lock. But his mind screamed in terror when he realised he couldn't remember the pattern. He twisted and turned the numbered dials, but it was no use when you couldn't see the numbers, nor remember the combination.

Tom fell to his knees. An old lump of rock he had often used to wedge the door open pressed into his thigh. The cold was around him again. Stacie was inside his head, begging him to come back to her, to keep his promise. But he didn't want to be in the cold and dark. He didn't want the grainy soil to cover his face, his body, to enter his mind like a worm burrowing a void in the earth.

The fight was almost gone out of him but still his fingers gripped onto the rock. He stood up and smashed the rock down where he thought the lock would be. It connected. He smashed down again and again until finally the rusted hinge holding it in place bent and snapped with a loud crack.

Tom dropped the rock and yanked the barn door open. The black hole before him halted him in his tracks. Inside the barn his sightlessness, if possible, grew worse. It was as though a hangman's hood had been placed over his head, covering his face, blinding his vision.

Terror twisted his heart and stomach in knots, but he forced his leaden feet to move, one step, then another. Forward, to the left. The generator was near.

Tomas. You promised …

'No. I didn't understand. I don't want to die, Stacie. I'm not ready yet.'

He felt her slender arm, a cold dead-weight, slip around his waist.

You said you loved me …

'I do Stace, I do …But this is too much.'

I trusted you to keep your promise …

Tom began to sob. He pulled at the dead arm trying to free himself even as her corpse-cold fingers dug into his flesh through his thin tee-shirt.

'Let me go, Stace …Let me go …'

Tom heaved himself forward. The generator was near: he knew it was. But now Stacie held on tighter. Her clawing hands fighting against his every move.

His hands beat at her, connected with air and nothing more, then he twisted and turned in her grasp until his frantically flailing arms connected with the generator.

'Get off me, Stacie,' he yelled. Anger now fuelling his determination.

His fingers probed the machine, searching for the trigger switch that would start the generator and illuminate the barn, the house and the grounds.

Keep your promise to me Tomas. It was my best work. You said so yourself.

The switch was under his fingers. He paused. A flicker of memory burst behind his blinded vision. *Stacie lying in the hospital bed, her wasted fingers gripping his as she extracted the promise from him.*

'You will take care of this? You promise?'

She had handed him a handwritten manuscript. He glanced down at the pages, the penmanship started out so clear and neat, but as he read on, the writing became more frantic, but was still good. Still the best novel she had ever written.

Soon after that she was gone and the wad of paper lay discarded. He remembered picking it up, placing it in the box with her other possessions. The same box that he had put in the study.

He recalled how he hadn't been in the office since: he wasn't ready to sort through her things, to admit that finally she was gone.

Tom flicked the switch, but there was now no need. His night blindness had gone, Stacie's ghost had released its grip and his memory had returned along with the dreadful grief that had been pushing him slowly towards madness.

The barn lit up, the grounds surrounding the house were awash with light, and the house, Tom knew, was now as bright as daylight inside.

Tom turned and walked calmly back to the car.

'Tom?' Patty called, emerging from the brightly lit cottage and turning off her torch.

'I turned on the generator.'

Patty looked afraid. Her eyes were wide open as though she had seen something in the dark.

'I'm okay,' he said. 'Are *you* alright?'

Patty glanced back at the house, a look of confusion and fear coloured her cheeks. 'I thought I ...'

She stopped as though she was too scared to voice what she had seen, but Tom didn't need her to explain. He knew already what had been in the house, waiting for him. Prompting him to recall a promise he should never have forgotten. A promise that had been pushed down and buried in as deep a pit of darkness as his wife's body had been.

'I have to get one more thing,' he explained.

'Tom?' Patty said, gripping his arm. 'Don't go in there ...'

'It's all okay.'

He walked into the house, and hurried upstairs.

At the door to Stacie's office he paused. It would be painful, but he still didn't have to deal with it all. Just this one thing. This one important deed.

He opened the door and switched on the light. The room was covered in dust, a cobweb grew in one corner like ivy overrunning a wall, and the windowsill was matted with dead flies.

Heart beating rapidly he stepped inside. Memories of the room flooded him: Stacie sitting proudly at her desk before her small old-fashioned typewriter, while the new-fangled word processor sat untouched; Stacie smiling at him as she brandished a page with the words 'THE END' typed neatly in the centre; a growing pile of paper as she worked on her latest novel; Stacie laughing as Tom tried to persuade her to use the word processor; so many happy memories and flashes of their life together.

The box was on top of the desk. Tom felt a chill in the air as he hesitated, but no, this time he would keep his promise. The world would know the words she shaped in those final months, days and hours of her life.

He lifted the cardboard lid and a plume of dust rose from the box. There in the box was the manuscript. The title page glared at him. It was called *The Promise*. He remembered the story now. A man lost the woman he loved, and failed to keep his final promise. The lover returned from the grave to exact revenge.

Suddenly Tom's phobia made perfect sense.

He picked up the papers and turned away from the room, switching the light off as he went.

At the top of the stairs the house lights began to flicker. Tom realised with horror that he couldn't recall the last time he had filled the generator with gasoline. His heart began to pound as he was plummeted once more in darkness. Clutching the manuscript against his chest he reached out for the banister. He wouldn't let the phobia beat him this time.

One foot at a time he started to make his way down the pitch black stairs. Suddenly, he felt something rush around him: that same cold malevolence that had hounded his nights. The darkness blinded and choked him. An icy hand pressed against the small of his back.

'No …' he gasped. 'I remembered my promise …'

His foot missed the next step and he toppled forward, tumbling down the narrow staircase. But even as he fell, Tom didn't let go of the manuscript. He *had* to keep his promise. Without his hands to break his fall, he hit the bottom hard and there was a loud crack as he impacted with the wooden floor. He gave a small groan and then lay still. The darkness finally claimed him for good.

Torchlight flashed around the small living room as Patty hurried back into the house and towards the stairs.

'Tom?' she cried.

His body lay at an unnatural angle, head and back twisted in obscene opposition. Patty knelt down beside him, the light from the torch picked out the horrified expression on his face that signified the moment of death. She took a moment to study him before she stood and walked back through the house to the telephone beside the front door. She made a call then headed back outside towards the barn. A moment later the generator kicked back in and the cottage lit up once more.

'He's dead then?' asked Stacie, climbing over the body as she came down the stairs.

'Yes,' Patty nodded.

Stacie prised the manuscript from Tom's dead fingers. 'I'd better burn this.'

Patty slipped her arm around Stacie's waist and kissed her lips. 'Pity. It really is the best book you've ever written. But it would be pretty damning evidence.'

Stacie stared at the wad of papers in her hand, then she released Patty, walked into the kitchen and placed them in the wood-burner.

'Are you sure?' Patty asked.

'The amount of insurance we have on him …I won't ever have to write again.'

Stacie lit a match and held the flame against the corner of the manuscript. The paper caught immediately and she watched the top cover turn black as the flame slowly ate its way through.

The Promise burned.

DNA Books

For Mark Edward Askren

The voucher arrived in the post inside a birthday card. Mark Edward Askren read the words carefully, unsure what the present was. All it said was 'DNA Books'.

The card was signed 'With love, Aunt Josslin' and this was indeed the biggest surprise. His aunt was rarely in one place for long, travelling as her considerable wealth allowed, often forgetting his birthday completely, only to send along a card and a large cheque once she realised. This present, however, was both on time and was indeed an actual gift that had possibly taken her more than a few moments to choose.

Mark turned the voucher over, on the other side he saw the small indemnity, *DNA Books direct into your DNA. Satisfaction Guaranteed Or Your Money Back. Book your appointment now!* Mark was intrigued. He loved literature, was impressed that Aunt Josslin had actually remembered this fact. The gift meant more to him than a fat cheque, despite the welcome top up to his savings it always gave.

On his laptop, Mark keyed in the website and a colourful page popped up on his screen, followed by an instructional video.

This looked wonderful! DNA Books promised to insert an entire catalogue of novels into your DNA. It was far better than VR, you could live in the fictional worlds you most loved, anytime, night or day.

After watching the video, Mark clicked the button that said 'Book Your Appointment'.

He ignored the disclaimer. It was the usual rubbish ... *DNA Books could not be held responsible for this issue, or that problem* ... Instead of reading the list of exemptions, Mark ticked 'Accept' and the terms and conditions disappeared. After that it only took a moment to arrange his appointment.

A few minutes later the address and appointment details ejected from his printer. Mark noted that the address was a local private clinic. His appointment was in three days time. He was very excited.

Three days later Mark lay on the operating table, an oxygen mask over his face fed a small dose of anaesthetic, while the DNA Books' surgeons implanted his literature directly into his bone marrow.

When he woke his pelvis was slightly sore and he felt a strange tingling sensation at the tips of his fingers and toes.

'This is all normal,' explained the doctor. 'It will take a few weeks to take effect, and then you need to come in to be shown how to access your literature at times convenient to you.'

'So I can choose to be any of the characters? To be truly interactive?'

'Yes,' said the doctor. 'You'll be able to feel everything that the book describes. So all of your senses will be tricked into experiencing all of the action. Love, lust, pain. You'll be able to taste food. It's a truly rounded VR experience like none other.'

Mark took the aftercare sheets home, but after the specified few days of rest he promptly forgot to read them.

A few weeks later, after attending his training appointment, Mark was regularly accessing his favourite stories. He sat on a comfortable sofa and submerged himself in fiction of all kinds. If his phone or doorbell rang he was rapidly pulled away from the world he was in and back to reality. Crossing into the book worlds and back again was so natural that it was very much like picking a physical book up and reading it, only to put it down again when you had enough. Mark rarely tired of the worlds he inhabited though, always seeing the novels and stories through to the very end before disconnecting his mind from the literature, back to the present.

Before long Mark's daily world seemed dull in comparison to the written worlds. He found himself more and more often slipping into a new book, only to emerge sometime later, a day or two of real time completely lost. On these occasions, he found a need for food and sleep, then he would return refreshed and continue where the story left off. It was like watching a movie inside your head, except that it was completely interactive just as the doctor had said. He was in it. He even began to feel the emotions the characters felt.

One evening Mark was skipping through his DNA library and he found something different from his usual preferences. He was a little surprised to see a horror novel there. His stated preferences had been for literary classics, action adventures and some erotica. He wasn't much of a horror fan, thinking it generally mass market trash, but this one looked interesting. It was a ghost story.

He dipped into the opening and found it to be well written and as the first character died a brutal death, Mark was hooked. Several hours later he had read most of the story and only two of the characters survived: one whose perspective he was in; the other was a female love interest to his character. The final mystery unravelled and Mark saved the girl, while sending the malignant ghost back into the darkness it came from.

After that Mark searched out more horror from the catalogue and was surprised to find quite a few gems in the literary section. Bram Stoker, Sheridan Le Fanu, Mary Shelley, all of these authors had created wonderful works that appealed to him more than he would have expected.

Then, hidden in the erotica, he found a tale that completely chilled his blood. It was about a man grooming women via social media – not a new idea but still a concern. Mark skipped through the character list, all of them seemed a little shallow, but the stalker himself seemed to have hidden depths.

He chose 'Peter' and the story unravelled. It was told in the first person, from Peter's perspective and this also surprised Mark. Most of the stories he had read were third person, so that you could see everything that the other characters were doing even when you were in the head of one in particular.

I watched Marina through a slit in the velvet curtains as she removed her jacket. She removed her jeans, dropping them casually onto the floor. I didn't like how untidy she was, I was sure this was something I could 'knock' out of her personality once she was mine. But it was early days, and she didn't even know I existed. When she stripped down to her underwear I felt that familiar arousal. Don't get me wrong I'm no perverse Peeping Tom, I like women. Especially the vulnerable, the weak, the type who I can control. Marina, I hoped, would nicely fit the bill.

A phone was ringing in the distance, Mark searched the text and realised it wasn't part of this story, then he pushed the sound away, submerging himself completely in Peter's world. As Peter, he lied, cheated and manipulated his way into the unsuspecting Marina's life and he felt a weird satisfaction from it. He felt no respect for the woman, she was an object, something he needed to possess, nothing more. This dark emotion, so far removed from anything he had ever felt, made him feel strangely invulnerable.

Marina was fooled. She thought I loved her: it made it so much easier to persuade and confuse her feeble mind. After a few days she was doing things my way and thought very little about it.

'What movie would you like to watch?' I asked her, testing my control.

She thought for a moment. A small wrinkle appeared on her brow. 'I don't mind. You choose,' she said eventually.

I felt the excitement accompanied by a major victory. She was mine now and I would do with her exactly what I pleased. I would use up her youth, her beauty, her confidence, until she was nothing more than the slave I truly desired.

Then I was going to kill her.

Mark felt that coldness seeping into his heart and mind. He was starting to believe he was Peter, actually enjoyed his mindset. And when the call of nature pulled him unwillingly from this world he resented it completely.

He began to order food deliveries in. The consultancy work he did from home suffered as he failed to log into the work systems and stopped filling in his timesheets. He ignored the phone when it rang, submerging himself so deeply in the story that outside influences stopped meaning anything. Sometimes sleep would force its way in and he would crash out of Peter's world, only to find himself covered in bodily fluids. Resentfully Mark would stagger to the bathroom, clean himself up, then go to bed for a few hours. When he woke again he would be straight back into Peter's world.

Marina loved me now, and everything she did was for my happiness. But I wasn't happy. I wanted to see her beauty fade, her soul wither, her lovely throat bleed.

Mark came away from the story. Excitement jumped in his blood at the thought of abusing Marina. She was everything that he needed. He never questioned why he had to kill her, but death was on his mind.

'I'm tired tonight,' Marina told me the next evening. 'If you don't mind I'm just going to bed.'

'The kitchen is untidy. You need to put the dinner plates into the washer before bed,' I said. My voice was firm and brooked no

argument.

Marina frowned for a moment. 'I thought I'd leave that until the morning.'

'No. Do it now.'

Marina's frown deepened. 'I don't want to. I had a hard day and I'm going to bed. If it bothers you so much, then you *clear up the mess.'*

I stood up then. Rage filled me but I kept a smile on my lips so that she wouldn't see what was coming. Then I slapped her hard across the face. Marina fell back against the door frame but she recovered from the slap far quicker than I had anticipated.

'How dare you touch me! Get the fuck out of my apartment. You freak.'

I wouldn't leave though. She was mine, she couldn't get away with defying me. Maybe Marina's usefulness was suddenly at an end. A shame really because I liked using her body so much.

I chased her into the kitchen. As she reached for the telephone I grabbed her by the hair, then smashed her lovely face hard against the fridge.

I let her go as she slumped to the floor. 'I hope that is going to be enough for you to realise you will *obey me,' I said.*

Marina sat on the floor in shock, then she turned her face upwards to look at me. A bright red mark was blossoming on her cheek bone. There would be a bruise there, showing my handiwork. I felt my cock harden. She was even more desirable damaged than she was perfect.

'Let's not fight anymore,' I said. I helped her to her feet. 'Clean the kitchen then come to bed and we'll make up.'

Marina walked around the kitchen in a daze, but she did everything I wanted her too. That night we had the best sex we'd had so far …

Mark came out of the story disgusted but aroused. He had felt his hand connect with Marina's face, had heard the sickening sound when he smashed her against the fridge. None of it made him feel good though, not in the way that the character Peter felt. It made him feel sullied. Cruel. He had never been a mean-minded person and when he dated, he had always been respectful to the woman in his company. This mindset of Peter's frightened him. It was too attractive and Mark was afraid that it would change him somehow.

But he couldn't leave the novel where it was. It had to finish, and he knew that Marina had to survive at the end, otherwise the story wouldn't be good.

He went to the bathroom, showered and brushed his teeth. Maybe his total submersion wasn't healthy? Maybe it was time to get back to the real world?

In the kitchen he placed a ready meal in the microwave. While he waited for it to cook he looked around the room. Strangely the layout in his apartment was just the same as Marina's. He had never noticed it before and it concerned him until he realised that it was likely he had superimposed his own world onto that of the book. His imagination had created it around the vague description that the writer had given.

The microwave pinged. Mark took out the plate. It burnt his fingers and he quickly placed it down on the work surface. Then, using a tea towel, he picked up the plate and carried it over to his small kitchen table.

Marina sat opposite him. She said nothing because she was bound and gagged.

Mark ate his food. Then he removed the gag and fed her some water. He couldn't leave her all day without a drink.

'Please Peter,' she said. 'Untie me. I'll do whatever you say.'

Mark's eyes fell on the kitchen knife that he had left by the sink. Marina had been difficult and so he had threatened her with it. Now maybe she had learnt her lesson. He hoped so. He wasn't ready to end this yet.

'Okay,' he said. 'But if you act out again I will have to punish you.'

'I promise. I will be good,' she said.

Mark stood and untied the ropes. There were dark red welts on her wrists where the rope had cut in. Mark smiled, the sight of her pain was arousing. He took her arm and pulled her into the bedroom.

Marina was passive as he took his pleasure. It wasn't what he wanted. He wanted her to cry out, show she was enjoying him, but afterwards the only reaction she had was quiet tears that rolled down her cheeks.

Even so, he gave her no sympathy. He turned in the bed and promptly fell asleep.

Mark woke and looked around his familiar room. Fractured light seeped through the blinds and he felt angry. Marina hadn't closed them properly again! He shook his head. What was he thinking? Marina didn't exist. Mark knew he lived alone. His mind was confusing reality with the novel he had been reading. He pushed back the covers and climbed out of the bed but when he looked back he saw the bedclothes were dishevelled. The other side of the bed looked as though someone had been sleeping there.

Mark dismissed it. He had to get back to reality and the first thing he needed to do was to call into his work number and get back on track again. After all if you didn't have money you had nothing.

In the kitchen Mark found Marina cooking breakfast.

'What are you doing here?' he asked. His conscious mind knew this wasn't right. That Marina didn't exist.

'I'm making breakfast for you. Like you told me to last night. Did I do something wrong?' Marina's face held genuine fear.

'You can't be here,' he said. 'You don't exist.'

The girl backed away towards the cooker and stared at him in horror.

'Please Peter. I'll do whatever you say. Don't hurt me again …'

'I'm not Peter,' he said confused. But part of his subconscious began to wonder.

Marina said nothing. She stared at him, clearly terrified.

'This is all in my mind,' Mark said. 'You aren't here. You don't exist. Whatever I do to you doesn't matter.'

Marina began to cry softly as he approached. Then, she turned and grabbed the carving knife she had been using to trim the fat off his bacon.

Mark laughed. She couldn't hurt him. This was all a confused dream. His mind was still partially connected somehow with the DNA Book he had been reading.

He felt pain as the knife slashed into his stomach, but Mark still laughed. It was truly amazing, how you felt everything. Just like the doctor said. Love, lust, pain and now as he bled on the kitchen floor, even death.

'Let's get this straight, you're saying your husband has been acting strangely ever since he received a present from his Aunt?' said the police officer. He had introduced himself as Sergeant Spelling.

Mark's body was on a stretcher, and Suzanna watched the paramedics wheel him out. Her deflecting blow had found a main artery, Mark had bled out before help could arrive.

'He believed he was a character in a book,' she explained. 'A serial killer. I was his victim. He even made me call him "Peter" and he was calling me "Marina" which was the girl the character was … abusing.'

Suzanna pressed a hand to her bruised cheek. Spelling noted her chafed wrists and several more bruises on her bare arms.

'We should get the paramedics to check you out as well,' said Spelling. 'And we'll need to take pictures of your injuries … for evidence.'

'He was going to kill me …' Suzanna said.

When Spelling had gone, Suzanna sat down on the sofa and closed her eyes. A vacuous space occupied her emotions. There were no more words on the page describing how she felt and so she felt nothing.

The page turned to a blank, signifying THE END.

Inside Suzanna's head, Aunt Josslin sighed happily. *This was better than travel any day.*

She closed the DNA Book and wondered what she should experience next …

The Night Bird

For Chloë Hickson

Chloë Hickson closed the door and looked around the expansive hallway. Ahead the wooden staircase was shiny and clean, the small Georgian-style table to her right was polished to a sheen. Just with one glance she could tell that Mrs Beatrix had been that day; the housekeeper prided herself on keeping everything perfect for Chloë and her father.

There was a notepad, left open and placed conspicuously on the table. This was not an oversight. Mrs B always left notes in exactly the same spot. She was as orderly as Chloë's father and just as meticulous.

> *Doctor Hickson,*
> *I have left a pie in the fridge for you and Chloë.*
> *I won't be here for the next few days because I'm visiting my sister and her family.*
> *Have a nice weekend. I will be back on Monday.*
> *Mrs B.*

Chloë left the notepad where it was and passed through the hallway and down towards the kitchen. On her left, the basement door was slightly ajar – not something her father would have normally overlooked but it was an indication that he was home and downstairs in his laboratory. She contemplated calling down to him but knew he wouldn't like it. Instead she closed the door properly without looking inside and then turned and walked into the kitchen.

She poured cold juice into a glass and sat down at the marble-topped central table. The kitchen was spotless, the expensive white units shone, and the black stone work tops gleamed as though they were freshly installed. She both hated and liked the way the house was always so immaculate. Sometimes she wanted to spill something and not clean it up. But such an occurrence would never be tolerated by either Mrs B or her father.

For devilment she splashed a drop of juice on the table top, but the small blot glared at her until she fetched a cloth to wipe it up with. When she finished her drink she dutifully placed the glass in the dishwasher and left the kitchen as tidy as it had been when she entered.

In her room she found her bed freshly made, dressing table top tidy: the bits of make-up she had left there had been put away in the small make-up bag she kept in the top drawer. Now Chloë pulled out the make-up and tipped it onto the clean surface. She stared at the clutter.

She lay on top of her bed, deliberately rumpling the throw, and moving the pillows until they were no longer perfectly placed.

At least in her room she could make some mess, as long as she tidied it before Monday that was.

She turned on her stereo and listened to music through one side of her head phones. Loud noise, blaring music, running around her room, or down the stairs, was not allowed. *Children should be seen and* never *heard*. But Chloë was no longer a child. She was 17. That was old enough to know she was tired of perfection. Sick of quiet. Bored with solitude.

There was a knock at her door. Chloë sat up on the bed.

'Don't come in dad, I'm not decent!' she called.

'Dinner's on the table. Mrs B left us a pie,' Hickson said.

'Okay. I'll be down in a few minutes.'

Her father rarely entered her room, which meant it was Chloë's only refuge, but even here she couldn't truly relax. She straightened the bed again and packed the make-up back into the bag, then stowed it once more in the drawer.

Downstairs the table was laid out with precision. The pie, now warm, was cut up and neatly placed on two plates. A plate of mashed potato and a bowl of vegetables were positioned on placemats over the pristine tablecloth.

Chloë sat down in her usual seat and waited patiently while her father poured exactly the same amount of water into each of their cups. Then he poured a small glass of wine for himself.

They ate silently. He didn't ask how her day had been, and Chloë never asked about his work. His 'work', whatever that involved, was obviously lucrative. Their home was perfect, expensive, and in the best neighbourhood. But she knew her father was a scientist. That when he wasn't in his place of work he was experimenting at home. Though Chloë wasn't permitted in the lab at all. In fact she had never even been downstairs to the basement because it was all 'off-limits'.

After dinner, Hickson and Chloë tidied the table. Then, as he always did, Hickson returned to his laboratory while Chloë went into the study to complete her homework.

Like the rest of the house, the study was dust-free. Chloë sat at a large leather covered table, on an executive leather chair. The only computer in the house was switched on, but Chloë was only permitted to look at things that would help her studies.

'Books are better and more accurate a reference than the internet,' Hickson would say.

When she asked why she couldn't downstream movies, or join the social network site that all of her friends seemed to favour he told her that these things weren't 'educational'.

When I leave here, Chloë thought, *I will never have my house tidy, and I will watch television all day if I want to.*

There was a television in the house though. It was in a locked cabinet in a small den, just off the kitchen. Sometimes Hickson would let Chloë watch specific movies and programmes he approved of. Nothing horror was allowed, nor romance – that might give her 'ridiculous notions' about love. Sometimes he would allow her to watch crime dramas where forensics were used to solve a murder. Together they watched science programmes, biographies of famous and important – in Hickson's sole opinion – people in history. All of these things conformed to his ideal of learning.

'Can I have driving lessons, dad?' Chloë had asked recently. 'All of my friends already have their own cars.'

'One day I may deem it necessary,' Hickson said. 'But for now the school bus is good enough.'

Chloë didn't point out to him that she was the only 17 year old still travelling to school that way, or that the bus was full of kids. She felt so foolish waiting at the stop that she had taken to walking the five miles there every day. Sometimes though, one of her friends would give her a ride home. She never brought them inside, nor talked about her father. She had become adept at answering questions with questions, switching the focus of conversations about herself back to the people she was with. This wasn't a difficult thing to do once you realised that what teenagers enjoyed most of all was talking about themselves.

Chloë finished her homework, packed her bag and went back up to her room. There she pulled free the novel she had borrowed from the college library. It was definitely something her father wouldn't approve of, but she had heard from her friends that it was good.

The book was about a mysterious underworld in a fantastical city – Chloë was hooked from the first page, and it took up the long and lonely evening until, tired, she closed her eyes, turned over and went to sleep.

It was still dark when Chloë awoke. She had been dreaming again. Some silly fantasy that involved flying. When she had researched the meaning of dreams she learnt that the flying dream usually reflected a subconscious urge to escape. But it wasn't the dream that woke her. There was some distant and uncharacteristic noise in the house. Even now she could hear the faint change of sound that disturbed the normal silence.

She climbed from her bed, pulled on her robe and walked bare-footed out onto the landing. She could hear the steady tick-tick of the house cooling and settling, the only noise that her father couldn't eradicate.

At the top of the stairs she saw the flashing of the house

alarm lights on the box near the front door. She crept downstairs, turned the interior alarm off and wandered through the house.

There was a palpable silence again. Something that Chloë felt was more imposing than all of the loudest noises in the world. It was a suffocating drone, like white noise echoing in the ears of the young. She craved the sound she was starved of.

In the kitchen she noticed that the security lights had flicked on in the garden. From the dark she looked out onto the glowing lawn. A cat leapt up onto the fence, then dropped back over the other side to the neighbours' garden. The lights next door lit up as the animal, presumably, passed the expensive heated pool that Chloë often envied.

She poured herself a glass of water and headed back to her room.

As she passed the door to the basement a shallow mewling sound came from below.

Chloë stopped. A noise, like a flock of birds beating heavy wings against the wind, echoed up from below.

Chloë took a step back: something was in her father's laboratory. She thought about calling him but stopped herself. *What was her father doing with birds in the basement?*

Chloë pressed her ear to the door. All was quiet again and she considered for a moment if her imagination had gotten the better of her. When no more sounds were heard, she turned away and began to walk back towards the stairs.

Help me.

Chloë paused. Had she actually heard a voice? She realised she was holding her breath when her lungs began to hurt. She exhaled and inhaled as quietly as possible as she returned once more to the basement door.

Her free hand reached for the handle expecting to find it locked. The door opened, however, with a barely audible click.

Chloë froze again. Her father always seemed to know when she did anything that was against the rules, and entering the basement was definitely 'Not Permitted'. She waited at the top of the cellar stairs, expecting to hear his heavy tread, or the rushed opening of his bedroom door, but no further noise issued from the house.

Help … me …

Chloë peered into the dark stairwell. Something was definitely down there. She fumbled for the light. The glass of water in her hand sloshed over her fingers, and onto the step, but Chloë didn't notice. She found the light switch and the staircase lit up.

The stairs were boxed in. There was a door at the bottom which she suspected would be locked. Her father would never leave his laboratory open for anyone to walk in. How many times had he told her that there was danger there: poisonous chemicals, acids, things she shouldn't touch?

Chloë found herself at the foot of the steps before she had even decided to take the chance. She stared at the door. It was fully made of wood and so she couldn't see what was on the other side. Part of her had hoped that there would be a glass panel she could look through; less of a crime than actually opening the door and going inside.

The handle was warm, as though someone else, moments before, had stood in the very same spot, contemplating entering. The hairs on the back of her neck stood up. A shudder ran down her spine, as someone *walked over her grave* … And as Chloë thought this she also wondered where that expression came from.

Help … please …

Chloë stared at the door, willing it to show her its secret, but her nerve had gone, she couldn't turn the handle. She might as well just return to her room, drink her water like the well-behaved daughter she had always been and never again think about the lab.

The handle turned in her hand.

Chloë jumped back, she barely managed to stop herself from dropping the water glass even as it sloshed more of its contents on the steps.

The door was unlocked and it opened before her. She felt herself propelled forward into a dully lit room. Ahead was a row of glass windows, through which she could see a long central table, Bunsen burners, a microscope, analytical machines and computers of all kinds.

The basement ran the entire length of the house. But that was to be expected. Her father would never waste anything, especially space.

She didn't go inside the lab, afraid that she would inadvertently do something that would bring her father's wrath down on her. Instead she followed the glass panels round until they brought her to another door.

She opened this one without hesitation: she had to see everything that was down here.

The room was in complete darkness. After a few minutes of searching Chloë found the light on the wall outside, not inside, the room.

There were cages all around the room. One contained a baby chimpanzee, another a white spaniel puppy, the third was a litter of kittens, the fourth was empty. The fifth cage, in the farthest corner of the room was covered by a thick canvas cloth.

Chloë was shocked to see the animals. Her father had never let her have pets, saying how untidy they were. He had also said that she wasn't ready to have such a responsibility, now she felt as though she didn't know Hickson at all. Did he experiment on these poor creatures? Chloë felt sickened by the thought that her father could do such a horrible thing.

She approached the first cage, looking in at the chimp to see what condition it was in. The animal looked healthy, but Chloë observed that it didn't wake. She thought about her father's need for silence. He wouldn't be happy if the animals had been making noises down here, plus, both she and Mrs B would have heard them. It was obviously drugged.

'You poor things,' she murmured. 'No wonder he doesn't want me down here, to see you all like this.'

She moved along the cages: all the animals were the same, sleepy, quiet and unaware of her presence.

She came to the fifth, and largest cage. With new found confidence that the animal inside wouldn't make a noise, Chloë lifted the cloth. She found herself staring at a bundle of rags in straw, and a heap of black feathers. Her mind made a kind of sense of the mess – torn up pillows, or quilts. Then, as she turned – believing the cage to be empty – the rags moved.

A human face with big round eyes looked up from beneath the blanket of feathers. It was a young man. Pale, fragile-looking as though he had been half-starved. Blue lines were visible under his eyes, and his hand trembled as he slowly reached out towards her.

The light touched his skin and he snatched his hand back as though he had been burnt.

'What are you doing here?' Chloë asked. She knelt down by the cage.

Was her father completely insane? Experimenting on animals was bad enough, but a human. A man, not much older than herself …

Chloë didn't know what to do. She felt she had to help, had to do something to free him from his captivity. She didn't know what though. She had never openly gone against her father, knowing that his decisions were always final. She feared his fury on a deep rooted level that was both irrational and logical, yet she had never really seen him angry.

The man peered back at her from the shadows. His eyes were a bright turquoise, and she noticed that the feathers seemed to be growing out of his head to fall like a long black mane over his shoulders.

'What *are* you?' she murmured.

He stared at her, and again she heard those words ringing in her head as though he could speak directly into her mind. *Help … me.*

Chloë glanced back at the cages around her. What was her father involved in? It was obvious what he was doing here, but she didn't want to contemplate it, because that would mean her father wasn't what she thought. That would make him a *monster*, wouldn't it?

'Can you talk?' she asked.

'Yes …' the man croaked from a throat that was dry and

unused.

Chloë realised she could help with water at least. She held out the glass, passing it through the bars.

'Drink this ...'

Crooked fingers grabbed at her wrist and sharp nails bit into the soft flesh of her forearm. Chloë yelped, the glass fell from her fingers and the man grinned at her. His mouth looked odd now, it appeared elongated and beak-like. And his big eyes seemed to grow rounder.

'You're hurting me ...' she said. 'I only wanted to help you.'

Suddenly her arm was free, she pulled back, shuffling away from the cage on her bottom until she reached the open door that led back towards the lab and the basement steps.

Help. Me.

Heart pounding, Chloë scurried to her feet, and out of the room. As she reached the bottom of the stairs, she examined her arm. The skin was pierced, sharp nail prints left a trail in her forearm. Although she was trembling she stopped and looked back. She had to close the door, turn off the light, and leave everything as she had found it or Hickson would know that she had been down here.

Once this was done, she opened the door to the stairwell. Her bare feet felt the water she had spilt earlier and so removing her robe, she mopped up the mess and carried on up the stairs, pausing to wipe away the drips at the top. There was nothing she could do about the drinking glass in the cage, but she suspected her father wouldn't get too close if the man was that dangerous.

Silently she closed the basement door and returned to her room.

The next morning Chloë felt sick. Her arm hurt, but when she looked she saw that the nail marks had completely disappeared. She had barely slept after returning to her bed, and when she had slipped into brief bouts of sleep, her dreams had been surreal and confused. She had imagined herself flying through the night sky, like a migrating bird. This time the flying dream was more real than it had ever been.

When she woke she remembered the man-thing in the cage. The more she thought about it, the less human he appeared to be. What was he? Her mind toyed with a name that made sense of what she had seen. He was some kind of birdman. She recalled how the light had hurt him, as though he was photophobic. It also explained why the cage had been covered up. *He is a Night Bird*, she thought, though she had no clue where the name came from.

'Chloë, you'll miss the bus,' her father said at her bedroom door.

'I'm not feeling well today, dad,' she said.

Hickson opened the door and looked in at her. 'You shouldn't miss school …'

When he saw her yellowish colour he came in.

'You don't look well,' he said surprised. 'Perhaps we should call the doctor?'

Chloë shook her head, 'No that's alright. I just think I'll sleep it off.'

A short time later Hickson brought her a glass of water and some pills. 'Take these.'

'What are they?'

'Just aspirin.'

Chloë took the pills and drank the water. She felt incredibly thirsty.

'I have to go into work,' Hickson said. 'But ring me if you need me.'

A short time later Chloë heard her father leave. She struggled from her bed and went into the bathroom. After she had showered and changed she felt a little better. The pills had taken down her fever and she no longer felt sick.

In the kitchen she poured herself another glass of water which she drank down and then refilled. After the third glass she felt rehydrated.

Alone in the house for the day Chloë felt restless. She didn't know what to do with herself. Now that she felt less sick, she considered going into college after all. She went into the study, picked up her books and homework and then returned to the hallway.

As she picked up her purse she noticed that the basement door was ajar again.

She had been certain it was closed when she passed earlier. She approached, feeling strangely nervous. Part of her wanted to believe that she hadn't seen the cages, or the lab, the night before. But she knew she hadn't imagined any of it, or the way the Night Bird had dug his talons into her arm.

She pushed the door closed and then on impulse, pulled it open again and went downstairs.

The basement was exactly as it had been the night before. Nothing had been disturbed. She wondered if her father had even ventured down there at all that morning. Surely he would need to feed the animals and the ... *Night Bird*. The name she had given him stuck now, became a natural link, as though it explained everything that he was.

In the back room the animals remained quiet. Chloë ignored them though, and went straight to the large cage in the corner. The cloth was back over the cage. Chloë knew she had left it turned up, but maybe the creature had pulled it down to protect itself.

With a trembling hand she raised the canvas. The rags were there, the creature remained asleep under them. She could see the glass now, stood near the bars as though waiting for her to take away the evidence.

'Thank ... you ... Chloë ...' he said, as though speech was not easy.

Chloë gazed back at the round, bird-like eyes, the beak had gone again: the creature was once more a man.

'I want to help. But I'm afraid ...' Chloë said.

She was afraid of the Night Bird, afraid of her father. How would she explain its absence when finally her father noticed it gone?

'He hurt my ...'

The man turned his head. Chloë followed his gaze to the

empty cage and she knew what he was trying to tell her. The Night Bird's mate had occupied this once. Now he was alone.

She ran from the basement, horrified that her father could have done something so cruel, so inhumane. Tears of sympathy, fear and anxiety flowed freely down her cheeks.

Back in her room she paced up and down unable to decide what to do. She couldn't leave the Night Bird to suffer the same fate as his lover, but how could she help?

Her arm was no longer hurting, the sickness had completely gone, but Chloë found herself drinking more and more water as the day passed. She took the Night Bird another drink, noticed how he stayed back from her this time until she pulled her hand clear of the bars. He was showing her that she could trust him and she was slowly becoming more and more certain that he had not intended to hurt her when he had reached for the first glass of water. Perhaps he had been so thirsty he had reacted on instinct.

She stayed by the cage for most of the day, but an hour before her father was due home. She took the water glass away and covered the cage.

'I'll be back later,' she promised.

When her father arrived, Chloë had prepared them a light dinner of chicken and vegetables. She placed everything where it should be on the table, conforming as she always did to his rules and ideals of perfection.

'That was lovely, Chloë,' Hickson said. 'My! I think you are finally growing up.'

He kissed her forehead in an uncharacteristic display of affection and then left her to go to his lab and his secret experiments.

The evening passed and Chloë's nerves became increasingly agitated. What was her father doing down there? Was he hurting the animals or the Night Bird? By the time she heard him leave the lab, and retire for the night, Chloë was upset and afraid. She wanted to run downstairs immediately and see if everything was okay but she had to wait, give her father time to fall asleep.

An hour passed before Chloë was sure that Hickson wouldn't hear her leave her room. She opened her bedroom door and listened. She could hear the soft whistle of Hickson's snoring. Satisfied, she crept back downstairs unheard.

This time Chloë didn't turn on the light in the back room, she knew it disturbed, or even hurt, the Night Bird, and so she merely used the light from the room outside to light her way to the cage. As she lifted the canvas, Chloë knew immediately that the creature wasn't well.

'What happened?' she said.

The Night Bird was less man and more large bird again.

It looked at her with sad eyes, sharp beak resting across feather covered arms that were ... no longer arms ...

For the first time Chloë looked for a way to open the cage, but could find no obvious lock. How it opened was a puzzle. Finally she gave up her search, and fell asleep beside the cage, only waking when the man tickled her arm with one of the feathers.

'Day ... light ...' he stuttered.

Chloë recovered the cage, then retraced her steps back upstairs. She had just closed the door to her room when she heard her father's shower switched on.

Long days followed short nights, and Chloë found herself spending more and more time with the Night Bird. She learnt that by day he was a man, but after sunset, a change occurred to transform him into the strange half-man, half-bird thing.

How did this happen, she wanted to know, but the man never told her and the bird only ever said, *help me* in her mind.

As the week passed, Chloë became increasingly concerned for his safety. It went beyond any feeling she had ever had. All of her life was about order and her father's control. She no longer wanted to do everything he said, but was still afraid to take that further step out of her comfort zone and disobey him completely. As it was she was already breaking so many rules she didn't know what Hickson would say if he ever found out.

242

And the Night Bird became sicker as each day passed. She brought him water and food, but something was hurting him. Perhaps it was something her father was doing, or maybe it was just the constant captivity, Chloë wasn't sure. She just knew that somehow she had to set him free.

On the seventh night she discovered how to open the cage.

On entering the basement Chloë glanced inside the lab as she always did. She noticed immediately that there was something black on the normally clear and pristine work surface. She had never opened the door to the lab, feeling no curiosity at all about its contents. It was unlike her father to leave anything lying around. That evening though, she had noticed he was quieter than normal. As though he had something on his mind. At times like these Chloë had learnt to be silent, leaving him to his own thoughts. Now his strange mood was to her advantage.

When she entered the lab she discovered that the black object was a remote control device. She picked it up, examined it carefully, then without thinking she took it with her to the cage room.

The Night Bird was in half-change again. He seemed in terrible pain, as though this half-state was a kind of limbo between two worlds. Chloë felt a close sympathy, as though she could experience the pain too. She imagined she knew what he was feeling: it was as though he were being torn in two, neither one thing, nor the other but both trying to coexist in the same body.

'Yes …' croaked the Night Bird. He pointed his arm-wing at the remote control she was holding.

'It can open the cage …' Chloë said, immediately comprehending his unspoken words.

She glanced down at the buttons but nothing seemed obvious and so she began to press them randomly to see how they worked.

The cage door creaked on the fourth try, and Chloë froze, waiting as she saw the front begin to slide upwards as though it were on runners. The Night Bird scurried out quickly into the darkened room, but it wouldn't approach the door where the light from the lab poured in.

Chloë stepped back through the opening. Now that she had opened the cage she didn't know what she would do with the Night Bird. What if he suddenly turned on her?

'Light …' said the Night Bird.

Chloë knew she had to make this decision. She had come too far to turn back, what else could she do but lead him outside to freedom.

'Okay …' she said. 'I'm going to turn off the lights as I go. Follow me.'

The Night Bird chirped his assent then Chloë passed back through the basement. She replaced the remote control on the table in the lab, then she turned off the light and closed the door. Once this was done she hurried towards the steps and when her hand fell on the switch at the bottom of the stairs, the basement was plunged into darkness.

Feeling nervous, she hurried up the steps and out into the hallway. The front door was just down the hallway, all she had to do was turn off the alarm and open it to let him out.

The Night Bird would leave and she could feel happy that she had saved him.

'Chloë? What are you doing?'

Hickson was standing in front of the alarm.

'Dad,' she gasped. 'You scared me.'

'Why are you up?'

'I … thought I heard something …'

Light slanted through the glass panels in the doorway and lit up the frown on Hickson's face.

'There is no noise,' Hickson said, 'except the noise you are making.'

'Sorry. I didn't mean to wake you,' she said.

Stay below! she thought, hoping that the Night Bird could hear her thoughts as much as she sometimes heard his.

'You didn't wake me,' said Hickson. 'I had a letter today from your college though. They said you hadn't attended all week.'

Chloë said nothing.

'What have you been doing at home all by yourself?' asked her father.

'I wasn't feeling well, dad. I didn't want to worry you.'

'Then I must get you some more pills,' said Hickson. 'I'll just go down into the lab and …'

'No!' Chloë said. 'I mean … I'm fine now. Feeling better. I just need a glass of water …'

Hickson folded his arms across his chest. 'What are you hiding, Chloë?'

'Me? Nothing, dad. I'm tired. I must go to bed and sleep now. Goodnight.'

Chloë turned towards the staircase.

'Wait,' said Hickson.

'Yes?'

'Have you been in my laboratory?'

Chloë was glad for the darkness in the hallway which hid the guilty flush that came to her cheeks.

'Of course not,' she said. 'I know the rules.'

She scurried up the stairs, heart pounding in her chest, all the time hoping that her father wouldn't go to the lab and see the Night Bird freed from his cage. When she closed her bedroom door, Chloë breathed a ragged sigh of relief.

A few moments later she heard her father shouting and the screaming siren of the house alarm erupted.

She ran down the stairs taking them two at a time. When she reached the hallway Chloë found her father on the floor, blood was pouring from his throat, and the front door was wide open.

She switched on the light, silenced the alarm, and bent down to see the wound on Hickson's neck. Blood pooled on the polished wood floor. It only took a moment for her to realise that her father was dead.

Remorse swamped her. She had saved the Night Bird, but in turn he had killed her father. Chloë felt sick and afraid. She had been misled, surely her father had merely been protecting her world from a monster that inhabited it. Now she had let that monster free.

As the neighbours came out of their houses, Chloë could see that they all thought she was some poor girl whose father had been a victim of an attempted burglary. She sat on the stairs and cried while someone ordered an ambulance and dialled for the police, saying nothing of what she had seen and heard.

As she looked out through the open door though, she saw the Night Bird, fully changed for the first time, soaring above their heads like the angel of death. The sight of him like this brought physical pain to her limbs.

She was drawn to the door, then over the step. The air felt cool and welcoming, and the noise and bustle as people rushed around her home trying to help, jarred with the normal quiet of her surroundings.

She felt that stirring of pain and sickness. She fell to her knees, arms clutching her stomach even as feathers burst from her forearm and grew in a black wave over her head, around her shoulders. The thin nightdress she was wearing tore as her arms grew wider at the shoulder, bat-like in their span, and then wings burst forth, forcing her upwards into the air.

With the change came memories. A cruel torture disguised as a cure, forced on her even as her lover cried and fought in a cage next to hers. She remembered who Hickson really was now. He wasn't her father, he bore no blood relation to her at all. He was merely the one who had captured them, lost and forlorn as they were. So trusting and in need of shelter.

Chloë circled above the house, the air gathered under her, lifting her higher, but now she was in control, she knew who and what she was.

The Night Bird, her Night Bird, Sven, waited in the distance, afraid that she would reject, or refuse to remember him.

Chloë looked down. For a while she had been part of the human world, had been given a chance to live in it, instead of being always on the outside. But full integration had never really happened. She had known all along that she was different. Had sensed the lies and deceit beneath the smiles and the routine that Hickson had forced on her.

Sven … how could she have forgotten him?

She remembered everything now and the sadness of leaving another safe haven bit into her heart and soul, but no matter. She had never belonged to that world.

She matched her flight to Sven's. Turning when he turned, rising when he rose, until the Night Birds – a breed of their own – could no longer be seen in the night sky.

The Puppet Master

Even though it was high noon the town was deserted as Mario rode into Oak City. His horse hesitated, rearing up as they crossed the town border. Mario took this as a good sign: he was on the right track. He held onto the reins, forcing the stallion into a short gallop until they were halfway up the high street.

There was no movement at all in any of the stores. Not that there were many: a small fabric shop, general store and a hardware shop were all that lined the main street together with the saloon, blacksmith's barn and sheriff's office. 'City' was something of an exaggeration. This town was like taking a step back in time. It reminded him of all the old towns, mostly deserted now in favour of the big cities. It was hard to comprehend that New Orleans wasn't too far from here: maybe a day's ride east. He had heard many rumours on his route but even so it was odd to find this place still here, but so empty. It made him feel on edge. Though that was never a bad thing given the circumstances.

He tied up his horse outside the saloon and looked up at the balcony on the second level. The curtains were drawn. The saloon was deathly quiet but that wasn't so unusual, given the time of day. The action wouldn't happen here until after sundown. Or at least that was the usual thing in these towns. Mario wasn't so sure about Oak though. There might never be any 'action' here again.

Mario had come to Oak looking for a girl. If Saskia was in town, this was where he was likely to find her and he was determined to find her no matter what it took.

At that moment a buzzard flew overhead and began to circle the town. Mario narrowed his eyes, squinting up into the sky. He watched the bird for a few seconds then unclipped his holster. *Time to get moving.*

He walked up the steps towards the traditional saloon doors and peered into the gloom over the top. The saloon was as dead inside as the town was outside. Mario pulled his gun, then pressed against one side of the swinging door with his right shoulder. The door creaked as it opened. He let his eyes adjust to the darkness before he walked all the way inside. He could see pretty well then and his eyes skittered from the bar to the stairs and over the empty tables and chairs. The old piano in the corner still had the cover up and the stool was positioned as though the pianist were still sitting there.

A floorboard groaned as he shifted his weight. He paused, looked up at the balcony above and noted that all the doors were firmly closed.

He leaned over the bar, checked that no one was lurking there, while glancing in the mirror to ensure that no one was behind him. Then he made his way up the stairs slowly, his back sliding along the wall so that he could see both the landing above and the bar area below.

At the top of the landing, Mario paused again. He could start at the end, on the last door, but who knew which one of these rooms housed Saskia? He didn't want her to realise he was there until it was too late. Making a quick decision, he opened the first door as quietly as possible. Inside he saw a whore and client, still attached, the whore on all fours, dress up around her waist, the man behind her, mid-thrust. Mario said nothing. The bodies didn't move.

He had seen this kind of thing before. It was like a paralysis, or like they were frozen in time. He walked in, got closer to the bed.

The man wore a pained smile. His eyes were half open, hips twisted in such a way that he appeared to be in the final moment of his ecstasy. His hands gripped the whore's waist in a death-like grip.

The whore's face was blank. Wiped clean of features. No eyes, lips, nose, just a smooth veneer of pale perfect wood.

Mario prodded the shallow cheeks of the man. His face began to crumble like lime whitewash subjected to intensive heat. Mario backed away. He closed the door behind him.

Saskia was here. No doubt about it now. The puppet was all the evidence he needed.

In each room he found a similar scene. The only thing that varied were the sexual positions. Sometimes the man was wood and the woman real, but most often it was the other way round. All of the humans were dead, disintegrating dried up husks that had been left to rot. They looked as though they were years dead, but Mario knew that this had all happened recently.

In the last room the set-up was more unusual. Mario noted the rich boudoir colours of reds and purples, the fancy Chinese screen that separated a bath tub from the rest of the room but what chilled him to the bone was the sight of the two men in bed with one woman. The woman was spread out on the bed, naked, hands tied to the metal headrest with purple sashes. Mario felt no sexual interest in the bare breasts: they were shrivelled like old figs. Her crumbling mouth was slightly open, while one man kneeled, his body falling to dust, above her face. His member dangled over her like tantalising fruit that had been left on the branch too long. The other lay between her legs, his bottom raised, as though he were caught in half thrust.

Mario couldn't make sense of it at first. There were no puppets: obviously they had been active elsewhere, but why were these humans dead? There were always puppets involved in that somehow.

Mario backed away, then caught sight of himself in the mirror behind the half-drawn dressing screen. He also saw the reflection of a puppet, bent over, watching like a voyeur through the gap in the hinges.

The sight of it made the hair rise on the back of his neck. This was a new high, even for Saskia. He pulled back the screen. Anger burned in his stomach and chest. The puppet, predictably, didn't move.

Outside in the street Mario gulped in air. So she wasn't there, perhaps the damage was done already and the town was beyond saving?

Mario had a theory. The puppets were alive at night and

they drained that life from the people they interacted with. He just had to find Saskia in order to prove it, and to stop this from ever happening again. The trouble was, he wasn't sure just how he was going to stop her.

Saskia had up and left him six weeks ago and she had taken something with her, something very important. Mario had to get it back. That was all he could think about.

'Hey. You.'

Mario looked up. He sighed with relief as he saw the sheriff standing outside his office.

'What were you doing in the saloon? It ain't open yet.'

'Sheriff, have you seen what's up there?'

The sheriff took some persuading to go inside but eventually he followed Mario into the bar. Mario waited downstairs as the man examined the rooms, it was now almost two and the afternoon was wearing on. He didn't want to be inside the saloon when the sun went down. That was when Saskia always did her work. That was when *they* lived.

'What the hell's happened here?' asked the sheriff as he descended the stairs.

Mario shook his head. His hands were trembling. This was the worst he had seen and no mistake, and he had been following her ever since this started. Saskia was getting more inventive, plus she was taking them a town at a time now. He just hoped he had arrived in time.

'Listen fella, I reckon you know what's going on. You'd better speak up or I'll be inclined to take you to the jail house.'

'I don't know anything,' said Mario. 'I'm just passing through. Wanted a drink. I went looking for the barman but I found … that.'

'Sheriff Haley?' called a voice outside. 'Grant? We need you right now.'

'My deputy …' Haley explained. 'Wait here.'

There was a creak upstairs.

'Sheriff, I'd rather come with you,' said Mario. He wasn't ready to face this yet.

They went outside to find a tall, thin, young man waiting in the street.

'What is it Shane?' asked Haley.

Shane turned his head and looked down the street. Haley and Mario saw then that a small queue of people had appeared outside the sheriff's office. Mario noticed that the shops were now open and he could hear the steady tap of the blacksmith's hammer echoing down the street.

'Where did everyone come from?' asked Mario. 'This place was dead not long back.'

Haley shook his head. 'It's a little weird. We've all been sleeping rather late recently. I can't seem to get outta bed much before noon. Fortunately neither can the rest of the town.'

'Too much excitement at night?' Mario asked.

Haley said nothing, but Shane looked sick. Mario knew they had suspicions but they weren't about to discuss them with a stranger.

'What do they all want?' Haley asked Shane.

'Same as usual. Husbands and wives gone missing,' said Shane.

Haley glanced up at the saloon. 'I think I know where a few of them are.'

Then Haley turned and walked back towards his office. His step was slow, tired, deliberate. Mario frowned.

'How long have you all been feeling … tired?' he asked Shane.

Shane turned to look at him as though he had only just noticed him. 'Who are you?'

'Just arrived in town. I found the bodies.'

'Bodies. What bodies?'

Mario nodded towards the saloon. Shane looked up at the balcony in front. The closed curtains did nothing to dispel the unease he was feeling. Then Shane turned and followed Haley leaving Mario alone outside the bar.

Inside the sheriff's office Mario found Haley and Shane talking to a man.

'My wife's no whore, Grant. You've known her all these years. Do you really think she'd willingly do something like that?'

Haley placed a soothing hand on the man's shoulder. 'I seen some weird stuff recently that I just can't believe. People acting out of character, going down to the saloon and taking part in things I'd never have dreamed. Hank, if Sara got tempted and went on in there, there's no telling what coulda happened. The thing is, I seen her body with my own eyes.'

'I want to see …' said Hank. He tried to stand but Haley forced him back into the chair.

'It won't do you no good. Let the undertaker deal with this Hank. I promise you, you don't want this to be the way you remember your lovely wife.'

Mario noticed the undertaker then, standing in the corner of the office. He looked so stereotypical, wearing a dark suit and with a sincere expression on his face as he took the sheriff's instructions and left the office, followed by Shane.

If I were making a puppet show of this story the undertaker would look just like that, thought Mario. This made him realise how tentative reality was these days. But then everything had changed so much.

'The rest of you, sit down,' ordered Haley and the other people there, waiting to hear about their loved ones, sat down in unison, like puppets whose strings had just been cut.

Mario felt sick and guilty. This was all his fault. He left the sheriff's office and headed down the street. He had to find Saskia and end this. It wasn't right. These people didn't deserve this punishment, no one did.

He went to see the shop owners first. The haberdashery was a good place to start. Puppets needed clothes after all and Saskia would want them to appear as real as possible.

'Can I help you?' asked the shop keeper, a portly man in his fifties.

'I'm wondering if you've seen this woman?'

Mario pulled his pocket watch out of his waistcoat and opened it. Inside the lid was a small portrait of a petite blonde woman of around twenty. The shop keeper looked at the picture, eyes narrowing as he squinted down to see it.

'Can't say that I have. What's she to you?'

'I'm looking for her,' said Mario. 'She's my wife.'

'Oh right. Sorry. Lots of wives going missing around these parts. No one knows what's happening, but the preacher says we have to stay strong in this darkest hour.'

Mario thanked him and moved on to the general store. Inside he found a young woman and an old man serving two sluggish customers. One was a rancher collecting sacks of grain, the other was a boy buying candy sticks. When they had been served, Mario stepped forward and showed the girl Saskia's portrait.

'Never seen her,' she said barely glancing at the picture.

'What about you?' he asked the old man.

'Nope,' he said with a lethargic finality to his voice.

Mario walked the entire street. Everyone he spoke to said they hadn't seen Saskia, yet he knew she must be there. All the evidence pointed to her sickness and obsession taking hold. He *had* to find her before nightfall.

He walked on to the church at the far side of town. Inside he found the preacher sleeping in one of the pews.

He shook him awake. 'Have you seen this girl?' he asked holding out the picture.

'Looks like a whore to me,' said the preacher. 'Try the saloon.'

Mario resisted the urge to shoot the man in the head.

No, Saskia!

Mario heard music burst out from the saloon. It was a familiar tune, one he had heard many times. It was the melody that Saskia played when all the puppets danced on the stage. He took a step forward, then realised his feet were moving towards the saloon all of their own accord. He had to get away, before the music got to him, but first he need to reach his horse.

The sun was going down and Mario began to panic. The

puppets would be waking and Saskia would be controlling them with her music.

He felt confused for a moment. Then remembered that his horse was roped up just outside the saloon. He let the music carry him forward again. He paused at the sheriff's office and glanced through the large window. The sheriff was locking the deputy up in one cell, while he locked himself in the other. Then they exchanged keys. Both men began to dance around the cell, like marionettes on strings.

At the fabric shop, Mario saw the portly old man locking up; he had wads of thick material hanging from his ears. He glanced at Mario sadly, then he walked away from the shop, down the street, far from the saloon.

At the hardware shop he saw the old man tie the young girl's wrists and ankles. Then he placed her on a mattress, covered her with a blanket and began to tie his own feet to the leg of the counter. All this time the man's legs twitched and kicked as though he couldn't control them.

Mario reached the bar a few seconds later. There was a crowd around the door. A young man gripped the rocker that sat on the porch, his knuckles were turning white with the effort of holding himself back from the bar. Inside he could hear the voice of a girl singing now. He recognised it, so rarely used in the old days, but now Saskia had really found her voice. His heart lurched in his chest.

Then he reached his horse, hand rapidly slipping into the sack attached to the back of the saddle. He pulled out the strings and the sound of Saskia's voice receded.

It was too late to do anything now. He had to let the night unfold and keep himself safe from the spell. He turned to see the preacher dancing towards him. His face was distorted, mouth open in a silent scream. Mario felt the man's terror, even as he watched him dance, almost joyfully, up to the swing doors.

At that moment a puppet appeared. It turned its blank face out towards him. Mario was sure that the eyeless face would still see him somehow.

The preacher fell into the marionette's arms and a dance of a different sort began as the faceless thing sat him down on a chair by the piano. The doll lifted its skirt and then sat aside the man.

Mario's horse reared as the half-screams, half-cries of pleasure poured out from saloon. He stroked its mane, just as he had once stroked Saskia's hair. Then he slipped the strings, up and around the animal's neck and felt the calm return to the stallion's shaking limbs. He held onto the strings, keeping the strength he needed around them both, then he mounted the horse, and rode out and away from the town with his thoughts and his memories.

His master, Federico, had taught him well. Mario manipulated the puppets with dexterity. Small though they were, they appeared to hold real life essence every time he picked up the strings.

'You have a real talent for this,' Federico had said. 'One day I will share all of my secrets with you.'

Mario carved the puppets during the day, while Federico performed the shows at night. But sometimes he would let Mario take over during a particularly simple dance routine, and the audience never knew. Mario loved his apprenticeship with the old man, but he often wondered why Federico never taught his skills to his granddaughter, Saskia, instead. She travelled with them, making small dresses and suits for the puppets to wear. Cleaning up after them both, making edible food as they travelled over desert and wastelands between towns.

As the old man's fingers became less flexible, Mario had gone from apprentice to partner, and then eventually he had taken over the show completely while Federico and Saskia had walked the crowd, hat held out, to take money. They travelled around Mexico like this for years, scraping a living, until eventually the old man couldn't travel anymore.

After that Mario would take the show to nearby towns. Then he would return with money to help them live.

'I have to show you something,' Federico said on Mario's return from yet another trip. 'It is what once made me great.'

By this time Federico was being nursed by Saskia, he couldn't be left alone. Mario knew that he was dying.

'Fetch me the box, Saskia,' Federico said and for once Saskia hesitated to fulfil his request. 'I said get me the box!'

Saskia scurried away, she was always subservient to Federico, and so Mario was surprised by her reaction to his request. She returned quickly though and she held out a wooden box to Federico.

'Thank you Saskia. You have been a good girl all this time. I now need to make sure that you are taken care of,' Federico said.

'Don't grandfather,' she begged. 'I don't want you to leave.'

The box was a rough, wooden casket carved with an S on the top. Federico now held it out to Mario, 'I want you to have this. Inside is the secret that I promised to share with you. You have been like a son to me and I leave you this legacy. Promise me you will look after Saskia?'

Mario stared at Saskia as she now sat calmly on the other side of the dying man's bed. He had always loved her, but had never dared to tell her or his master.

'I will marry her,' Mario said. 'We will work together as always to keep the puppet show going.'

Federico closed his eyes, a small tear slipped from his eye and he passed quietly away while Mario clutched the box firmly to his chest.

'Aren't you going to open it?' asked Saskia.

'I want to marry you tonight,' Mario said.

Saskia said nothing, but she dutifully stood and she went to the trunk at the bottom of the bed. There she retrieved a white dress. It was beautiful and Mario knew it was something she had made herself. It was as though she had been waiting for this moment and had prepared for it. He left her to dress, while he fetched the undertaker, and then the two of them went straight to the church as Federico's body was taken away to prepare it for burial.

'This is for you,' Saskia said as they stood before the priest. 'You must never take it off.'

She tied a cord bracelet around his wrist and Mario remembered that Federico had worn one similar for all of the time Mario had known him.

After they were married, Mario forgot about the box. It was the last thing on his mind as he took Saskia, now his wife, home. As they prepared for bed, he stowed it in the chest where he kept the parts for his puppets.

After Federico was buried they set out once more to take the puppet show all over Mexico.

A few years passed before they came to the town that changed things. Mario was happy when they had left Mexico to start their new life in New Orleans. Saskia was a good girl, easy to control, and they took the puppet show from town to town making a very good living. Mario's skill grew. He felt empowered every time he picked up the puppet strings. The marionettes did everything he wanted them to, just by the mere flick of his wrists, and so he decided to make some of them life size.

They rested in New Orleans while Mario obtained the wood and carved the new dummies. Then Saskia made the clothes. Mario had seen a picture card, taken from a cigarette packet, which showed a row of dancing girls in Paris. He asked Saskia to make the puppets look like the girls.

Then he set about making the cart they travelled in into a full size stage, with an area above where he could stand unseen and manipulate the puppets.

'Use this string,' Saskia suggested as Mario laced up the first doll. It was thin and almost invisible, but incredibly strong. Mario didn't ask her where the cord came from, but he used it and hung the dolls up on the cart and began to practice the show.

Using the marionettes was easier than he thought it would be. They took on a life of their own every time Mario touched the strings. At the end of each performance, Mario could barely recall doing anything, but the dolls danced the Can Can much to the delight of the crowd.

Their reputation grew, at each new town the crowds were bigger and the money began to flow easily into the hat as Saskia went around the crowd. They travelled up and down the Mississippi and beyond.

At Dakin City, a small town that aspired to be big, Mario had left the puppet cart in the stables owned by the blacksmith, and Saskia and the puppets were in his room in the town's one small hotel. Saskia had some costume repairs to do but that day the show had been a huge success.

Mario was wired as he often was afterwards. He needed to relax, wind down and so he went to the saloon, as he sometimes did after a good day. A little whiskey and a card game was all he needed to help settle. Saskia never minded this, nor did she complain if he came back late. She was the perfect wife. All any man could ask for.

He didn't notice the tension in the air when he walked into the bar. He wasn't good with people, he only understood puppets and Saskia never made any demands of him.

'Hey Mister, you the guy with them life size puppets?' asked a man at the end of the bar.

'Yeah,' said Mario. 'Whiskey straight up.'

The barman sloshed the amber liquid into a shot glass. Mario placed the money on the counter and slugged the drink. Then he turned around and looked at the room. This saloon was set out pretty much like any other. A few tables and chairs, one group of men with a card game in the corner, another group sat with a few of the saloon girls. The girls drank and giggled as the men refilled their glasses from a bottle in the centre. Over in the corner a guy with a bald head was playing something vaguely recognisable on the piano, while on a small stage a woman sang almost in tune.

'So, these puppets … you ever use 'em for anything else?' asked the man at the end of the bar.

'What do you mean?' asked Mario. 'They're just puppets.'

'Yeah,' laughed the man. 'I caught your show, all that swirling around of skirts, frilly underwear.'

Mario shrugged, he didn't understand what the man was implying but he felt strange. It was almost as though there were something dark in the air brewing.

'Where you keeping 'em then?' asked the man.

'Why?' Mario replied.

'I'd like to see one, close to.'

'We have another show tomorrow, come by and I'll let you see them, and the strings and stuff.'

'I'd like to see one now,' said the man.

'Now Jake,' said the barman. 'We don't want no trouble tonight. These folks have come here for fun.'

'I ain't causing no trouble,' said Jake. 'I just wanna see a puppet.'

Mario finished his drink. He was feeling uneasy now.

'Tomorrow, buddy. Come by and I'll let you see one. Night gentlemen,' Mario said then he left the saloon.

He went to the stables and checked on his cart and stage, making sure it was all safe, and then he returned to the room at the hotel.

Saskia was sitting in a chair by the window when he came in. She was surprised that he was back so early but she said nothing. She watched him change for bed, then he came back to her and began to stroke her hair for a while.

He liked to brush her long, blonde locks before bed sometimes. She didn't mind. It was soothing and her hair felt good afterwards. When he had finished they went to bed.

'You know I love you don't you?' he said as they curled up for sleep.

Saskia knew it was true, but she was already dozing and so didn't reply.

A few minutes later the door burst open.

'Now that's one puppet I'd like to play with,' said the man called Jake as Mario sat upright in bed.

There were four men in the room, one of them was Jake. He glared past Mario at Saskia cowering under the bed covers.

'What are you doing?' yelled Mario, 'Get out of here!'

But the men came in and closed the door instead. Two of

them grabbed Mario, pulling him out of the room.

They held him down but he didn't care about his own safety, all he cared about was his wife. Saskia was being hurt, he had to do something. Mario twisted and turned, fought and kicked, but he couldn't get free.

Saskia would be destroyed. He couldn't have that.

He managed to pull one arm free and he hit out at one of his attackers. Then one of the men hit him so hard that Mario's head slammed back against the floor. He drifted into unconsciousness.

When he woke the men were gone. He ran up to his room and found Saskia lying listless. She was bruised and hurt and she wouldn't talk to him, or tell him what the men had done. The room was wrecked and his puppets destroyed. Some of them were covered in semen, dresses ripped from the wooden bodies, wigs torn from the smooth heads and the painted faces scarred beyond recognition. Mario felt sick. He looked at Saskia. Other than a few bruises and cuts she seemed unhurt.

'What did they do?' he insisted.

Saskia refused to speak.

As they drove away the town was quiet: the people were nowhere to be seen. Mario barely noticed. All he cared about was taking Saskia away to safety. He felt guilty: a total failure of a man who could not protect his wife. Mario had never even fired a gun in his life and didn't own one. All he could think about was that he wished he had learned.

'We'll go back to Mexico,' said Mario. 'I'm going to buy a gun.'

'No,' said Saskia. 'We must carry on with the show. That is where your skill is Mario.'

Mario said nothing. He wasn't used to her disagreeing with him. He couldn't face the thought that what had happened had changed their relationship in some way. He loved Saskia and would do anything to save their happy life.

'We're going back to New Orleans to make more puppets. These ones will be different Mario. This time you will open my grandfather's box.'

Mario was surprised by the force in her voice. He clicked his tongue, sending the horses speeding along across the desert. As the sun rose he glanced down at his wrist and saw that the bracelet she gave him on their wedding day had gone. He felt an overwhelming sense of loss. It was as though this were the most important thing in the world. He thought it some omen that life had been irrevocably changed.

They returned to New Orleans and Mario did all that Saskia asked. He wanted to please her. Wanted to help her forget what had happened. But the one thing he shouldn't have done was open the box her grandfather gave him. That was the day when everything really changed.

Mario returned to Oak just before dawn. The music was still drifting from the saloon but he was still holding onto the puppet cord and he had weaved it into the horse's mane.

Outside the saloon he saw the bodies of the dead entwined with puppets. A wind picked up and Mario saw one man's hat fly away. He stared down at the shrivelled face of the man. He looked more jerk beef than human, but he recognised the face nonetheless. It was the sheriff's deputy, Shane.

'I found them,' said Saskia as Mario pushed open saloon door. 'They won't be hurting anyone else ever again.'

She was standing by the piano. Mario looked around the room. He saw the preacher still sitting in the chair, the marionette astride him. His face looked as though all of the life and blood had been sucked from him.

'All of these people. You killed all of these innocent people,' Mario couldn't think of anything else to say.

'Not innocent. These men were like those others. These women were all whores.'

'What happened to you?' he asked. 'We were so happy. Then all of this changed. I wanted to just forget what those …'

Mario broke down. He staggered against the bar and stood shaking until Saskia came to him. She stroked his head and put her arms around his shoulder.

'What now?' he said. 'You will kill me too?'

Saskia shook her head. 'I found this,' she said.

Mario looked at her outstretched palm. He saw the broken remains of the cord she had placed around his wrist on their wedding day.

'You should never have removed this,' she told him.

Mario's mind was a whirl of emotion, Saskia had kept this all along and he had thought it lost. His mind flashed back to the box. The one that Federico had given him, but never really explained. How he had opened it only once, the night before Saskia had disappeared with all of the puppets.

The S on the lid had been important. He had known that all along and so when he had seen the heart inside, with the marionette cord tied around it, Mario had finally understood. Federico's magic lay in realms that Mario could never quite comprehend. The heart of his real granddaughter beat on inside, while the marionette copy of her walked and lived and held her memories believing she was human. This was Saskia's heart.

'Where is the heart now?' he asked.

Saskia took his hand and placed it on her chest. He could feel the slight pulse. 'Where it belongs,' she said. 'I found the men. Aren't you happy that I killed them?'

Mario shook his head. *So many lives, Saskia.*

'I love you,' she said. 'Now that I have my heart I understand what that means.'

Mario stroked her arm and wrist. Saskia didn't realise what he was doing until the first puppet string was tied.

'No!' she said but Mario took her other wrist and as the cord bound her she no longer had the strength to resist.

Once the puppet was restrung, Mario took the wedding bracelet and began to weave in some of the remaining cord, then he tied it once more around his own wrist. He wouldn't have to use the strings now. Saskia was his to command once more.

He looked around the saloon then turned his arm in a flowing motion. He swept his hand over the room. Saskia gasped and turned, her hands outstretched. He heard her heartbeat grow louder, filling the room as the puppet whores disintegrated. Mario knew that they would never rise again, night or day. Their mistress, Saskia, had been bound to him again and he would make sure that he never lost the cord, no matter what happened.

They went outside. The town was dead and there was nothing more he could do. He felt the regret for his uselessness once more. He would have saved them, but Saskia was more important.

'Time to go home,' he said.

'Yes, Mario,' said Saskia smiling.

As they rode away from Oak City, Mario smiled. He had finally learnt the lesson that Federico had really wanted to teach him. He had graduated to puppet master and he would never let the puppets get away again, particularly not Saskia. He stroked her hair as she sat in the saddle in front of him.

'Happy?' he asked.

'Yes, Mario. I love you.'

Had he been facing her he might have seen the torment in her eyes. A drop of linseed oil traced a path down her face. No one really wants to give up control of themselves, not even a marionette with a human heart.

Copyright Information

About the Author

Award winning author Sam Stone began her professional writing career in 2007 when her first novel won the Silver Award for Best Novel with *ForeWord Magazine* Book of the Year Awards. Since then she has gone on to write 15 novels, 5 novellas and over 40 short stories.

Sam's first screenplay, *The Inheritance*, which is the first story in *White Witch of Devil's End* (a *Doctor Who* spin off anthology movie about white witch Olive Hawthorne - first seen in the Jon Pertwee era, *The Daemons*) will make its DVD debut in November 2017.

Sam has since written two more screenplays which are currently in pre-production.

She was the first woman in 31 years to win the British Fantasy Society Award for Best Novel. She also won the Award for Best Short Fiction in the same year (2011).

Sam loves all genre fiction and enjoys mixing horror (her first passion) with a variety of different genres including science fiction, fantasy and Steampunk.

Her works can be found in paperback, audio and e-book.

Sam currently resides in Lincolnshire with her husband David and cat Leeloo.

For more information visit **www.sam-stone.com**

Other Titles By Sam Stone

Other Telos Horror Titles

DAVID J HOWE
TALESPINNING

FREDA WARRINGTON
NIGHTS OF BLOOD WINE

PAUL LEWIS
SMALL GHOSTS

STEVE LOCKLEY & PAUL LEWIS
KING OF ALL THE DEAD

SIMON MORDEN
ANOTHER WAR

GRAHAM MASTERTON
THE DJINN
RULES OF DUEL (WITH WILLIAM S BURROUGHS)
THE WELLS OF HELL

RAVEN DANE
ABSINTHE AND ARSENIC
DEATH'S DARK WINGS

CYRUS DARIAN STEAMPUNK SERIES (Forthcoming)
1: CYRUS DARIAN AND THE TECHNOMICRON
2: CYRUS SARIAN AND THE GHASTLY HORDE
3: CYRUS DARIAN AND THE DRAGON

TANITH LEE
BLOOD 20
DEATH OF THE DAY